SHAMELESS

SHAMELESS

a novel by

Vonetta C. Pierce

WWW.QBOROBOOKS.COM

An Urban Entertainment Company

ISBN 0-9777335-1-3
First Printing October 2006

10 9 8 7 6 5 4 3 2 1

Cover Copyright © 2006 by **Q-BORO BOOKS**
Cover Design: Candace K. Cottrell
Editors: Candace K. Cottrell, Pashen Solomon
Proofreader: Tee C. Royal

Q-BORO BOOKS—WWW.QBOROBOOKS.COM

Dedication

To Zaria Ayanna
Mommy's little princess
For all the nights you crawled into my lap and fell asleep
while I was on the computer.
Thank you, Munchkin

Acknowledgements

Where do I begin? First and foremost, I thank God and my Lord Jesus Christ for His guidance, providence, and unfailing love and mercy.

I could not even begin to acknowledge anyone without first recognizing the young lady who motivated and inspired me to write—Miss Daaimah S. Poole. Thank you for your invaluable support, your advice, and, ultimately, for your friendship. You made me feel like it was a reality and you have taught me so much. You are indeed one of the many jewels in Philly's literary crown.

To those in the industry

To Mark Anthony and the rest of the Q-Boro family, thanks for taking a chance and providing me with the opportunity; the best is yet to come. Mark, I believe we have similar visions as to where urban fiction can possibly go. Thanks for taking a chance on something out of the ordinary; I appreciate your sincerity and helpfulness. Thanks also to Karen Q. Miller and Jamise Dames for your advice and phone calls. To Kia Morgan, for helping me to make my writing become more alive. Thanks to Pashen Solomon, my editor, for your expertise. And to my cover designer and editorial director, CandaceK, girl, what can I say? Thanks for your patience with me and for lending your talents and creativity to my work. You are irreplaceable!

To my family
I love you all. To John and Janice Pierce, the hardest-working parents I know; thank you for teaching me the value of being educated and industrious. Thank you Mom for instilling in me a love for literature and the cultural arts. Your poetry is beautiful and to be shared with the world. To my sister Cyndi, thanks for putting up with me and always being there. To Joe, Keith, and Kevin, thank you for being the best big brothers a girl could ever have. Thanks Keith for your marketing savvy and encouragement.

To the Howard High School of Technology
Shout out to my Book Club and all of the students who have inspired me and contributed ideas as I put this novel together, especially my self-proclaimed "agent" who was with me every single page—Sade Thomas-Clarke. Where would I have been without you? Also to the students who supported me, I can not *possibly* name you all, but I especially want to recognize Aniqua, Laren, Tierre, Hazan, Torrie, Dom, Vernita, Corrine, Crishonda, Kourtney, and the rest of my students. Special shout-outs to my 7th period TSS and PS babies Limaris, Winisha, Kyleen, Marvin, Courtney, Miah (keep writing, girl!), Myishea, Vicky, and Aneika. Thank you to my dear friend Lori Hayes for your support and the comraderie. To staff members Ray Theilacker and Daniel Simmons for helping me find my voice,

and pushing me to go beyond the ordinary. Thanks to Marv, Mike, Troy, Kev and the rest of the crew. Last but not least, special thanks to Marv. If you never gave me *Got a Man*, I don't think my writing career would've ever started!

To all of my friends who either helped or encouraged me in some way

Thanks to my sisterfriend Sheila Fisher, who believed in me and celebrated every small victory from day one when I had the idea to write a book. Thanks to Nate for all of your input. Thank you Bryan for my gift; we have grown into a season of maturity. Shout-outs to so many other friends: Karen, Rashida, Nicole, Ayanna, Troy, Claire, Kelley, Lisa, Larry, Michelle, Charlene, Lashawn, Lillet. . . . the list is endless.

To the church families who have nurtured my spiritual growth

I pray God's richest blessings upon Mt. Carmel and Sharon Baptist Church in Philadelphia. Thank you Pastor Albert F. Campbell and Pastor Keith W. Reed for your exemplary leadership.

In Conclusion

To those who are fighting daily battles with AIDS, cancer, and other diseases, keep fighting the good fight. To those in the Armed Forces defending our freedom at any cost, thank you as well. So often, we get wrapped in our tiny little worlds, that we forget that there are those who are fighting real battles every day. Thank you for reminding me to count my blessings.

To my grandmother, the late Lina Christine Pierce, who passed away during the writing of this novel, the heavens have gained another angel.

To every young person and to all of the students whose lives I have touched; I hope that this novel will enrich your life. To everyone else, if I have left anyone out, please charge it to my head and not my heart. One love to the Zeta Phi Beta Sigma family, UMBC, Wynnefield, and the city of Philadelphia.

Sorry to have been so long, but my heart is just overjoyed. Thanks y'all.

Blessings always,

Vonetta Cherisse Pierce

PROLOGUE

"First, the bad news. . . ."

_____Jasmyn

I could feel my heart beating through my chest. My breathing became rapid and I felt beads of sweat emerge along my hairline. Calm down, Jazz. It's not the end of the world; thousands of people get diagnosed and live ordinary lives. Look at Magic Johnson. I could really use a cigarette right about now.

"Ma'am, can I get you something to drink? Water? Ginger ale? Orange juice?" a male nurse asked as he led me to the patient consultation room.

Juice? Water?! What the hell is that gonna do? What was I supposed to do—wash the virus away? Yeah, okay. I guess they would try to be polite after dropping a bombshell on me.

"Yes, I'll take some orange juice, thank you." I wanted to say, _"I'll actually take some Tanqueray with that orange juice. And while you're taking drink orders, Isaac, I'll take an apple martini on the rocks, a sex on the beach with a lime twist, not one, but two Bahama_

Mamas, and pass the Courvoisier too!" But no, I'm not going to get smart with these people. I'll be nice.

I took a deep breath and examined my surroundings. The fluorescent lights were an annoyingly bright yellow—too bright if you ask me. Safe sex posters and pamphlets made up the décor. One poster was of a young Hispanic girl, maybe fifteen years old, holding a STOP sign up in front of her boyfriend with the caption "No Glove, No Love." I shook my head. *Oh, no. I am definitely out of my element in this place. What am I even doing here? I figured I needed to stop putting it off and get an AIDS test. Don't these people see I'm a grown-ass woman, not some teenager wanting birth control, a pregnancy test, or free condoms?*

I wanted anonymity, and at my doctor's private office that wasn't possible. And since I went to middle school with one of the billing clerks, Dr. Angelini's office was definitely out of the question.

So there I was in the Barbara O. Randolph State Center for Health Services, otherwise known in the hood as the "free clinic," tapping my foot and having a nicotine fit.

"Ms. Simmons, would you be so kind as to complete this sexual history form?" the lab tech in a white coat asked me. "Public health policy mandates us to contact any individual who has been exposed to a person with a sexually transmitted disease. We are going to need the complete names, addresses, and phone numbers of any persons you have had sexual contact with in the past seven years. Unfortunately, the HIV virus remains dormant so long we can not be sure of when you actually contracted the virus."

"Yes, of course." I reluctantly took the clipboard and slowly walked to the chair at the furthest side of the waiting room. I still couldn't believe that I, Jasmyn Chantel Simmons—an attractive, fit, sexy 22-year-old woman—was HIV positive. With tears burning, I closed my eyes and thought back to the eleventh grade, when I lost my virginity, and started to complete the forms.

Let's see, there was Terrell—my first. After him . . . okay, now tell me how in the hell am I supposed to remember eleventh grade and whatnot? All right, there was my first real boyfriend, Manny. Then, of course, there was my junior prom date, Jason. Okay, that's three people. All right, let me see, twelfth grade. That's when I really didn't care who I got with 'cause I was so depressed about my dad. Shoot, I even hollered at corny Mike and fat-ass Marquise. Then I met Dre and his cousin, Kenny. All right, after that summer with Kenny, I left for school and met James, Darnell, and Tony during freshman year. Then sophomore year, I messed with Shannon, Charles, and Damon. Then Brandon, Kyle, Maurice, Hassan, Antoine, Lamont, J.R. Hmmm, let me see who else. Um, Omar.

I could barely read the names because of the tears in my eyes. How could I have been such a slut? I mean, I never considered myself a straight-up, official ho. It wasn't like I had a "For Sale" sign between my legs or anything like that. I always got a lot of attention from guys. If I let these people see this list I knew exactly what they'd think. I was so stupid when I was a young girl, letting all those guys hit it—and only using condoms half the time. I shook my head, dabbed my burning eyes with a tissue, and continued writing. *Darnell, Shareef, who worked at the casino, and that nigga who claimed he played for the Sixers—I can't even remember his name. And, of course, my baby Tarik.*

I stopped writing to look at my reflection in the window of the lobby doors. *Let me not lose my composure here. I can't let these folks see me looking a hot mess.* I slicked my shoulder-length black hair back with my moist palm and sucked it up. Facts were facts, and it was time to face the difficult truth. The days of rolling sevens and elevens were over. I suppose fate dealt me just what I deserved. My past had finally caught up with me, and it was about to catch up with a whole lot of other people too.

Looking at the list I had made of more than twenty names stirred up a lot of memories—memories of my younger days when I used men to satisfy my ego and affirm my beauty. Those high school and college days when I used my body to get what I wanted.

After twenty minutes of writing, I sighed and handed the clipboard to the white lab coat guy. Peering at the name embroidered on his uniform, I could make out "R. Barnes." I wondered if this guy had ever gone through anything like this before. He must get into everybody's business working up in this place.

"Thank you, Ms. Simmons." He took the clipboard. "May I call you Jasmyn?"

Is he crazy? Not only did I just hand him a list of all the men I remember sleeping with, but now he wants to be my friend.

I shot dude an evil look and said, "Sure, that's fine, umm, it's—uh, Mr. Barnes?"

"Call me Robert."

I rolled my eyes. *Whatever you say, Robert!*

"Now Ms. Simmons—uh—Jasmyn, I know making this list may have been painful, but I'd like to know, has there ever been a time in your life when you think you might have exposed yourself to a person who was infected? Now, if that is too personal you don't have to answer, but I thought I could perhaps help you sort out some uncertainties."

I looked away, clenched my jaws tightly, and ignored him. *Too personal? Okay, let me see, I just wrote down a list of just about every dude I've ever been with, my entire sexual history, and now you are telling me that you hope you're not getting "too personal?" Last I checked, people were in this clinic because it hurt when they went to go pee, so that's what you do. Make people pee in little cups, take their blood, and inspect their private parts. No man, that's not too personal at all!* I came to the conclusion this guy Robert was an idiot. I reached inside my purse for a cigarette, but came up empty-handed. Damn, I just smoked my last one this morning.

Mr. Barnes continued to probe for a response. "I really don't want to offend you, but I think I can be of help. I counsel many HIV patients here on a regular basis."

"Well, Mr. Barnes—uh, I mean, Robert—I'm only twenty-two years old. I've never used drugs, so more than likely, I got it from unprotected sex." I glanced over at the "This is a Smoke-Free Facility" sign. I really needed a smoke. I only started craving Newports whenever I became nervous or really upset.

"Yes, well, there's nothing to be ashamed of. Most of the clients I am starting to see are young women just like you. Unfortunately, AIDS is plaguing our community, and people of color are seriously being affected. In fact, one of the fastest-growing groups of new AIDS cases happens to be—"

"Ex-cuuuuse you. I don't have AIDS yet." I had to set homeboy straight. I knew a thing or two about the whole HIV thing.

"Yes, yes. I apologize. You can in fact have the virus—"

"—And not the AIDS disease itself. I know!"

I could tell he was getting annoyed with me. "I see you know a lot already, so I won't bore you with facts and figures. If you'd like, I can have you speak with one of our female staff counselors if that would make you feel any better. Meanwhile, by state law, the clinic is required to contact the men you have listed on your sexual health history form. Are you okay with that?"

I nodded. "Do what you have to do."

Better y'all tell them than me. Some of the crazy men I've dated would probably choke the hell out of me if I drop some news on them like that. I could imagine that crazy phone conversation: "Um hello, Tony? It's Jazz. Remember that summer we went to Atlantic City and spent the whole weekend in the hotel? Yeah, you do? And remember, when you told me you were allergic to latex? Yeah? Well tell your wife the two of you need to get an AIDS test because I'm HIV positive, okay? By the way . . . how are things with you? Fine? That's great. Can't talk now, gotta call twenty other men. Bye!" Click!

Mr. Barnes noticed my inattentiveness and cleared his throat to regain my attention. "Well, let me go get Mrs. Calderon. I think you'll enjoy talking to her."

"If you say so." By this point, tears were streaming down my cheeks. He excused himself, took my chart, and returned five minutes later with a young, pretty Hispanic woman.

"Jasmyn, this is Nina Calderon, one of our staff counselors. I told her you might be interested in discussing your situation with her, woman-to-woman."

I looked at Miss J-Lo with a bit of contempt. I mean, did he really think I was going to spill my guts to anyone in here? I shook my head again—in part disbelief, and part desperation. I knew I needed to talk to somebody, and Nina might be as good as anyone else. Considering I had no sisters and only a few close friends, talking to a stranger might make it easier when it came time for me to talk to my loved ones about this ordeal. Besides, the more I looked at her, the more I noticed she seemed down-to-earth, like she had been around the block a few times herself. She gave me a "you-can-trust-me-sis" kind of look and I surrendered.

"Jasmyn, I know this must be the most difficult thing you've ever had to face. Let me assure you, I know exactly what you're going through." Then, she lowered her voice and moved closer toward me. "I've also tested positive for the virus, but look at me, I'm living proof you can carry on a normal life. I've known for three years already."

My eyes widened in disbelief. After three years, I would at least expect her to be skinny like a crack-head or at least have blotchy skin or something, but she looked fabulous. If she were about six inches taller, she probably could've been a model.

Nina turned towards Mr. Barnes after turning the corners of her mouth upwards into a smile. "I think we've got it from here, Rob. Thanks."

"Okay, Nina." He then extended his hand for me to shake. "Pleasure meeting you, Jasmyn. Good luck to you, hon," he said and promptly walked away.

"Jasmyn, do you have time to chat? How about we go into my office?"

"Okay," I tearfully replied and stood up. I gathered my purse and a handful of tissues. We went to a secluded office down the hall.

Once inside, I immediately felt warm and at ease. It was painted a soft ivory color with various works of abstract and ethnic art on the walls. I glanced around at her pictures. It was obvious she was a family woman, as evidenced by the various photos: a picture of a young boy and girl in front of a Christmas tree, a gorgeous husband, and an adorable black puppy. They looked happy in every shot. No sadness. No regret. No tears. I made myself comfortable on her dark green leather sofa as she closed the door.

"Make yourself at home, Jasmyn. Would you like some tea? I can brew a pot. I don't like to think of myself as a shrink, but some clients feel comfortable reclining on that sofa."

I looked at her with slight uneasiness. She smiled, handed me a fresh-smelling pillow, and directed me to take my shoes off. Nina turned on the hot water in her coffee pot and sat back in a large armchair. I accepted her offer. "With sugar and lemon, please."

"Of course," Nina smiled. "There's no other way, is it?" She walked over to the pot and made the tea just how I liked it. Its peppermint aroma was inviting and soothing.

We giggled in amusement. For a minute, I felt like I was at a friend's house, but the manila folders and charts on Nina's desk plunged me back into reality.

"So, before you begin, let me tell you a little about myself, just to break the ice."

She went on to tell me she was twenty-nine years old with two kids, had been married for six years, and learned she acquired HIV from an ex-boyfriend who she was with before she met her husband. Her husband and children were not HIV positive. She had a master's degree in counseling and worked out five days a week, as well as maintained a daily regimen of medicine to keep her immune system healthy. She also stated many people are living full healthy lives with HIV, and, yes, she and her husband Antonio were intimate. He had always loved her and vowed to be with her "in sickness and in health." She said they learned how to express love and intimacy in alternative ways that don't necessarily involve penetration. I appreciated her openness and honesty.

"Well Jasmyn, now you know a little more about me, tell me about yourself and how you think you may have come into contact with this virus."

I looked at her, raised my eyebrows and smirked. "How?!"

We both chuckled a bit. Then, she said, "Girl, I think I know how! But maybe you can tell me a little bit about your past."

"Well, how much time do you have?" I began to let my guard down, and to my surprise, I didn't even feel the need for a cigarette.

"I have all the time you need."

Thoughts of all the things I went through since college started to flood my head. I experienced so many ups and downs. In twenty-two short years, I learned many lessons about life. I didn't have anything else to do, so I decided to lay my soul bare in front of this stranger.

"Well, to be honest, Nina, I think it all started back in college. . . ."

_____*Kyle*

I just walked in the door after working all day. Not five minutes later, the phone rang.

"Can you get that, Kyle?" Tiana yelled. "I'm doing something."

"All right." I darted over to and answered the kitchen telephone. "Hello?"

"Yes. Good afternoon. Is this Mr. Kyle Anthony Clayton?" the voice on the other end asked.

"Yes it is," I answered back with slight hesitation, unsure of the voice.

"Mr. Clayton, this is Robert Barnes from the Department of Public Health, Randolph Health Center Number Five. I need to inform you that you have recently been listed as a person who has had sexual contact with an individual who has tested positive for HIV."

I almost dropped the phone. "What? What person? You're jokin', right?!" I panicked. *This can't be happening.*

"I understand this is difficult news to accept, but

I am legally required to inform and advise you to be tested immediately. We offer free, confidential testing at any of our district health clinics. If you would like, I can arrange—"

I quickly interrupted the cat. "Hol'up, hol' up, hol' up man. Are you telling me I got . . ." I looked around to make sure no one could hear me and lowered my voice. "Man, are you saying I might have H-I-V?! From who? And when did all this happen?"

"Well sir, I am not saying you are infected. I'm just letting you know we conduct HIV screenings every day. This particular young woman came to visit our office a few days ago. She provided us with names and my job is to go down the list and call those previous partners. It protects the patient. I'm sure you understand."

I totally blocked dude out. H-I-V. Just uttering those three deadly letters brought a sense of doom over me as I instantaneously thought of all my girlfriends from high school and college. Without warning, my breathing became labored and my blood pressure began to rise. I felt as if I just completed an hour in the weight room. A bunch of thoughts ran through my head. *How could this be? I've always strapped up. I ain't no homo. I ain't never been locked up, and I damn sure ain't one of them D.L. dudes who sleep with their woman and still let a man run up in 'em. I never got with any hookers or strippers, never had any dirty broads. All of my females have been clean. Think Kyle, think. You're about to get married, man.*

My thoughts were disrupted by the voice on the other end. "Mr. Clayton, patient privacy laws do not allow me to divulge that information. However, as

I was saying, we can offer you testing and counseling at no cost. Now according to our records, the center closest to you would be . . ." Mr. Barnes might as well have been talking to himself.

I put the phone on the counter and faintly heard what he was saying. I began having instant replays of every woman I'd been with since high school. I was always a good guy. I mean, all guys sow their wild oats, don't they? Now some stranger is telling me I might have caught the bug from some slut from God-knows-when and I can't even know who the chick is?

"Babe," Tiana called from the hallway. "Who was that on the phone?" Regaining my composure, I played it off. "Uh, no thank you, we're satisfied with our long-distance company." I hung up on Mr. Barnes who was saying "Hello? Hello? Is anyone there?"

I caught my breath, relaxed for a few seconds, and redirected my attention toward my beautiful fiancée, admiring her butter pecan complexion and dark brown naturally wavy hair that was gathered back in a low ponytail. "Nobody, baby. Just a telemarketer." Damn, I'm lucky to have a woman so fine.

Tiana laughed and shook her head. "Those companies must call you every month, right babe?" I glanced down at the issue of *Modern Bride* she had rolled up and tucked under her arm and nodded with a smile. If only Tiana knew what that phone call was really about, she probably would have cussed me out, threw all my clothes in my car, and set it on fire the way Angela Bassett did in *Waiting to Exhale*. *But, wait—I didn't sleep with anybody, so I should be straight!*

Jayda rode her scooter across the kitchen floor and bumped into my leg. "Beep-beep!" she said with an innocent laugh. All I could do was look at her and hold back my tears. She had been through so much already with her biological father and she hadn't even turned two yet. It pained me to know I might possibly bring even more drama into this precious little girl's life.

I wished all of this was a big practical joke. I tried to blame my best friend. Leave it to Shawn to play a prank. But, there were no hidden cameras. Shawn was nowhere around. This was my hard-core reality.

I vowed to find this mystery woman. It took me too long to hook up with the love of my life. I've had girlfriends before and even hooked up with a few chicks at Marshall State. Nevertheless, I didn't consider myself all that much sexually active when compared to a lot of guys I knew who slept with different women each week. Let me see, there was Simone and Renee back in high school, but they were virgins. At Marshall, there was Aliya, Jasmyn, Damaris . . . um who else. . . . oh, Latoya. Then, of course, Tiana, my angel. This is why I picked a church girl in the first place. They're supposed to be clean, right? What if she was keeping secrets from me? We've been together for a couple of years. I'm going to make her my wife and adopt her daughter. This is all supposed to work out. It couldn't possibly be her.

I gave myself a headache stressing over the "what-ifs?" As I absorbed it all, the recollection of my days of "wilding out" at Marshall brought themselves to the forefront of my memory. Well, the two girls in high school were virgins, so they're probably out. I got with Tiana right after my senior year of college, but she was with one person before me, so more than likely it's not her. I guess I'm left with those Marshall broads. Marshall held good memories and prepared me to become a software engineer at a prestigious telecommunications firm. It's ironic that I was always the one giving advice to my boys and discouraging them from making poor decisions, but now, I couldn't figure out what to do for myself. The only thing was to walk through those Marshall memories.

In the meantime, I went to change out of my work clothes and kissed Tiana and Jayda goodbye. I needed to go clear my head.

PART ONE:

THE COLLEGE YEARS
"I just wanna 'do me' . . . ."

Jasmyn

I rolled over and slowly opened my eyes, realizing that, once again, I was not in my own bed. Spotting the posters of Donovan McNabb, Janet Jackson, and Jay-Z on the wall, I knew I was in Damon's room. Damon was on the football team and had to be in the weight room on Saturday mornings by seven-thirty, ready to lift. I wore him out last night and knew his trainer was bound to yell at him. I laughed to myself. _That's what he gets . . . leaving me by myself in this nasty room._ Damon and his roommate did not know the meaning of vacuum, nor that the purpose of hangers was to hang clothes.

I heard the faint sound of Alicia Keys playing on FOXY 104.9 FM. I sang along in my head as I scanned the room for my clothes. Luckily, this happened to be one time his roommate Brandon was not asleep in the other bed. Brandon was in his girlfriend's room. She lived in Leidy Hall, which was also my dormitory. Damon and Brandon stayed in McKennan, one of the newer dorms built for the

athletes. Brandon was on the swim team and was a
senior. Damon, also a senior, was a star running
back for our college—Marshall State University—a
mid-size college located forty miles outside Philadelphia. Now me? I was no athlete. Hmm, let's say
I was an "athletic supporter." Not a jock strap, mind
you. I enjoyed the company of physically fit, strong,
popular men. My best friend Crystal called me a
future NFL and NBA groupie. She told me all the
time I was gonna be one of those chicks hanging
out by the back gate and locker rooms before the
end of the fourth quarter, but that wasn't the case
with Damon.

We met last semester in my dorm lobby while he
was hanging out with one of his boys. Ever since
the end of April, we were officially a couple. We
stayed together all summer and I didn't cheat on
him once. Well, define "cheat." I may have hung
out with one or two male associates, but I didn't
call that cheating. Damon was good to me, but I'd
started to feel like I needed to meet other guys.

I looked on the floor near the foot of the bed.
My fuchsia bikini panties were strewn on top of
one of Damon's Timberlands. My jeans were
draped on the back of his chair and my shirt was
on his desk. I looked around and finally noticed
my bra was between the headboard and the corner
of the mattress. An unused condom was on the
floor next to the bed with a slight tear in the corner. We used one during the first round, but during our second and third rounds I told him I'd
much rather feel him skin-on-skin. I'd been on the
patch for years, so pregnancy was never a real concern.

I was nineteen years old, had been sexually active for three years, and was pregnant twice. Both times I miscarried, so it was no big deal. Of course, I think that time I was messing with Shannon last year, all the fighting, yelling, and pushing matches we had had something to do with my last miscarriage.

Shannon was the reason I definitely didn't take any mess from these dudes. Our last rumble left me with a scar on my leg. We fought over phone numbers he found while digging through my pocketbook. He claimed he was looking for my lighter, but I knew he was trying to be nosy. I was already hot with him because I lost the baby. He had the nerve to choke me and throw me on the bed. With all the fighting and knocking stuff around, I managed to scrape my calf on the jagged edge of the bed frame. Needless to say, I was on my cell phone with the quickness. Although Shannon and I made up, he promptly received a visit from my cousin Scoop and a few of his boys from North Philly. They were on campus within an hour and a half. Storming past our security desk, they came to Shannon's room where we were both asleep, woke us up, and proceeded to beat his ass. Now, Shannon has transferred colleges and last I heard, he was somewhere far, very far, upstate.

Anyway, Shannon was officially "Black History." My main objective for now was to get dressed and go back to my room to shower and go back to sleep. I pulled my clothes together and prepared to get dressed when I heard keys rattling at the door. *Awww . . . Damon, poor baby, Coach must've told him to go back to his room. Well good, that means when he comes in, we can lay here for a little while longer.* Halfway dressed, I decided to stand up and surprise him.

"Heyyy baby," I purred with arms outstretched. I was stunned to see Brandon walk in with a duffel bag over his shoulder. He immediately stopped in his tracks.

"Jaaasmyn? Um, hey. What's up?" Brandon looked at my half-buttoned top and eye-catching panties. He may have been a white guy, but he was definitely taking in all my Nubian beauty.

"My bad, Brandon." I sat down on Damon's bed feeling real embarrassed at first. I took the comforter and tried to cover the bottom half of my body.

"Um . . . uh, I'm sorry Jasmyn. I guess I should've called first. I didn't know Damon was having company." Brandon lowered his head. I noticed his cheeks were flushed as he hurried to his side of the room. I heard him throw his duffel bag down and take off his shoes. Yeah, Brandon was definitely a cutie. He had the look that made you wonder if he ever acted before. He reminded me of Brad Pitt and the guy who played Joey on *Friends*, both of whom were fine white guys in my book.

I rethought my decision to return to my dorm room and decided to climb back under the covers of Damon's bed. I yelled over to Brandon, "Do you mind if I just get a little more rest before I head back over to Leidy?"

"Sure, I don't mind."

Of course he didn't mind. Most men wouldn't! I'd never been with a white guy before, but I'd always wondered what it would be like. I knew Damon wasn't coming back till after eleven. The team always went to breakfast after working out on Saturday mornings.

"So how's Ashley?" I asked.

"She's okay. I hung out over there last night, but we got into this huge argument. She caught a major attitude because I told her I was going home to Baltimore next weekend and wasn't taking her with me."

Puh-leeeease. Is that all? Shoot, I love for a man to be out of my hair—so Jasmyn can do Jasmyn. I can be me and free to do what I want. Just like I was about to do.

I turned on a sympathetic tone. "Wow, Brandon. I'm sorry to hear that." Then deciding to switch the vibe, I put on my suburban girl voice. "Hey, what you over there doing? It sounds mighty quiet!" I joked.

"Just laying here. Thinking . . ."

"Thinking? Awww, about Ashley?" I sweetly asked.

"Yeah, I guess. But, I'm getting tired of her drama-queen episodes. I've been thinking of being single again. What 'cha think about that, Jasmyn? I'm crazy, huh?"

Not really, cute white boy. I smiled a devilish grin and contemplated my next move, which would take a lot of guts. I pulled back the covers and took off my top.

"Jasmyn? You still there? Are you asleep?" Brandon asked.

I walked over in my bra and panties and sat on the edge of his bed.

"You know, Brandon, I've always thought you were handsome."

Seducing this man was going to be a piece of cake. Men, I don't care what color they are, act so stupid when they know they're about to get some.

He sat straight up and gazed straight at my chest in awe and admiration. He began stumbling over his words. "Um, uh . . . Jasmyn?" He nervously looked around. "Don't you think you should put some clothes on?"

"Have you ever been with a sista, Brandon?" I ignored his suggestion, straddled him and stroked his face, all the while remaining on top of the covers. The thrill of being caught made my adrenaline rush.

"Actually, one or two." he confessed. "I've always thought you all were sexy. But uh . . . I don't think, um, my uh, roommate—"

"Damon?"

"Um, yeah, Damon. He's not gonna be happy—I mean I can't, uh, you know, do this to him. I mean, Jasmyn—I have a girlfriend, and you know . . ."

Oh yeah, look at him—stuttering and everything. This is going to be too easy.

Ignoring him, I leaned against his chest and laid his head back on the pillow. In his ear I whispered, "Brandon, do you think I'm sexy?"

Feeling his manhood through the covers and being quite impressed, I didn't wait for a verbal reply. His nonverbal reaction was all I needed. I kissed him on his mouth and he held nothing back.

We did what came naturally and all the while I wondered why I was doing it. Maybe I had an addiction. I liked Damon, but Brandon was a cutie too and when an opportunity presents itself, I don't let it get away. I knew it was a slut-move, but I couldn't help myself.

"Hold on, baby." I went over to Damon's side of the room and picked up the condom we didn't use last night. I returned to Brandon, handed it to him, and said, "Here, let me help you put this on. . . ."

If I was going to sleep with two guys within twelve hours, roommates at that, the least I could do was use protection.

Thirty minutes later, satisfied at my conquest, I took a quick shower and put my clothes on. I reflected on my accomplishments of finally doing it with a white guy, doing two guys on the same day, doing my man's friend behind his back, and managing to escape. It was nothing personal against Damon—he was still my boo, but I had to do me, you know? As I walked back to Leidy I glimpsed at my cell phone for the time. *Ten-forty. Twenty minutes to spare. Damn, the things I could've done in those twenty minutes. . . .*

My fantasies were abruptly cut short by the ringing of my cell phone. The words "DAMON cell" flashed on the caller ID.

"Hi boo," I answered the phone. "I miss you. I've spent all morning thinking about you."

I asked Damon to hold on while I fished through my purse to find my last cigarette. I lit it and began to feel calm and relaxed.

"Okay boo, I'm back. So tell me, how was practice?"

_____ ___*Kyle*

"Yo man, did you line my edges up right this time?" I swear I hate bootleg barbers. They always charge too damn much and half the time they mess your head up with their dirty-ass clippers. My boy Moe was a bootleg barber on campus. He lived in Leidy Hall, which was two dorms down from mine, and usually gave me my weekly shape-up in his room.

"Fifteen dollars, kid." Moe snatched the towel from around my neck as he tossed his clippers on the desk.

"Fifteen?! Nigga, that's the 'round the way price. Come on, Moe man, I only got five."

I picked up his hand mirror and had to admit my Caesar cut looked pretty sharp now that he trimmed away the excess growth. Moe had skills, but he thought he could charge outrageous prices, as though he was Puffy's personal stylist .

Moe stepped back, looked at his work, and proudly proclaimed, "Yo family, I lined you up nice. You know all them Banneker freaks gonna be on you." He snapped the towel at me, yelling "Go 'head, Cat Dad-day! Pop ya collar, son!"

Banneker referred to Benjamin Banneker Residence Hall, a dorm famous for housing some of the tightest females on campus.

"Aiight. Thanks, man." I handed Moe a five-dollar bill and gave him a ghetto handshake. I sat down on the side of his bed and picked up one of his video game controllers off the floor.

"Which one of y'all wanna get spanked in some Madden?" I challenged. Since I have two younger brothers at home, Jamir and Ty, I was a beast on PlayStation 2. My specialty was Madden NFL. Every time a new version came out, I perfected my skills in it, learning all the strategies needed to win.

My boy Shawn broke open a Black and Mild cigar and proceeded to empty its tobacco contents into a nearby trash can. "Yo, Kyle, I got you."

"Ay yo, I got next!" Moe's roommate Raheem added.

Shawn continued to open a tiny pale blue cellophane pouch and poured its potent, addictive contents inside the cigar's wrapper. After making sure he had enough weed, he licked the wrapper closed and sealed each end by pressing it closed with his already dark, smoked-out lips.

"Where you goin' tonight, cousin?" I asked my long-time childhood friend.

"Probably the Kappa party over at the S.A.C. Y'all tryna roll?" Shawn offered. He lit the blunt and began smoking, filling the air with the distinct odor everyone from the 'hood is familiar with.

"Hell yeah!" Raheem and I responded. Moe was on his cell phone, but he looked in our direction and responded with a nod.

S.A.C. was short for the Student Activities Center, the campus hangout where there were stores, a café, an arcade, game room, and a large ballroom where parties were often held.

Shawn gently held his blunt and continued to puff slowly. Sparking up was a common practice for Shawn and the rest of my boys.

"Ay, yo. Puff, puff, pass, nigga!" Moe looked up, directing Shawn to pass the blunt around.

By then, I'd become so used to the scent of weed, it didn't bother me like it used to back in the day. I know if Mom-Dukes or, for that matter, anyone from my church back home would've seen us sitting here in college passing around blunts, they would probably have passed out.

Shawn and I were best friends for as long as I could remember. We grew up in Hilltop, the Overbrook section of West Philadelphia. We lived on the same block and attended high school together. Our families were close and attended the same church. In fact, Shawn's mom was my godmother, and my mom was his.

Since we'd graduated three years before, we'd been tighter than ever. When it came down to choosing a college, there was no doubt in my mind I was going with my dog. The longer we stayed away from home, it felt like the more ill stuff we got ourselves into. That included getting high, drinking alcohol, and partying two or three nights a week. We often took road trips to other schools— Lincoln, Cheyney, Temple, Delaware State, and even Morgan, which was in Baltimore.

"Did y'all know Marshall rejected blood donations from that blood drive last week?" I asked.
"They found a whole bunch of hepatitis and HIV
in it."

"Nah, son," Moe replied. "I ain't hear about no
shit like that."

"Yeah, kid. It was in the campus newspaper."
Apparently, out of all my friends, I was the only
one who kept up on current events. I also held the
highest grade point average out of all my boys—a
3.2. As a computer science and business double
major, I couldn't afford to mess up.

Ignoring my campus news, Raheem nudged my
elbow with the slowly shortening blunt held tightly
between his thumb and middle finger. "Toke this,
nigga. Dis dat ole' chronic shit for real." He smiled
and threw his head back, enjoying every puff.

"Naah, I'm all right." I rejected his offer and focused on the game and beating Shawn. I was
Daunte Culpepper from the Minnesota Vikings
and my team was stomping all over Shawn's Miami
Dolphins. I smoked with my boys from time to
time, but I still wasn't totally down with the weed
thing. I'd seen too many of my boys get high and
turn into totally different people. It was true what
they said about marijuana: it was definitely mind-
altering. When I smoked, it messed with my memory. I couldn't study or take tests.

Shawn laughed and screwed up his face at me.
"Go 'head, Kyle! You Madden-Tecmo Bowl-playin'
mutha —"

"Aiight! Damn, if it will shut you the hell up!" I
quickly interrupted Shawn. I put the game on
pause and snatched the blunt from Raheem's fingers. I'd be twenty years old the next month. Yet,

like a young boy, I still gave in to peer pressure. But I had to laugh to myself at Shawn's reference to the old-school handheld video game. Tecmo Bowl went way back like Connect Four and Operation. Back in the day my older cousins used to let me play theirs all the time.

I slowly inhaled and exhaled a rapid puff of smoke. I inhaled once more; this time it was a nice, slow drag.

As I released the smoke, I handed the blunt back to Shawn. I looked over at my roommate and announced, "Yo, Shawn, I'm 'bout to be out." My voice took on the crackly deep characteristic of every weed smoker. I took the game off pause and began wildly pressing various button combinations on the game controller.

"Nigga, we're only in the second quarter," Shawn protested. "I'm down by seven."

"Nah, family." I paused the game again. "Plus, I can spank dat ass anytime."

Shawn put out his blunt on the lid of an empty Heineken can and placed the game controller back with the rest of the PlayStation 2 equipment. He stood up and announced he was leaving with me.

Shawn and I told them we'd call them later before walking to the party tonight. I gave myself one last peek in the mirror, smoothing my fade. I gave my boys some dap and said goodbye.

Marshall wasn't a predominantly black college, but damn if it didn't feel like one from time to time, especially in dorms, where there was a high

percentage of black students. One good thing
about attending a racially mixed university was
that I experienced what it was like to attend a
school with people who didn't look like me. My
high school was ninety-five percent Black, so it was
good to see something other than brown faces all
the time.

Another advantage was that I was surrounded
by beautiful white, Latina, and Asian women—all
the flavors: vanilla, caramel, and butterscotch.
There were always women ready and willing to experience some chocolate.

In my few short months there, I'd had five white
girls, three Puerto Ricans, and one Japanese babe
try to get at me. They either flirted with me on
campus or tried to get me to be their study partner
in class. I hadn't hollered back at any of them so
far. I was a junior and had one girlfriend on campus: Aliya. She was on the track team. We were together five months until I found out she cheated
on me with half the team. So I vowed this year to
stop attending meets and events just to avoid her.
Anyway, Aliya was last year's news. I was a year
older and wiser.

Besides, I left part of my heart back home in
Philly.

I had a soft spot for nice, pretty, church girls.
There were several of them at Mt. Zion, where I attended. However, there was one—the perfect female—Tiana. She was like a sister to me, and I
didn't think she ever figured out how much I really
dug her. Besides, she never thought more of me
than a "play brother," so I decided just to do me
and stay single. I thought maybe I'd get to holla at

Tiana one day, but for then, there was a campus full of dime pieces waiting. I just had to pick one who wasn't a slut like Aliya.

When Shawn and I arrived back at Banneker Hall, we chilled. He went to sleep and I decided to study my accounting. It was around seven-thirty on a Thursday night and I knew we wouldn't be going to the party until ten. In college, Thursday seemed to be the official kick-off to the weekend. I knew I might as well try to do something right since my grades were slipping. With all the women, alcohol, and other distractions, it was hard to maintain the GPA I'd effortlessly earned in high school. I even read the Bible back home, but I didn't even know what I did with the one I brought to school.

The phone rang, interrupting my concentration on the assets chart I was reading.

"Young boy!" Raheem's voice greeted me on the other end. "Where punk-ass Shawn at?" he joked. Raheem and Shawn were "smoke-out" buddies. Shawn knew even though we were like brothers, I didn't enjoy getting high and drinking nearly as much as he did. I guess you could say to an extent, I was still a "good boy."

"That nigga's 'sleep!" I laughed.

"Well look, what's up with you taking your boy in town?" It figured. This fake-ID carrying dude probably wanted a ride to the liquor store. Raheem always used Shawn as a ride to this place and that place. If it wasn't "Was'sup man? Let me get a ride to Acme," it was "Yo, let me hold your whip tonight so I can go see my shorty at Lincoln." Shawn was always dumb enough to oblige, but this time, I wasn't going to wake him up.

"Come on, man," Raheem continued to beg. "It'll be real quick."

"Man, look, I'm trying to study." These niggas had averages barely over a 2.0, so studying was not a priority for them. I doubted any of them would graduate on time.

"Come on, K, man. Stop bitchin'! I'mma give you gas money. Damn! Just come on. Let that fat-ass nigga Shawn sleep. He'll be up by the time we get back."

What does the Bible say in Romans chapter seven? "When I would do good, evil is present with me." Or something like that. It's funny how Bible verses have a way of popping in your head at the craziest times. I guess when you've been brought up in the church all your life, some things won't easily go away.

The Bible verse left my mind just as swiftly as it entered. I reluctantly gave in to Raheem's request for a ride. "All right, Heem man, be downstairs in my lobby in ten minutes."

"All right. One." Raheem hung up.

Another night of drinking and wilding out was about to begin. I just wondered how deep I was going to get.

_____*Jasmyn*

The phone in my room rang and I didn't want to answer it. I let it ring. On Mondays, I tried to concentrate on studying and didn't answer my phone much. I was more than halfway through college and didn't want to flunk out. I thought it might have been Kyle, a guy I met at the Kappa party the other night.

Kyle had a caramel brown complexion and reminded me of the R & B singer Usher. I watched him post up on the wall with his boy Shawn who messed with my friend Crystal. She had a man back home, but as she put it, "they have an understanding" while she was away at school. They were both on the heavy side and looked cute together. My girl was a diva like me and she could rock a size eighteen/twenty like it was nothing. When we went to the mall, she could turn it out in Lane Bryant, for sure.

Anyway, Shawn was with his boy Kyle and I no-

ticed him looking at me, so I introduced myself to
him. It wasn't like we hadn't seen each other before, so when we met, we clicked automatically.
For the rest of the night, we danced and talked.
After the party, we chilled in his room with Shawn
and Crystal. Their friend Raheem went to the
liquor store earlier that night and brought back
some Henessey, Heinekens, and Jack Daniels'
Lynchburg Lemonade. We drank quite a bit, except for Kyle, who only finished half of his Jack
Daniels. Everyone had Friday classes, but I didn't
make it to any of mine.

As for Damon, he had been acting funny the
whole week since I slept with Brandon. I don't
know if he told Damon or what, but whenever I
saw him on campus with Ashley, I gave him a flirtatious grin that made him get nervous and look
away. I acted normal around Damon and even
spent the night over there two more times the
week before while Brandon was in the room.
Whenever I got up to use the bathroom, I made
sure Damon was asleep so I could walk over to
Brandon and kiss on him. After the last night I
spent over there, which was Saturday, I called
Damon and told him I wanted to chill for a few
weeks until final exams were over. The truth was, I
wanted to get to know Kyle better, but with a popular guy like Damon, I had to keep our relationship under wraps. If I wanted to see either of
them, it was going to have to be during a late-night
rendezvous meeting. Public on-campus displays of
affection would be out of the question. Lucky for
me, I didn't see any of them on campus and I ate
early in the dining hall before most people came.

On top of that, we lived in separate dorms, none of which were right next to one another.

I had a single room because I loved having my privacy. I was getting some reading in, but couldn't seem to remain uninterrupted because for the third time, the phone rang. I tried to ignore it, but couldn't any longer.

Whoever this is, it must be important. They didn't even try to call my cell phone. The only people who called the room and not my cell phone were the Office of Financial Aid, pizza delivery guys, and one other person—Jerome.

I looked at the caller ID. I made special arrangements with the phone company and with the dorm director that, along with a private phone line, I'd like to have caller ID service. True ball-ettes like myself could not survive without this great invention.

"STATE OF DE" flashed on the caller ID screen.

I live in New Jersey. I go to school in Pennsylvania. There is only one call I would be getting from Delaware.

My brother Jerome.

I picked up the phone.

"You have a collect call from an inmate at Smyrna Hill Correctional Facility. Will you accept the charges?"

Didn't I always? "Yes," I said and immediately looked at my watch so I would know exactly how long I talked on the phone.

"What up, girl?" I had to admit, Jerome's voice was always something I looked forward to hearing every week.

"Heyyy, man!" I yelled into the receiver. Prison always seemed to be a loud, chaotic place. Smyrna was no exception. "Damn, it's loud on the pod tonight, huh? What? You decided to call early tonight? It's not even eight o'clock yet."

"I know. So what's up? You coming down to see your big brother next Sunday since you dissed me yesterday?"

"Boy, ain't nobody diss you. I had a date Saturday night. I wasn't even in my room most of the day."

"I know. I called you." Damn. I felt a little guilty because I really should have been there for Jerome. I was the only one who came to visit him on Sundays.

"I saw you on the caller ID, but it's not like I can call the prison, now can I?" I joked.

Jerome sucked his teeth and huffed. "Whatever, Jazz. Ya ass always got jokes. So, when you gonna hook me up with one of them college babes? I know ya'll got mad females up there."

"Negro, don't nobody want you," I laughed. I knew I had a mouthpiece on me, always getting smart with somebody.

"Well, see if you can send me some pictures of 'em."

"We'll see. But they've got better things to do besides writing you and your boys."

"Well look, I get private visits in a few months so you gots ta hurry up. A brother getting lonely with these magazines, ya feel me?"

"Okay, Jerome. I don't want you creeping around with no niggas in there. If you drop the soap, leave it on the floor!" Jerome and I started cracking up.

"Come on, Jazz. You know your brother better than that. You know I'mma be in here for a minute.

I still got another year till I'm out on probation, you know. Then, I'mma have all the—"

"I know, all the women you can possibly get!" Jerome loved the opposite sex as much as I did.

We talked for a few more minutes. I always limited our calls to ten minutes. He called at least twice a week and I visited him at least twice a month.

No sooner had I hung up, there was a knock on my door. It was Crystal. I told her to come in.

"Girl, you done studying?" she asked. One thing I could say was Crystal respected my Monday study time.

"Just about. I was almost done highlighting this Sociology chapter when my crazy-behind brother called."

"Awwww. . . ." Crystal picked up the framed picture of me and Jerome from back in the day dressed up on Halloween as Michael and Janet Jackson. "Girrrlll," she started laughing hysterically, "you and this old Rhythm Nation key hanging off that earring . . . and look at Jerome, with that one glove and white slouch socks! I bet you thought y'all were the hottest thing in South Philly!"

I snatched the frame and playfully shoved her. I gave her a sneer and told her, "Fall back, cousin. Don't hate. You know if Jerome wasn't locked up, you'd be all on him. At least I'd trust him with you and not some of these chickenhead broads running around here." The fact was, Jerome was a good-looking guy who always had lots of female attention. I guess it ran in the family.

"I know you can't wait for him to come home."

"Yeah, I mean, since my dad died, it's like our whole world was rocked. Who expected him to go to work and not come home?" I thought back to how wonderful my life was a few years ago.

We had the near perfect black suburban life: two successful working parents, one son, and one daughter. We lived the classic urban fairy-tale: lower-middle class family works hard, moves out of the ghetto, and goes from being a public-transportation to a two-automobile family. Like the Jeffersons, we "moved on up" out of our South Philly rowhouse and over the bridge to our deluxe four bedroom single-family home in an upwardly-mobile town called Willingboro, New Jersey. Then, exactly two years to the date after we moved, my dad died.

"I mean, Crystal, we said 'bye to him for one of his weekly runs . . ." I felt tears welling up and I started shaking my head as my voice quivered. I cried about this at least a hundred times and Crystal had heard this story at least fifty times. That was why she was my best friend. ". . . and I mean, he drove that truck all over the country week after week. And we always said 'Daddy, make sure you drink your coffee and stay awake' and next thing you know, my mom got a call from his boss saying he fell asleep on the interstate outside of Chicago—all 'cause that fucking department store needed their shipment before six a.m. Who the hell do they think they are?!" I began yelling and crying uncontrollably. "Crystal, I was only sixteen! I lost my daddy because some big executive had to have a delivery on time. And you know what it was? Socks and ties! Can you believe that mess? My dad died trying to rush some stupid-ass socks and ties halfway across the country! My dad never saw his baby girl go to the prom, graduate from high school, go off to college—none of that! He won't be around to see me get married, have kids—nothing!"

Crystal put her arm around me as consolation and hugged me tight. I really needed that hug. My mom wasn't around anymore to do it. After Daddy died, she had a nervous breakdown and has never been right since. I mean, Jerome and I suffered our post-traumatic stress disorder, but my mom just went to a whole other level. When she became suicidal we placed her in Meadowpines Mental Health Facility a few miles from my home in Willingboro, New Jersey. After about six months, she got out, but in the past few years, she's had several relapses, going through bouts of depression as well as anxiety attacks. The doctors thought she had a hormonal imbalance prior to Daddy's death, and that the tragedy of losing a loved one was so severe, it pushed her over the edge. As such, she couldn't sustain a decent quality of life for herself, let alone maintain the responsibility of owning and keeping up a large home. She spent so much time in and out of Meadowpines, I think being around the nut cases in there made her a little bit more 'thrown off' each time she got out. Now we refer to her as Adrienne; she doesn't feel like a mother-figure with any type of authority anymore.

As usual, Crystal tried to comfort me with religion. "It's gonna be all right, Jazz. God knows all about it. He wouldn't put more on you than you could bear . . ."

I looked up at her with that "Don't-even-go-there" look. Crystal knew that me and God didn't mix well together.

First, her God took away the two most important people in my life—one physically and the other one mentally. When my brother tried to hustle to keep a roof over our heads, he got arrested because he refused to snitch on his boys. For carrying with the intent to sell, he should've received a few years max, but being that he was on the interstate in Wilmington, Delaware, they threw the book at him. Not only did he get charged with drug possession with the intent to deliver and sell across state lines, he was also charged with forgery for some counterfeit money his boy gave him to deliver along with the drugs. To top it all off, he was driving a vehicle which had the VIN scratched off. His boy Lee, who he was with, was carrying a gun and was a repeat offender, so he got an automatic felony charge and was sent to a New York federal prison. Once you combined drugs and guns, the charges became deeper. Luckily, Jerome only received six years total, but because it was his first offense and he had good behavior, they managed to cut it down to three and a half years. So far, he has served two and a half years, which means Jerome is not scheduled to get out of jail until next year. With more good behavior and possibly an East Coast-Johnnie Cochran type of lawyer, he could probably get an appeal, get that last year knocked off, and maybe get out early and do two years of probation.

"Crystal, please. Don't go there. I don't even

feel like hearing none of that 'keep-your-head-up' mess right now. I'll be all right," I assured her.

"Look, Jazz, I'll go down there with you this weekend coming up if you want. You need to put money on his books, don't you?"

Besides knowing that Jerome was incarcerated and even helping me out by putting some of her own money in his commissary, Crystal also knew about Jerome's secret money stashes. Before he went in, he stashed sixty thousand dollars in different places. Places no one, not even the police, would think to look, such as under the spare tire in the trunk of the Honda Civic my dad bought me for my sixteenth birthday. He also stashed it in plastic bags under mattresses, inside a hole he busted in the wall behind a painting, inside air vents, and even under the lid of our piano. I'd be the first to admit our family has a little more cash than the average black family. My mom was a loan representative at a bank and earned a decent salary.

From truck driving, my dad saved a lot of money, and, consequently, in his will, there was a huge sum of money left to help take care of household expenses. For the first year after he passed away, we were pretty well-set financially speaking, but the closer it came for me to go to college, the more Jerome started to worry that the family would need more money. He didn't want me to have to work my way through school and take out student loans. That's when he hooked up with one of his former buddies from South Philly and began selling drugs. He started small—just a few bags of weed here and there, just enough to bring in a couple hundred dollars a week. Soon, guys began asking him to do major drop-offs as far as D.C. and Virginia. Eventually, he got into the cocaine and heroine game with some guys from New York. He started doing bigger sales, making larger transactions, and more money.

One night on his way to do a drop-off in D.C., they were pulled over in Lee's Lexus. The car was searched and, of course, the rest is history. They both got arrested and locked up immediately. Since the worst thing in the streets, in the drug game, in jail, and just in the hood period, is being called a snitch, Jerome and Lee took the rap for the whole thing, never revealing who they worked for. Call me a rat, a snitch, whatever. If it's going down and I'm with one of my girls, and I'm doing a favor for say, Crystal, or another one of my friends, and we get pulled over by the cops—oh, best believe, I'm name-dropping like a mug. 'Cause if this chick goes down, I'm taking every chick with me. I guess it's different for men because the old schoolyard saying really does apply: "Snitches get stitches and body bags in ditches."

Crystal gave me a half-hearted smile. "Aww, girl, you gonna be all right, you'll see, watch. Your brother will be out sooner than you think. You'll be so busy celebrating, you're gonna have to give me some of your men."

I broke my seriousness and asked lightheartedly, "Gim-me?! Excuse me, but um, 'gimme' got shot!"

"Okay, my bad—you won't have to give them to me. I'll just borrow a few!"

"Girl, please. You are a trip! You know you can't

keep up with me!" We both laughed and I appreciated my friend cheering me up and taking my
mind off my brother.

Crystal and I chilled in my room for the next
couple of hours. She filled me in on her latest hap-
penings with Shawn, as well as her boyfriend
Corey. I, in turn, gave her the update on Kyle and
Damon. I never told her what went down with
Brandon, though. I had to keep that filed in my
personal triple-X-rated-too-hot-for-TV files. Even
though Crys was my girl, she was still a female, so
she had that hater potential inside of her. If it ever
got out what I did with Damon's roommate, my
rep would be shot, and there was no telling what
repercussions I would face from Damon. I may be
bold and aggressive when it comes to the bedroom, but truth be told, I am well aware of what an
upset man, especially one of Damon's size and
strength, is capable of doing. I didn't want to get
anybody beat up again. Last time, my cousins were
fortunate; they didn't catch any assault charges for
attacking Shannon. I found no need to push my
luck again.

While we were having our usual talk, I kept thinking of how much I needed to get into Crystal's
head in order to find out everything I could about
Kyle. From messing around with Shawn, surely she'd
been around him a few times. I wanted to know his
past in order to be in his future. He had a sensual
aura about him that was unavoidable. It was as
though women were drawn to him because he didn't
look like the pursuing type.

"You know what, girl? I think Kyle is playing
hard to get, but it's cool. You know me, I'm up for

the challenge, no doubt." I slapped hands with Crystal in our usual fashion. "And watch, when I do get him, I am definitely going to keep him around for a while. I think me and him look good together."

"Girl, you stay messing with these men, don't you?" Crystal shook her head, smiling to herself. "So, you not with Damon anymore? With his fine self. Girrrl, you crazy 'cause it's plenty females on this campus on your boy."

"Well, they can have him. I'm not sweating him. You know Jazz don't sweat nobody but Jazz, o-kayyyy?!" I laughed and slapped fives with her again.

I looked at the clock, which read nine-twenty. A soft knock came at the door. Crystal got up to answer it. It was Kyle.

She flashed a mischievous smile at me, singing, "Jazz, you got com-pa-nyyyy."

I nodded to say okay and gave her a look signaling, "Girl, it's time for you to go!"

She took the hint. "Well, let me get back upstairs to my room. My show is about to come on anyway. I'mma see you later, girl." She waved and turned to my new man. "See you, Kyle. Tell your boy he better call me," she said jokingly as she left.

"All right, Crystal. Call me," I said behind her. I looked at Kyle, who had walked in, dressed comfortably in a pair of gray baggy sweatpants, a gray hoodie, fresh pure-white sweat socks, and slide-in flip flops. He looked like a casual, laid-back guy who still had a little hood in him at the same time. Kyle struck me as one of those nice-dressing smart guys who wasn't a cornball, but ten percent thug, ninety percent everything else. Inside I wanted to explode with excitement because my new boo came to see me. He was empty-handed, so I knew the last thing we would be doing was studying, which was good. I was tired and ready to chill for a while before going to bed. Hopefully, this would become an everyday occurrence and Kyle would spend every evening with me.

_____*Kyle*

It was eight-thirty on a Monday night. I was getting tired of looking at my Microsoft A+ book. I was good enough at computers; programming didn't come too hard for me. *I will be so glad when next May rolls around and I can walk out this piece with my dual bachelor of science in information systems and business management, strut into any Fortune 500 company, and demand a corner office with a window and a starting salary of no less than sixty thousand as a software engineer or programmer.* Once I was settled for about a year or so, I planned to get married, buy a nice house in the suburbs, and have a kid or two.

Finding Mrs. Right was going to be a task in and of itself. There were so many fine women at college, I constantly asked myself, "How can a brotha choose?" After Aliya, I told myself I wasn't going to get serious with any more broads on campus. I pretty much kept that promise. Since Aliya, I was with one other person—some chick named Latoya.

She was some girl I hooked up with after we met at a Black Student Union party. She was from West Chester University, another local college. We went to her apartment, did our thing, and never spoke to each other again. I used protection, so as long as I didn't get any phone calls telling me I was going to be a daddy, I was cool.

I closed my book, got up, and checked myself in the mirror. I brushed my waves forward and smoothed my eyebrows. I was an attractive, intelligent young man, so why was it I couldn't find a decent woman? The Bible even says, "He who finds a wife finds a good thing." Now I wasn't exactly trying to get married tomorrow, but I didn't want to be a forty-year-old bachelor either.

This one honey named Jasmyn had been trying to get at me ever since I met her at the Kappa party the previous week. She was best friends with Shawn's girl. I saw her here and there and my boys and I agreed she was a certified dime piece, but there was something about her that seemed shady. Call it feminine mystique, I don't know. Maybe it was her eyes, her sexy walk, or the way she seemed to command the attention of any guy whenever she walked into a room. Whatever it was, she had me hooked. We'd been talking for a few days and I could tell already that she was starting to dig me, so I decided to go see her.

In a side-by-side comparison in the looks department, Jasmyn was definitely no Tiana. Jasmyn was brown-skinned with straight shoulder length black hair that was no doubt a weave—a tight weave, but a weave nonetheless. When I met her, she was dipped out in fresh Baby Phat jeans, stiletto boots, and a rabbit fur vest over a tight red shirt which showed off her curves. Her thighs and butt were thick and "borderline" plump—not so big that I would call her "fat," but then again, if she started eating one too many meals, she'd be a prime candidate for Jenny Craig. All in all, Jasmyn had a naturally pretty, girl-next-door look—sort of like Rudy Huxtable from the *Cosby Show*, but all grown up.

Now Tiana, on the other hand, was light-brown skinned with dark, wavy hair. Her skin was the perfect shade of caramel. She looked like a short Tyra Banks and had model-type looks, without the model-type arrogant, stuck-up personality to match, which I was glad about. Tiana was slim, petite, and carried herself like a true lady. On the other hand, she could flip the script and kick it with the guys. Back home, besides hanging out at church, we used to all go out to the mall, the movies, or summer barbecues at someone's house. Tiana was truly like a little sister to Shawn and me. She dated a few nuts along the way, but luckily had never stayed with any of them. I wondered if she had a new "friend" she was seeing since she hadn't called lately to say "hi" the way she usually did at least once a week.

Come to think of it, I hadn't spoken to Tiana in almost a month. Being that I had not been home in the past three or four weeks, I wondered how she was doing. She was a year younger than me and attended Temple University, so she could commute from home via public transportation and save money. Even though Tiana was an only child, her dad lived out of state and didn't help her and her mom out a lot with tuition. Tiana was studying to be a pediatric nurse, so she took academics as seriously as I did.

Before I headed out to see Jasmyn, I decided to

give Tiana a call on her cell phone. I took advantage of the privacy because Shawn was over at Raheem and Moe's sparking an L. Surprisingly, she picked up on the second ring.

"Is this my baby, Kyle?" she squealed in a sisterly fashion.

"Was'sup, shorty!" Tiana and I threw out playful, flirtatious nicknames from time to time. I never knew if she was as serious with hers as I was with mine.

"So what's going on out there in Exton? You be-having yourself, right?"

I grinned. *I am for now.* If Tiana were there—I mean, I love the Lord and everything, but the "no fornication" rule I'd been having so much trouble with since I turned sixteen—well, let's just say I would have had problems controlling myself around her. Just talking to her brought on such mental stimulation and emotional arousal, I knew I had to promptly end the conversation before it became apparent that my interest in Tiana was as more than a friend. The older we became, the more sexually and intellectually attracted I was to her. Like most young people who grew up in our church, we walked a fine line between the world's standards and God's expectations. I tried to keep it as street as possible, but still maintain some level of integrity. I followed as many of the rules as I could in the Bible. I prayed every day or at least when I remembered to. I always said grace, even around my friends when I did it real quick with my eyes half-open. I tried not to curse that much, and Tiana hardly ever did. Now, the sex-before-marriage rule was one almost everyone I knew had broken.

No matter how much you tried to live for God, it was hard to pass up a good looking member of the opposite sex. As long as I didn't get out of control and had sex within monogamous relationships, I figured God would be okay with it. I wondered how many guys she had been with. As my mind wandered, I began envisioning how my first time with her would be.

My fantasy was cut short when suddenly Tiana posed the question, "So Kyle, where's your girlfriend this evening?"

"Girlfriend? Chill, ma. . . . You know I ain't got no time for these homely-looking, broken-down broads up here." I began to chuckle.

"Kyle Anthony Clayton . . ." Tiana said, sounding like somebody's mom.

"Why you gotta call out my government?" I joked, referring to the way she distinctly pronounced each of my names.

"Because I can." I could tell that she was grinning, even through the phone. Tiana had beautiful white teeth.

"Well, like I said, why you wanna know?" I asked. She must have had a reason for delving into my personal business.

"No reason, I just figured with all those females around, you and Shawn must be getting into all kinds of mess! And don't even try to lie, Kyle, talking about all those so-called 'homely broads' on campus. Have you forgotten my cousin Reesie also goes there?"

"Oh yeah, that's right." I actually did forget about her cousin. "Well look, my girl must be with your man!" I decided to flip the script on her.

"Well," Tiana's lighthearted demeanor lessened as she took a more serious tone. "Kyle, I actually did meet somebody. I think he might be the one."

I could tell she wasn't joking. It surprised me that Tiana thought she met the guy who could be 'the one.' I was certain that in time, I would find out the real deal. Obviously, my heart sank a bit in disappointment. At the risk of appearing soft, I decided to man up and play it off like I was happy for her.

"Oh, word? That's what's up! Congratulations. What's his name?" I asked out of curiosity.

"His name is Chauncey and he goes to Temple too. I met him on my way from class last week."

The name sounded familiar. It wasn't a name you ran across every day. I remembered a guy named Chauncey who lived around my way back in West Philly. I hoped it wasn't the same one because he was known for having a reputation for running game on young girls and having a big mouth which got him into trouble. I made it a point to ask Shawn about him later to see if he remembered him too. But, suffice it to say I was polite and would wait to find out if the Chauncey I knew was the same Chauncey that was her new so-called man.

Tiana went on to tell me how Chauncey approached her as she was leaving class. He complimented her outfit and hairstyle and they began talking. Chauncey mentioned he was a fourth-year student, lived in Cheltenham, a suburb of Philadelphia, and drove a Range Rover.

". . . and yes, by the way, he does go to church." I guess Tiana thought telling me he went to church was supposed to make me feel better. It didn't

work because I was hating on dude right about
then. After knowing her for half my life and being
like a brother to her, Tiana was like a straight-up
'wifey' to me in my head. To see some knuckle-
head come along and push up on your imaginary
wife was hard to take. Out of all the guys Tiana
dated over the years, I never heard her refer to
somebody as "the one", especially after only knowing him a week. That in itself angered me further.
No other female I dated could hold a candle to
her. I always compared females in my head, which
was probably another reason I was still single.

"Well, baby-girl, that's cool. I'm happy for you,
Tee. Just make sure he treats you right. I don't
want me and Shawn to have to come down there
and get in his grill for disrespecting our sister." I
wasn't much of a fighter, but for Tiana, I would
definitely square up.

Tiana and I talked for another twenty minutes
or so about school and our families. She went on
to tell me about the stuff she was doing with her
sorority, Gamma–something or other.

Last year, Tiana joined this new lavender and silver colored sorority at Temple. She used to be real
psyched about it, wearing all this gear and doing
some annoying cuckoo-bird-sounding call, "G-U!"
I wasn't mad at her though. I knew a lot of females
who were into that Greek nonsense. My aunt was
in the blue and white one—Zeta-something—and
my grandpop was an Alpha and a Mason too, I
think. All I knew was he had a lot of black and gold
plaques and paddles with the letter A, as well as
this tip-top secretive stuff with the letter G on it for
the Masons. I, for one, wasn't down for pledging. I
thought it was stupid to let someone yell at you

and disrespect you, beat your ass and two months later get geeked 'cause you "earned" some weak-ass shirt with fraternity letters on it. I couldn't understand how all of a sudden, you could be "brothers" or "sisters" and begin doing secret handshakes with the same person who beat you. I can't front because I liked the step shows, and the Greek parties were always the shit. I listened to Tiana go on and on about the Gammas. I started to tell her about my new female friend, but decided to wait until I knew exactly what time it was with Jasmyn and had made sure she wasn't a psycho.

We hung up and I thought about going back to study for a few more minutes. I decided against it and took a fleeting look at my alarm clock. Seeing it was already five minutes to nine, I decided to freshen up and pay Jasymn a visit. I jumped in the shower, threw on a clean t-shirt, some fresh sweat pants, and a hoodie, tied on my do-rag, and made my way next door to Leidy Hall.

When I arrived, I flashed my color-coded Banneker Hall photo ID to front-desk security. Marshall State was pretty relaxed about visitation. If you lived on campus you could pretty much go into any dorm and visit until eleven. After eleven, you had to be signed in by a resident. If you didn't live on campus, you had to be signed in and escorted to a room.

I remembered Jasmyn saying she lived on the second floor. When I got upstairs, I asked this Indian girl if she knew where Jasmyn Simmons lived. She pointed to the end of the hallway. Jasmyn lived on a single-sex floor, which made me comfortable. If she lived with guys on her floor, I would start to wonder whether or not she was messing around with any of them.

I walked down the hall to room 201 and stood nervously outside the door. What if she's in there with a guy? What if she doesn't like surprise visits and snaps on me? What if she looks tore-up and busted?

I heard Jasmyn and another girl, who sounded like Crystal, talking and laughing, so I decided it was safe to knock. Crystal opened the door and I caught a glimpse of Jasmyn looking sexy in a yellow wife-beater tank top and a pair of navy blue cut-off jogging shorts. Jasmyn may have been thick, but she had a nice pair of legs. The muscle cuts in her thighs and calves told me she probably was a dancer.

Crystal and Jasmyn said goodbye as I became more nervous. I would have honestly chilled with both of them, but Crystal's departure signaled to me that Jasmyn welcomed my visit and the opportunity for us to be alone

_____*Jasmyn*

I walked to the door as Crystal left and kept it open. Kyle stood in the doorway. What a gentleman, he didn't just invite himself in.

"So what's up? You're not too busy, are you?" he asked.

I walked back over towards my bed, leaving the door open and shook my head no. "You can come kick it for a while. I know you've been missing me."

Kyle walked over toward me.

"Can I get a hug?" I opened my arms and he walked into them.

Kyle fit my image to the fullest. He was smart, good looking, and drove a nice car. Getting him was going to be easy. It was obvious he was on me because he was at my door. I went over to visit him at Banneker once, but we just talked since Shawn was there. So far, we hadn't even kissed and I was surprised, knowing how fast I tend to move.

Kyle sat down at my desk and I teased him, "You can sit on my bed you know—it's cool. I'm clean."

He laughed, looking around the room at my burgundy bedspread with matching sheets and decorative pillows. I hung matching curtains myself.

"You have a nice room Miss Jasmyn. I see you're a neat freak. That's what's up."

"Yeah, I can't stand to be in a junky room."

"So who's this?" he asked, picking up a framed picture of Jerome in his high school cap and gown.

"That's my brother Jerome I was telling you about." I told him I had a brother, but I didn't tell him where he currently resides.

"Oh aiight, I guess he does look like you. I was going to say 'don't tell me you got a man!'" Kyle continued glancing between my face and Jerome's in the photo. "Yeah, you can definitely tell y'all are related."

"Of course, baby, I ain't got no man. Please, I'm trying to get a 3.0 this semester." Now part two of that statement was true. I was shooting for a 3.0 but, technically, Damon and I hadn't broken up yet—even though we'd only been together since May and it was now almost Thanksgiving.

"Oh, okay. I guess you're telling the truth," he laughed.

"I am telling the truth!" I reached over from the chair I was sitting in, picked up a pillow off the bed, and smacked him with it. "Now, nigga, what?" I stood up like I was ready to fight him.

"Girl, you don't even wanna see me in a pillow fight!" He picked up a pillow and whacked me on my butt with it.

"What? Oh, so you gonna hit me on my butt? O-kay!" I reached up and hit him with the pillow right on top of his head.

We started laughing and played like that for a

few minutes, pillow-fighting and wrestling. I got him to the point where he was pinned underneath me on the floor.

"Now what?" I announced. "Say my name! Say my name, nukkaaaa!" I laughed and gently pressed my knee into his stomach. I knew he was letting me win and though we were playing, it felt erotic and I was getting turned on rather quickly.

"All right, get off me, get off me!" Kyle yelled humorously, refusing to surrender.

"Say my name and I'll get off you," I demanded teasingly.

"All right, all right," he laughed because I was tickling him at the same time. "It's Jaaass-myn! It's Jasmyn!" He caught his breath and tickled me back.

I hopped off of him and threw my fists up like a champion. "Ha! I laid the smack down on that West Philly ass, didn't I? Now, what!?" Then mimicking Will Smith in the Muhammad Ali movie, I proclaimed, "The champ is here!" and ran around my room imitating Rocky. We both fell out laughing.

Kyle rolled his eyes. "Now you know all of the best athletes come out of Philly—not Jersey!" Kyle was definitely proud of his city—our city.

"Kyle, I'm from Philly too, man—South Philly, holding it down," I boasted.

"Yeah, but um . . . y'all moved to New Jersey, am I right?" It was obvious he paid a lot of attention to the details I shared with him. With that last statement he tackled me, landed me on my back, and started tickling me. He smelled like baby powder deodorant and fresh Irish Spring soap like he had just taken a shower.

Oh, I had his game figured out. Acting like he just rolled over there all laid-back and casual in his sweats, knowing good and well he purposely showered and threw on fresh, clean clothes to come over there. Even his breath smelled good—like spearmint chewing gum.

I went along with his playfulness and quickly ran my hand across my arm to make sure I could feel the imprint of my birth control patch. I was supposed to change it every Monday night and wanted to make sure I did it already. After I felt the outline of the patch, I felt another imprint, but this one came through Kyle's baggy sweatpants. I leaned forward and kissed him as he kissed me back and softly caressed my shoulders and arms.

We laid on the bed, pinned together, kissing and exploring each other for the first time. I ignored the muffled ringer of my cell phone, which somehow, in the midst of our tussling and play-fighting, had made its way underneath my pillow.

A few minutes later, the voice mail alert went off. I'd have to check it later. Then it occurred to me. The muffled ring tone re-played itself in my head. It was the custom ring tone I pre-set for Damon and my other male associates. Kyle was definitely my new flavor of the month, but his number wasn't saved in my phone yet. After tonight, I would have to see if he was worth it.

Oh shit. Damon.

The ringing started again. I could barely focus on kissing Kyle. I knew he was ready to go to another level, but he stopped. "Answer your phone," he quietly suggested.

I dismissed the phone, telling him, "It's Crystal

trying to see what we're doing. She is so nosy!" I lied. I couldn't think of what else to say.

Kyle softly began kissing me again and tugging on the jogging shorts I was wearing. His hands worked their way under my shorts and inside my underwear, stretching the elastic in my waistband.

"Let me turn some music on," I said tenderly. I walked over to my CD player and got ready to pop in some R. Kelly. I heard a knock on my door and at the same time my cell phone rang again with the same ring tone.

The knock got louder, so I walked over and looked through the peephole. Aww damn. It was Damon. What is he doing here? Don't tell me this nigga tryna stalk somebody. I had to think fast and play it cool or I would lose them both.

I turned up the music to drown out the knocking.

"Sorry about that baby," I said as I sauntered back over to the bed where Kyle was reclined. "I had to make sure the CD was on the right track. You know how R. Kelly be havin' so many songs on one disc!"

Kyle was either deaf, dumb, or just trying to act like he didn't hear the door. He just looked at me and said, "It's cool. I ain't going nowhere." I knew I was mad at God and all, but I shut my eyes and prayed really hard. *God, pleeeaaase, let Damon leave. Please don't let anything jump off.*

I turned the lamp off and made my way into Kyle's arms.

Boom. Boom. Boom. A heavy-handed fist knocked on the door. From the other side, I heard, "Jazz! I know you're in there. Open the damn door! "

Now I knew, even over the music blaring, Kyle

had to hear that. There was nothing left for me to do but play stupid with him or open the door and play innocent with Damon. I chose option one and decided to deal with Damon later. I wanted a Newport, but knew I couldn't light a cigarette because the aroma would destroy the mood. I fought the nervousness and shook off the craving.

Kyle proceeded with caution and asked if I had protection. I did, and against my personal preference, decided to let him use it. In time, if he was like any other guys I dealt with, he would eventually want to go without it. He looked at me and said, "Jazz, you know I dig you. I hope you ain't tryin' to play me."

I gazed into Kyle's eyes and slowly kissed him. The knocking finally stopped. "Baby, you don't have anything to worry about."

I breathed a sigh of relief that Damon had left and focused on giving Kyle what I knew he really wanted. And I wanted it too.

_____*Kyle*

"Yo man, I'm about to mark this chick off the list of the future Mrs. Claytons." I motioned a director's "cut it" gesture with my hand in front of my throat.

Shawn puffed on his blunt. "So it's a wrap then, son?"

Shawn and I were in our room. I recounted the details of what went down in Jasmyn's room the night before.

"Let's just say she's not exactly girlfriend material," I replied.

Jasmyn was a nice girl, but I peeped her game early on when she ignored her cell phone and the guy knocking on her door. She tried to play it off, so I just went along with it, playing stupid. Since I saw she was a player already from the jump, I made up my mind I wasn't going to allow myself to get too close to her.

"So just tell me, was it good or what?" Shawn inquired. He was a typical dog. "I know y'all got it on

the first seven days. Without an original receipt, a .
at the lowest selling price. With a receipt, returns of n
and unopened music from bn.com can be made
Textbooks after 14 days or without a receipt are not return
are not returnable.

Valid photo ID required for all returns, (except for credit card purchases) exchanges and to receive and redeem store credit. With a receipt, a full refund in the original form of payment will be issued for new and unread books and unopened music within 30 days from any Barnes & Noble store. For merchandise purchased with a check, a store credit will be issued within the first seven days. Without an original receipt, a store credit will be issued at the lowest selling price. With a receipt, returns of new and unread books and unopened music from bn.com can be made for store credit. Textbooks after 14 days or without a receipt are not returnable. Used books are not returnable.

Valid photo ID required for all returns, (except for credit card purchases) exchanges and to receive and redeem store credit. With a receipt, a full refund in the original form of payment will be issued for new and unread books and unopened music within 30 days from any Barnes & Noble store. For merchandise purchased with a check, a store credit will be issued within the first seven days. Without an original receipt, a store credit will be issued at the lowest selling price. With a receipt, returns of new and unread books and unopened music from bn.com can be made for store credit. Textbooks after 14 days or without a receipt are not returnable. Used books are not returnable.

B. Dalton Bookseller
10202 E Washington Street
Indianapolis, IN 46229
(317) 839-4150

Where   15.00

Ret 12/9/00

SUBTOTAL   15.00
SALES TAX   .90
TOTAL   15.90
AMOUNT TENDERED
CASH   20.00

TOTAL PAYMENT   20.00
CHANGE   4.10

Thank you for shopping at
B. Dalton Booksellers

exchanges and to receive and redeem store credit. With a full refund in the original form of payment will be issued for new and unread books and unopened music within 30 days from any Barnes & Noble store. For merchandise purchased with a check, a store credit will be issued within the first seven days. Without an original receipt, a store credit will be issued at the lowest selling price. With a receipt, returns of new and unread books and unopened music from bn.com can be made for store credit. Textbooks after 14 days or without a receipt are not returnable. Used books are not returnable.

Valid photo ID required for all returns, (except for credit card purchases) exchanges and to receive and redeem store credit. With a receipt, a full refund in the original form of payment will be issued for new and unread books and unopened music within 30 days from any Barnes & Noble store. For merchandise purchased with a check, a store credit will be issued within the first seven days. Without an original receipt, a store credit will be issued at the lowest selling price. With a receipt, returns of new and unread books and unopened music from bn.com can be made for store credit. Textbooks after 14 days or without a receipt are not returnable. Used books are not returnable.

and poppin' 'cause she look like a bona fide freak just like her girl Crystal."

"No doubt." I slapped five and uncharacteristically flexed my bravado for Shawn. I kept my "I-ain't-sweatin'-these-broads" game face on when it came to Shawn. He's always been more hard-core than me, not giving a damn about anything or anybody. Don't get me wrong—he was a nice dude—but Shawn just did Shawn, and that was all there was to it.

Shawn laughed and congratulated me by saying, "Say word! That's my boyyyyy!"

The truth was I did have sex with Jasmyn. I felt guilty and prayed to God afterwards for forgiveness. I believe part of the reason I went through with it was because I was salty about Tiana and her new man. The sex was good and I was tempted to go without protection so I could experience even more of her. After the deed was done, I got up and went back to my room to go to sleep. I never brought up the mystery man I heard outside the door.

"Man, let me tell you how that chick had some dude banging on her door!"

"What? Family, you can't trust these hoes nowadays." Shawn had a point there. Females were as slick as males. In fact, they were more on top of their game than we were. I didn't know Jasmyn all that well yet, but I saw what she was capable of, and I definitely would keep my eyes open. I didn't want to get into providing too many details about my sexual encounter with Jazz or the incident with the dude banging on her door, so I changed the subject.

"Ay yo, guess who I talked to last night?"

"Let me guess. Tiana." Shawn knew how I felt about her and that I couldn't care less for these other females. "I never figured out why y'all never hooked up. I mean, I know I don't go to church like I used to, but even still, when we at home and see her at church, it's like the two of y'all have some kind of chemistry-vibe."

"Well, that don't mean nothin' 'cause she's got a new man!"

Shawn was shocked. "Get the fuck outta here!" The more smoked out Shawn was, the worse his mouth became.

"Man, I know, right?" I agreed with him in an equally disbelieving tone. "Yo, you remember a cat named Chauncey who used to live on Fifty-Ninth Street back in the day?"

"Tall, dark-skinned, with a low cut, used to run his mouth. Yeah, I remember him. I don't think he stays around there anymore. I never liked dude."

"Well, Tiana said her new friend's name is Chauncey. I didn't want to tell her about the Chauncey from around our way. You know with her being from Southwest, she didn't know cats from there."

"Unless it's another Chauncey," Shawn offered.

"Now how many black guys do you know named Chauncey?" I knew he would be unable to respond.

Shawn continued to smoke and went to the doorway to make sure the rolled up damp towel he laid was secure. If not, our Resident Assistant would write us up for smoking and marijuana would definitely get us in trouble with campus police, risking expulsion.

"I'm saying," Shawn continued, "even if it is the same Chauncey from around the way . . . what you gonna do about it? I mean, I know that cat is foul, but Kyle, man, you'd look like a straight-up nut if you start hating and telling Tiana she shouldn't mess with the dude."

"I know. Man, I think when we go home next week, I'mma feel her out to see if she is really serious about Chauncey. I mean, what's up? She could've gotten with me. I'd know how to treat her."

"That might be true, but you got your hands full right now with Jasmyn. You might as well chill with her for a minute. She looks good, she's smart, knows how to dress, and has a fat butt. I mean, for real, for real, what more could you ask for?"

Shawn did make a good point.

"I would say forget the nut who was banging on her door. If she didn't get up to answer it, she's probably really feeling you, dog." This may have been true, but there was something that didn't feel one-hundred percent right with Jasmyn.

"It's only been a little over a week," I said. "I'll see where it goes with her."

"Plus, you hit it once, so you know you probably can hit it as much as you want," Shawn declared, putting out what was left of his blunt.

I probably did have full, maybe not exclusive, but nevertheless full access to the booty. She seemed as though she enjoyed it. She wanted to do it a few times and begged me to spend the night. I think I made the right choice by leaving early, though. That left her wanting more. Plus, when I heard dude banging on the door, I knew she might be trying to play me by having a boyfriend, so I figured my best bet was to lay low and let her sweat me for a minute.

_____Jasmyn

"Daaaag, Jazz. Girl, it stinks in here. You got that mess smelling up the whole hallway!" Crystal let herself in and commented on my overcooked microwave popcorn.

I chuckled and tossed the steaming hot bag in her direction. "Here, you want some?"

"Hell no, I don't want that nasty popcorn," Crystal screwed up her face and moved away from it.

I got up to throw the bag in the trash. "So, what's up, girl?" I knew Crystal stopped by for a reason other than to say "Hi."

"You know why I stopped by, girl. What Inez and them Spanish chicks say? 'I want the chiiiis-me, nena!' I came by for the low-down on your boy. What's up? I know you let him hit it!" Crystal swore she could spit a little Spanish here and there because her roommate Inez was Dominican. In a way, I was glad we weren't roommates because she'd be in my B.I. twenty-four-seven trying to get gossip out of me. "So, what's up?" she pressed on. "Did y'all do it or what?"

"It?" I was amazed Crystal was twenty years old and still referred to sex as "doing it" and "the nasty." I looked at her and asked, "What do you think, Crystal?"

Crystal eyed me up and down. "Uhn . . . well, knowing you . . . ," she chuckled. "We know how you get down, sleeping with guys right from the jump!"

"Excuuuuse you smut?!" I said sarcastically. "I'm not the one with two boyfriends." Crystal wasn't sure if I was joking or not, but that didn't matter to me. Crystal was not about to sit up there and try to clown somebody. I put her fat ass in check. She was still my dog and even though she came at me wrong, I wasn't mad at her. I gave her a rundown of everything that happened last night, from our pillow fights to our first kiss, to Damon burning up my cell phone and banging on my door like a madman.

Crystal expressed concern about Damon. "Girl, you ain't shook? I would be scared if a guy that big was trying to track me down! What you do, make him mad or something?"

"I ain't do nothing to that negro!" I lied. "Girl, please. Damon knows better than to try to shake me! Look, we both know I got people back in Jersey and Philly who would be glad to teach Damon the same lesson Shannon learned last year."

We continued to talk a while longer. Around ten o'clock, I told her I was waiting for Kyle to stop by after he finished getting his shape-up by Maurice.

"Maurice from upstairs?! Girl, you didn't tell me Kyle knew Moe," Crystal stated, with a sly grin.

I shook my head. "What's up with all the grinning? Don't even try it, Crystal. Ain't nothing popping between us," I lied. "So don't even start no shit!" I added.

I shot her an evil don't-start-the-drama look.

"My bad," Crystal laughed. "It's funny how small this damn campus is! I mean, come on, Jazz, you don't have to lie to me. I know you and Moe have a little something-something on the side."

"Have you bumped your head? I am not jumping off with Moe, or nobody else for that matter. I left Damon alone and now I'm messing with Kyle—and that's it, period." I was annoyed that Crystal had the audacity to try to call me out like that.

The phone rang. It was Kyle telling me something about going back to Banneker to work on some class presentation for tomorrow. We agreed to wait until then to get together. I was relieved because I had other plans for the night which didn't include him. I might want to visit Maurice. First, I had to get rid of Crystal, so I pretended to prepare for bed.

I stretched my arms and released a loud yawn. "I am so tired! Crystal, I'm going to wrap my hair up and go to bed. I have one class tomorrow and need to pack for the Thanksgiving weekend."

Crystal began walking to the door. "All right, I guess I can take a hint. Maybe I'll see what's up with Shawn. I called him before I came down here and he didn't pick up his phone. I don't know where his behind is."

I gave Crystal a hug and told her that if I didn't see her tomorrow to have a nice Thanksgiving break. She lived in Coatesville and had a shorter ride than I did. I told her I'd call her sometime during the break.

_Kyle

A few days passed and Jasmyn called me every day. She never brought up the incident of the mystery man at her door. I assumed maybe she had a crazy ex and didn't want to get me involved in any drama, so she played it off. I mean, she couldn't possibly have had a man because we'd spent too much time together. I was over at her room every night.

Tonight though, I didn't feel like going over there. I was there every night this week. I decided to let her visit me the next time we saw one another. The only thing was, it was time for another shape-up and my barber lived in her dorm. I didn't want to sweat her, so I decided to call him to see if he could cut my hair tonight. I told myself when I went to Leidy to go straight upstairs to Moe's room and not stop at Jasmyn's if I could help it. I didn't want to get too caught up with this chick. I had yet to get to know her outside of what she likes to do in bed and the kind of music she likes to do "it" to.

Being that I am a one woman man, I made it my business to create an opportunity for us to get to know one another better; maybe I'd take her out to the movies or dinner since we'd never been outside her room to kick it. But I missed being with my boys and my hair was screaming for a trim, so I knew I'd have to see Moe. I called and let him know I'd be over around nine.

Around a quarter to nine that evening, Shawn and I were studying and listening to the latest Ludacris and Ja Rule CDs. Shawn wasn't much of a studier, but as long as there was music in the background, he was more inclined to read uninterruptedly. I encouraged him by reading myself and not conversing with him much. He really needed to pull his grades up and if I could help my boy do that, I would. We put in two hours of studying then decided to take a break and roll over to Leidy.

"Shawn, it's almost nine. You goin' over to Leidy with me to Moe's?"

"Yeah, but I think I'm gonna stop and see my young girl downstairs."

"What young girl?" I laughed. He swore he was a pimp with a capital P, looking like a broke Gerald Levert. That was my boy, I'd give it to him—he was handsome—but he could stand to do a few sit-ups.

"Man, you ain't the only one pulling these hoes, aiight?!" Shawn beat his chest.

I fell out laughing. "All right, Shawn. You da man, you da man." I gave him a pound and slipped a hoodie on, my do-rag, and a fitted Iverson cap. I was a huge basketball fan and Allen Iverson of the Sixers was my favorite player. I loved to rep Philly whenever I was away from home, whether it was sporting team jerseys and caps or bumping the sounds of famous Philly musicians Eve and Musiq Soulchild.

"Look, you don't know this jawn; her name is Danine. She's in my Adolescent Psych class." He was a psychology major, no doubt because it was an easy major and the one most selected by students who were undecided.

"Okay, well don't hurt 'em playa." I laughed it off and headed over to Leidy Hall. Shawn said he'd get up with me later at Moe's.

Moments later at Leidy, no sooner as I flashed my ID at the front desk, I spotted Jasmyn in the lobby at the vending machine. She looked over at me and tried to blow up my spot. Right then, I knew she was ghetto. She was wearing a brown silk head wrap, a pair of sweat pants, and a baggy t-shirt.

"Ahn ahn! Whatchu doin' here?!" she asked loudly. The ghetto-fabulosity in her voice echoed through the lobby as others looked to see who was yelling.

I tried not to think of how loud she was and went over to give her a hug.

"Where you heading?" she continued. "You'd better be on your way to room 201 to see me!" she added in a not-so-playful manner.

I removed my hat and lifted my do-rag slightly. "You see this?" I motioned towards the side of my head. "I'm going to see my boy Moe to get a shape-up. I never let more than a week go by without a trim."

Jasmyn's eyes widened when I mentioned Moe's name. "Oh I know him," Jasmyn said. "You're talking about Maurice from Brooklyn? He lives upstairs and cuts hair, right?"

I wondered exactly how well she knew Moe, or

Maurice, as she referred to him. "Yeah, that's my boy—we've been cool since freshman year."

"Oh okay, he's cool. I know him," Jasmyn stated. "Well how long are you going to be upstairs?"

"I'm not sure. Why, what's up?"

Jasmyn raised her eyebrows at me. "What's up?" She moved closer and stroked my forearm with her hand. "What's up is I'm trying to see you tonight," she whispered, "especially since Thanksgiving is this weekend and I won't see you for the next five days."

I was digging her flirtatiousness, but at the risk of getting caught up I pulled away and said, "Look, Jazz, it's getting late. I've got one class tomorrow before I go home." I knew if I stayed with her, I wouldn't be able to wake up on time. "Plus, I have a group presentation to do," I added. "I am trying to see you though. What time are you driving back home to Jersey? Maybe we can go catch an early movie before the traffic starts up. I mean we haven't been on an official date, so what's up?"

"Okay, I guess so. Let me think about what I have to do tomorrow." Jasmyn pondered for a few seconds and then replied, "All right, that's fine. I think I'm rolling out around twelve or one o'clock."

"That's cool 'cause I don't have much to pack and my class ends at ten-thirty," I said.

My body really wanted to skip that shape-up and follow Jazz to her room, but my mind was telling me to take my black behind up to Moe's for my haircut and then return to my dorm immediately. I was determined to exercise some self-control, listening to a little voice that must have belonged to God. I gave her a sensual embrace without being too lewd and seductive. As we walked upstairs she kissed me goodbye at the second floor landing and I jogged up to the next floor.

When I arrived at Moe's door, he greeted me with "You're fifteen minutes late!" I looked and one of our other boys Dave was in the room. Apparently, he just got his hair cut. He was on the basketball team and lived in McKennan. We all met during freshman year and were still cool.

"I know, man; I had some business to take care of. My bad," I apologized, removing my do-rag and sitting down in his chair.

As soon as Moe sat on his stool, Dave began pumping me for information. "So, word is you got a new young babe." No doubt, the Tom Brokaw and Peter Jennings of the ghetto, better known as Raheem and Shawn, told my business.

Raheem was watching Comic View on BET, but decided to join in. "Yeah, what's up?"

I stared at them in amusement, shaking my head. "Y'all niggas better go 'head. Look, I'm just doin' me, cousin, ya feel me? Now come on, Moe. Hook my head up like you was getting ready to do."

Moe turned his clippers on and Dave threw me a towel to put around my neck. "So, you ain't gonna tell us about your new girl? You know Shawn already told us how you hooked up with that thick honey from the Kappa party the other week. Jasmyn, right? She lives downstairs, don't she?"

It didn't shock me that Shawn told my personal business to these cats. But it was cool since we were boys. I knew Moe could be a hater from time to time, so I watched what I said around him. I also remembered how Jazz's eyes widened when I told her my boy Moe lived upstairs. It was almost as though she had a slight sparkle in her eyes. I didn't know, if Jazz was digging him or if they used to talk, or what. But I had no plans on worrying about that tonight.

I decided to indulge their curiosity a bit. "Yeah, I've been talking to Jasmyn for a couple weeks, you know. Ain't nothing serious, nah mean?"

"You hit it yet?" Raheem questioned.

"Of course he hit it," Moe offered. He then turned the clippers off and tapped me. "Ain't that right, dog?"

"Yo man, just finish shaping me up, dammnnn." I shook my head and smiled. Females may be known for being busybodies, but I could name plenty of dudes who were just as bad.

Raheem added, "I knew he did. That night I said to myself, 'That babe talking to Kyle look like a straight freak and damn if you and Shawn ain't leave the party with her and her girlfriend."

"Oh yeahhhhh," mentioned Moe, agreeing as always. "I was saying the same thing, Heem!"

I sat back and listened, deciding it was best to talk as little as possible.

"Yo Moe, you know how much of a freak Kyle's girl is, don't you?" Raheem shot him a sneaky glance and nodded his head.

Moe continued to carefully outline the edges of my hair along my forehead. I noticed he had ignored Raheem. I tried to act like I didn't peep Raheem's last comment, knowing he liked to stir up as much trouble as anybody I knew.

"Man, go 'head! Ain't nobody worried about Kyle's girl." I was shocked to hear Moe say that when just a minute ago he was in such a hurry to tell me he knew I slept with her.

Raheem, who by now had bloodshot eyes and was rolling his next blunt, stumbled over towards us. Unfortunately, I saw him transform into this person so many times before—intoxicated, high, and ready to run his mouth. Mr. High and Lifted was his alter ego.

I looked at him while my head was tilted to one side and blinked rapidly, turning away from the smoke being blown in my direction. He got in my face and said in a low voice, "Yo Kyle, man, did Moe ever tell you the time . . ."

"Yooooo!" Raheem was interrupted when a loud voice invaded the room, accompanied by two loud knocks at the door. Shawn let himself in as he banged on the door "What up?!" He gave Moe and me some dap and spoke to Dave and Shawn, who were now engaged in a game of NBA Live on the PlayStation.

I nodded at Shawn and said, "So you finally made it, I see." I quickly changed the previous conversation from whatever Raheem was about to spill and directed it toward Shawn.

"Yeah, I had to go holla at my young girl," Shawn smiled proudly. If I didn't know better, I would think he just finished having sex with her.

"Oh aiight," Raheem piped in. He handed the blunt to Shawn, who took a few puffs and motioned it toward me and Moe. I shook my head to say 'no thanks' while Moe set his comb down and took a hit. He handed it back to Shawn, knowing Dave couldn't smoke because he was an athlete and took random drug tests. "I was going to tell your boy Kyle about the smut he's messing with— Jazz, Jazzmeen, or whatever the hell her name is," Raheem slurred.

I felt Moe lose slight control of the clippers. I jerked my head as he shouted, "Damn it Kyle, watch it! If you get cut nigga, it's your fault!"

"My bad." I straightened my head and focused my attention on Raheem. "What's up with you calling her a smut, man? I'm saying, Heem. What's up? You know something I don't know? Holla at your boy!"

Raheem snickered. "My bad. I'm just saying, your jawn tried to get with your boy Moe back around the beginning of the semester."

"Man, you run your mouth like a damn female, I swear." Moe snapped at Raheem. He then looked at me and continued where he left off. "It ain't nothing, Kyle. Don't listen to that smoked-out nigga."

I really didn't know what to think at that point. It was starting to make sense now, why Jasmyn was all starry-eyed at the mention of Moe's name. If they were together, I couldn't get mad since she wasn't my girl. Just to think we might've dipped our spoons in the same bowl was too much to handle.

Shawn jumped in. "Yo Moe, man, don't tell me . . ." He began to laugh hysterically. ". . . that you," he looked at Moe and then turned to point at me, "and this dude . . . smashed the same girrlll!"

"Yo! Shawn, be easy brotha," Moe insisted. He remained cool and calm. "I ain't never say I hit that!" He didn't say he hit it, but smiled nonetheless.

Curiosity was brewing inside me and I blurted, "So did you smash or not?!" I got angry as I looked at Moe with intensity, waiting for a response.

"No, nigga! I didn't! So don't even worry about it," Moe defended.

Smokey-lipped Raheem busted in the conversation again. "Yo, Kyle man, you wanna know what went down for real?"

Moe continued to shape me up and shook his head in disbelief that we were still discussing him and Jasmyn.

Shawn chimed in "Yeah, tell us—I mean, inquiring minds want to know, ain't that right, dog?" He threw me an elbow in jest. I ignored him and put my fake "I-ain't-even sweatin it" grill on.

Raheem continued, "Moe and I were moving in the first weekend we came back, right? We peeped shorty and her peoples helping her move suitcases and what-not up the stairs. Moe asked if she needed help. She said her uncle had it so we left it at that. Later that night, we were chilling in the lobby and saw her coming downstairs wearing a little half-cut baby doll t-shirt and a pair of short-shorts. Everybody in the lobby was eyeballing her—the brothers, white dudes, Asian and Spanish cats, even other females."

"And?" I asked. What was the point of this story? Raheem should work for *Entertainment Tonight*. He loved telling everybody's business but his own. I had a mind to blow up his spot and tell everyone what he told me earlier this month: that he was failing all his classes and not graduating on time. Then again, that wasn't really news. We all figured that out when we found out he hadn't bought books since fall of sophomore year.

Raheem continued, "Well, she must've peeped us looking at her, 'cause next thing we knew she walked over to the couch where we were sitting and sat next to us. She hollered at Moe and then—"

"And then, nothing!" Moe interrupted.

"And then, what?!" I demanded. By now, fury and jealousy had me heated. I was insistent and unwavering. But I kept my cool.

Moe jumped in annoyed "And that was it, ai-ight?! We kicked it for a minute, she was feeling me, but I wasn't with it. I started seeing her with some big, black, diesel football kid. Like I said before, I didn't really have no rap for her. She tried to get at me another time and I still wasn't feeling her. That's it. Ain't nothing pop off." He was adamant in proving his innocence.

I didn't know what to say, so I let Moe finish cutting my hair in silence. "It's cool, Moe. I mean, you didn't have to front like you ain't know her. You still my people, though." I gave him a ghetto hand-shake and tried not to think about it.

I guess Dave sensed the tension because he stood up and said, "Yo, I'mma get up with y'all later. I see y'all got some things to discuss." He left and we watched a rerun of *Oz* on HBO for a little while, enough time for Shawn and Heem to get another smoke in. I even took a few puffs to allevi-ate the stress which was setting in. Around ten-thirty I decided to roll out. I remembered Jasmyn asked me—or more like demanded me—to stop by. In all actuality, I wanted to go back to my room to prepare for my presentation tomorrow and pack for the long weekend.

I said my goodbyes and shook Moe's hand to let him know everything was still peace between us. My cell phone rang and, sure enough, it was Jazz. I decided to wait until I got in the hall to answer it.

"Hey, what's up Miss Lady?"

"Hey, you still upstairs with your boys? You coming down to see me?" Jasmyn asked.

Based on my tiredness, the things I needed to do for tomorrow, and the fact I just learned she tried to hook up with my boy, I wasn't really in the mood to lay up with her. "I have a presentation to do and I need to pack for tomorrow. But, I'mma get with you then to do that 'date' thing. We can both drive since we're going home afterwards. I'll call you around twelve-thirty. Think of where you want to eat."

Jasmyn sounded slightly disappointed, but not enough to the point where she would beg me to come over. It made me think she wasn't on me as much as I thought. I hoped Jazz wasn't that hot in the behind where she would have some brother on standby in case I wasn't there to chill with her.

_____*Jasmyn*

The next day, Kyle and I decided to go to TGI Friday's after our morning classes. I was glad afternoon classes were cancelled. I told him I'd meet him in the parking lot around twelve forty-five. I have plans that weekend, which included visiting my mom and Jerome, checking on my uncle who was staying at our house, getting my hair braided, as well as stopping by the nail salon to get a fresh set of tips. When I get my hair and nails done, I go hard—the whole nine. Money is no object when it comes to keeping my looks up to par.

I packed everything and contemplated calling Damon to wish him a happy break, especially since I hadn't seen or heard from him. I decided against it, figuring it was best to "let sleeping dogs lie" as they say. No need to stir him up. It was going on twelve-fifteen when I got a knock on the door. I checked the peephole and opened it cautiously and let him in.

"Are you crazy?" I whispered, looking down the hall to see who might have been watching us.

"No! Are you crazy?" Moe shot back. "What's up, love?" He slid his arms around my waist and leaned forward to kiss me. I allowed him to do so, but began to feel strange because now I knew Moe and Kyle were friends. It was different than messing with Brandon, Damon's roommate, because they weren't really close. Besides, Brandon was my white-guy experiment. Kyle, on the other hand, was boyfriend material—intelligent, well-groomed, and handsome. He was definitely worth ending a relationship with Damon. Moe, on the other hand, had a slick, enticing coolness that was irresistible. Maybe it was his Brooklyn accent or his cute-thug look wearing Sean John and Avirex outfits, tatted-up arms, and neatly-done cornrows. Whatever it was, I had to decide how long we were going to keep our fling a secret.

"Maurice," I whispered as he softly kissed my neck. "Look baby, I can't stay here long, I told Kyle I'd meet him in about twenty minutes."

Moe just ignored me and unzipped my jacket, slowly removing the sleeves off my shoulders.

I tried to appeal to his friendship with Kyle. "Look Maurice, you know I'm feeling you, but I can't let you go out like that with your boy.

"Jazz, let me tell you, Kyle doesn't suspect a thing! Raheem, Shawn—none of those cats know the deal. Raheem tried to act as a private eye, but I told him it was a wrap with you. I said, 'I ain't feeling her!' and they believed me!" Moe grinned.

"Oh, so that's funny?" I teased.

"You know what I mean, baby. Kyle is my dog for

real, but when I saw you holla at him at that party, it made me want you even more. You know our thing is tight, we are way way on the low. So it's cool. You know we got that understanding, right?"

"I know. You do you and I'll do me—and we'll catch each other on the flip side."

"Exactly. You know, we can just do our thing whenever. I ain't really worried about Damon, Kyle, or none of those cats. I know when they're not around, their girl Jazz is with me." He planted a passionate kiss on me and I wanted to take him right then and there.

I nodded. "True, but I don't want us to get caught."

"Don't I always sneak down here when no one else is up? Trust me, it's all good."

We chilled for a few minutes and he left. I allowed at least five minutes after he left to walk out. I felt like there was a Spy Cam pointed at my room and, sooner or later, I would be busted.

With Moe gone, I headed to meet Kyle. As I got closer to my car, I eyed a yellow sticky note on the windshield. I thought maybe it was Crystal leaving me a goodbye note. The parking lot was half-empty and on the other side I saw Kyle circling around in his car looking for me.

Then I noticed something strange. As I approached my car, there was broken glass near the front passenger tire. The entire passenger window had been busted out and all my CDs I kept in my sun visor were scattered across the seat and keyed up. To top it off, there was one long scratch along the driver side door that went from the front all the way to the gas tank.

My heart was racing and I began to shake. As

Kyle circled closer to my car, the tears flowed. I couldn't think of Kyle, our date, Moe, nothing. My mind was going a mile a minute trying to figure out who had done this.

I yanked the note off the windshield and read it as Kyle got out his car. I couldn't believe my eyes. In big bold black letters, it read:

WATCH YOUR BACK JASMYN OR NEXT TIME I WON'T BE SO NICE!

I crumpled up the note, ran into Kyle's arms, and started crying. After a half-hour of him comforting me, I agreed to let him take me to TGI Friday's in town to get some lunch. We had a nice time and I mellowed out a bit, smoking two cigarettes after we ate. I lied, telling Kyle I had no idea who would be after me when all the while, I thought of the people it could've been.

Damon, Brandon, Brandon's girlfriend, Moe—was he jealous of me and Kyle? What about Kyle? He might have done it. What about Crystal? She's not off the hook either.

Kyle and I decided to call campus police when we got back, file a report, and call to get the window repaired. Being it was the day before a holiday, no repair shops were available, so I had to settle for driving to New Jersey with outdoor air conditioning. Luckily, it wasn't raining. Kyle promised to call later to see how I made out with the window repair. I told him my uncle knew a lot of Spanish dudes in North Philly who would fix my window for fifty dollars.

My mind was still unsettled at what I'd faced earlier that day. With a vandalized car, I was going to have a lot to do over the holiday in order to get it fixed up.

* * *

I arrived home glad to be in non-hostile, familiar surroundings. My mom's brother Jeff and his wife had been living in our house. They kept up the mortgage payments while my mom was away. She was due to come out of Meadowpines sometime in the next year before Jerome got out of Smyrna. She was on anti-depressants, but because she slit her wrists one time, she was on intensive suicidal watch. She went from one mental disorder to another—manic depression to schizophrenia to everything in between.

Thanksgiving break went by rapidly. I spent Thanksgiving Day with my grandmother in South Philly. The Friday after, Uncle Jeff took my car to get the window and scratches repaired. I was thankful for that. I suppose since they didn't have children, Uncle Jeff and Aunt Tammy treated me like a daughter. I used some of Jerome's stashed-away drug money to go shopping on Friday with my Aunt Tammy. Between Macy's, The Limited, and Baker's shoe store, I spent close to four hundred dollars on new boots and a few new outfits.

On Saturday morning, I went to Meadowpines to visit my mom. She was alert and acting normal for a change. I didn't stay long because I had scheduled a Saturday visit with Jerome that afternoon and didn't want to miss it. I drove the almost two-hour drive from Willingboro, New Jersey to Smyrna, Delaware. It was worth it, though, because I loved my brother to death. He was my heart. I put some of his money stash, along with money Uncle Jeff gave me, towards his commissary—enough to last him until Christmas and buy a few pairs of sweats and extra soup since it was getting cold.

By Sunday, I was eager to return to school to see Kyle, but more so to find out who was after me and had damaged my car. I had three and a half weeks left until final exams and winter break. I remembered telling Damon I would hook up with him after final exams, but since he was my number one suspect for the broken window incident, I nixed that plan. He would have to realize we were through— no questions asked. With some new gear and a fresh set of goddess braids, loosely spiral-curled at the ends, I headed back to Marshall, determined to have a drama-free end of the semester.

_____Kyle

"Yo baby girl, I need to speak to you for a hot minute."

Once again, I spotted Jasmyn in the lobby of her dorm on my way to Moe's. A few weeks had passed since Thanksgiving break and the whole broken window episode. Since then, something inside was telling me that Jasmyn attracted a lot of drama, so I decided to step to her about it. The past month with her had been like a soap opera. First, there was the banging on the door when we were in her room. Then, I found out about her once upon a time liking Moe. The icing on the cake was the broken window. Since she had it repaired, she no longer brought it up and I didn't make an issue of it either. But I was noticing how her cell phone rang a lot and she wouldn't answer it around me.

Finally, the day before, when I was in her room while she ran downstairs to the laundry room, I looked in her cell phone's address book and found close to fifty names of guys, including a

"Maurice" with Moe's phone number. I also noticed how often he appeared in her call history. Before I stepped to him I thought it would be better and wiser on my part to step to Jasmyn.

Moe was the type of cat who fought at the drop of a dime, and before I got into it with him, I'd just as soon cut him off and get a new barber and chill partner. I kept a few dudes up in my cipher, so to lose him wouldn't be that bad. It wouldn't be so foul if I hadn't been sleeping with her three or four times a week and taking her out to dinner every weekend.

Jasmyn was at the soda machine as usual. *Her ass is gonna get fat if she keeps coming downstairs buying soda and chips every night.* She walked over to me with a bag of Funyuns and a bottle of Pepsi tucked under her armpit.

"What's up, boo?" she sweetly asked as she grabbed one of my hands, trying not to drop her food.

I was caught off guard by her laid-back demeanor. Normally, she would've called me out, yelled my name, and made a big deal about me visiting her. Lately, it was like she could take it or leave it.

"Look, Jazz," I carefully planned out my words. "I think we need to have a talk. I've been noticing some things going on and I'm not really digging it."

Jasmyn led me to a sofa in the lobby, far away from other people, so they couldn't hear our conversation. "So, what's on your mind, baby?"

All right Kyle. Don't fall for the okey-doke. Don't listen to her sweet talk. And for God's sake, don't go to her room tonight. "Jazz, don't take this the wrong way, but you've got a little too much drama for me. It started with dude banging on your door that night I came to see you."

Her eyes widened. "What dude?" *Now she's playing me for stupid.*

"Come on ma, we both know there was a guy banging on your door the first night I came by to chill in your room."

"Oh, but, um, let me tell you. See, what had happened was—"

"And—" I said, cutting her off before she could make a fool of herself, "—the whole broken window thing. I wouldn't be surprised if it was the same cat who was banging on your door!"

"No, 'cause the campus police even told me there were some car thefts around town in the past few months and they could've been the same people who got me." Apparently, Jasmyn was an expert in lying with a straight face.

"All right Jazz, look, forget it. You think I'm stupid, yo. I already know you've been talking to my boy Moe behind my back."

That's when Dr. Jekyll and Mrs. Hyde came out. Jasmyn's facial expression and posture changed as her split-personality emerged. "What?!" she stood up and began to make a scene. "Ahn, ahn nigga. Ain't nobody talking to your boy. What you think this is? I know you better go 'head somewhere poppin' all that ish. I ain't the one, hon-eyyy!"

People started to look at us and I began feeling embarrassed, more so for her display of chicken-head-itis than for myself. She had to live in this building and face these people every day; I didn't. I knew that turning your back on a person was one of the most hurtful, disrespectful things you could do, but I decided to do it anyway. I got up and walked away from Jazz, but she began bugging out again. "Where the hell you goin', Kyle?! We ain't finished!"

Something told me this female was psycho. She was cute and all, but damn that. I wasn't about to get played. And I'd be damned if this chick was going to stand there and cuss me out. I left her there yelling in the lobby looking all stupid like a Jerry Springer guest. I went upstairs and decided to confront Moe. I hadn't told Shawn about any of my suspicions yet, because he would've gone back to Moe and Raheem real quick. Jazz continued yelling obscenities as I walked in the opposite direction toward the stairway leading to Moe's room. Thank God she didn't try to chase me down like a madwoman.

When I arrived at Moe's door, I took a few deep breaths. He wasn't expecting me, but I knocked anyway. He was studying for an exam and Raheem was downstairs washing clothes. I decided to keep it brief and speak my piece as fast as possible.

"Yo, what up kid, what's good?" Moe gave me a ghetto handshake and invited me in.

"Yo, what up Moe? I ain't gonna keep you man 'cause I know you gotta get your study on, but I need to holla at you about something real quick." I maintained a serious tone and avoided smiling. I glanced around his room. Other than being a typical sneaky cat, Moe was a likeable brother. He kept a tidy room with his hats hung on a rack and his sneakers and boots neatly stored in their boxes. All of his clothes were hung up and things were in their proper place. His walls were uncluttered, aside from posters of Kobe Bryant and Tupac.

Moe sensed I wasn't there to be sociable. "That's peace. What's up son?"

"Look man, before you say anything, I already know about you and Jasmyn. I know we've only been kicking it for about a month, but, I mean, how you gonna go out on me like that, cousin?" I asked.

"Man, I ain't gonna even lie. I don't really know what to say, dog. I mean, like I told you, I met her early in the semester, and I wasn't really feeling her. But then she started coming around me more, you know, sticking her chest out when she walked by me, hugging and rubbing all up on me and shit. So finally I was like, aiight, bet! I knew she had a man and everything—some cat named Damon on the football team—but we just kept our little thing on the low, ya nah mean? Yo word, we ain't have nothing serious man. In fact, when y'all two had started talking at that Kappa party, I ain't even trip. She was just some chick I visited every now and then. I'm telling you, man, I never really was around her all that much. Yo son, I'm for real." I was surprised that Moe was so apologetic.

Nevertheless, I gave him a look that showed my lack of concern. I wasn't in the mood for explanations, and, as far I was concerned, he could continue sleeping with that dirty smut.

We sat in silence for a minute, but it felt more like an hour. I didn't have much to say, but deep down, I didn't want to break up our two-year friendship over some twisted broad who couldn't decide who she wanted to be with.

Moe finally spoke. "Look man, I'm not tryin to let some whack-ass chick come between us, 'nah mean? I'm saying, I know you're mad right now. All I can say is I'm sorry."

I extended my hand to meet his open palm. Damn, why did I always have to be Mr. Nice Guy? "Aiight man. But look—on the real—I still think it's gonna be a wrap for me and Jasmyn."

"Man, you don't have to worry about me trying to holla at her again. 'Cause I know it was foul the way I tried to play you. I mean, it's plenty of tight females on campus I could get with. For real though, we're done." Moe tried to pacify me. Little did he know I was not worrying about Jazz. It was too late. I'd look like a sucka if I got with her after knowing my boy had already hit it.

I left his room and went back to Banneker. When I arrived, Shawn was there and I gave him the rundown of the whole situation.

"Yooooo, that is some ill 'ish." Shawn stated.

"I know, I know." I cut him off. I didn't want to prolong any discussion of either Jasmyn or Moe.

"I can't believe all this time Moe was diggin' Jasmyn out. Man, I know you must be mad as hell."

"I am, but it ain't much of a loss. I mean, we kicked it, but she's not my girl or nothing, so it's cool."

Final exam week ended at last. I was psyched to leave. I couldn't wait to get up off campus. Ever since our confrontation in the lobby of her dorm, Jasmyn had called me every day leaving me "I'm sorry, can we talk about it?" messages. I was tempted to let her scratch my itch, but I resisted, buckled down, and stayed to myself for the most part. My hair was woofin' a bit because I hadn't been back to Moe's for a cut. Shawn still kicked it over there as usual. I, on the other hand, just spoke to him whenever I saw him on campus. Even though we were still cool, I wasn't quite ready to go back around him like I used to. I figured when New Year's rolled around, I'd have a change of attitude toward everybody—Moe, Jasmyn, and even Tiana.

_____*Jasmyn*

Winter break went as fast as it came. Four weeks of vacation felt more like four days. I was so busy helping fix our house up for Christmas and running back and forth between Meadowpines and Smyrna. Jerome was scheduled to get out next year and I could hardly wait. Mom was scheduled to come home this spring. I hoped those years in Meadowpines did her some good. My dad's insurance was going to pay for a visiting nurse, which eased my worry of how she would fare while I was away at school.

Back at school, Moe had totally cut me off and Kyle wasn't really talking to me either. I never found out who smashed out my car window, so I guessed that would remain an unsolved mystery. I was starting to believe that I was going to be spending the spring semester manless.

I did everything short of sending myself as a naked singing telegram to Kyle to try to regain his attention. With Valentine's Day a week away, I decided to give it one last try.

The Saturday before the fourteenth, I pulled out my Visa card and called Crystal to go on a shopping spree with me to King of Prussia, an upscale mall located a few miles outside Philadelphia. The shops made the half-hour drive worthwhile. We went to Nordstrom's where Crystal, who usually kept a few dollars in her pocket, treated herself to a Jones New York blouse. I went all out and bought a risqué red negligee and matching robe. Next, we went to Neiman-Marcus and I purchased a slinky pair of Kenneth Cole stilettos to go with my negligee. I wanted to look as alluring and desirable as possible.

This semester, since they both were business majors, Crystal took two courses with Kyle: Technical Writing and Public Relations. Therefore, she was my spy who kept a watchful eye on Kyle. She let me know when he talked to other females, who they were, and how long they spoke. She discreetly followed him across campus whenever she could and let me know if and when a female stopped to have a conversation with him. From her findings, coupled with the pillow talk bigmouth-Shawn gave up, I learned although several women on campus wanted to hit on Kyle, he was not giving them any play. This was enough fuel to spark my big comeback in Kyle's love life.

When the big V-Day arrived, I didn't go to class and focused my attention on nabbing him. I was definitely a spoiled brat; I wanted my way and would do whatever it took to get it. It wasn't my fault; my daddy and big brother spoiled me!

I woke up early and went to Banneker, bringing

a bag of red rose petals I'd purchased. I knew it was corny, but I still sprinkled them outside Kyle's door. I then waited for him in the lobby and when he came downstairs, I presented him with a bag containing a freshly toasted bagel with cream cheese and a chocolate-frosted donut, two of his favorite breakfast foods to eat when he's on the run.

"What is this?" Kyle asked.

"What does it look like, silly?" I laughed. "Duhhhh! It's breakfast. Happy Valentine's Day, Kyle! I've missed you!" I threw my arms around him as he returned the embrace.

"Thanks. But look, I already told you we were a done deal. You know I'mma still speak to you around campus, but that's about it. We're just friends, all right?" Kyle was unwavering in his tone. This was going to be harder than I thought.

"Well, look Kyle. I'm feeling you on that." I stepped in closer to him. "But I know you don't have a girlfriend."

Kyle nervously shifted his weight from one foot to the other, while avoiding eye contact with me. "Look Jasmyn, I have a class in fifteen minutes, so whatever you've got to say-hurry up with it!"

"I know," I continued. "I planned a special evening for us tonight, seeing as how it's Valentine's Day. If you're not busy, I'd love for you to stop by. I'll make dinner—I mean you don't mind a frozen meal from the microwave, do you?" Kyle began to turn his lips upward into a half-smile. I nudged him, and added, "It's Seafood Newburg! So, come by around seven." I smiled and added, "You know you want to."

Kyle looked at me, thoughtfully considered my

offer, and then broke into a grin. He gave me a hug. "Okay, Jazz, but, just a friendly dinner, all right? Nothing else!" He gave me a "you-know-what-I'm talking-about" stare.

"Okay, baby—I mean, Kyle. I'll see you around seven."

"Seven-thirty," he contested.

"Okay, whatever you say. Thanks, Kyle," I added tenderly. "You won't regret it." I leaned up and placed a soft peck on his cheek. He looked slightly aroused, grinned, and turned to leave.

It was a new year and I was turning over a new leaf. No more games, no more manipulating guys. The drama and the stress weren't worth it. Seeing my mom and brother over the holidays made me realize stability was important and something that I needed in my life. Adrienne and Jerome asked me about my love life, and I responded by telling them I had a few "friends." The more I pondered the thought of having a monogamous relationship, the more I liked the idea. I thought I was finally ready to settle down with one guy and Kyle was that guy.

It was a few minutes before seven and I stepped out the shower, preparing to get dressed. I realized I left my purse-size bottle of Clinique Happy perfume in my car. I used it often to freshen up the interior. My hair was styled in a slick genie ponytail. My MAC foundation and Viva Glam lip gloss were perfectly applied, giving the sheer natural illusion that I wasn't wearing make-up. I planned to wear a short black leather skirt which barely touched my knee and a black and cream striped wrap blouse. I threw on a pair of jeans, sneakers, and a velour hoodie and grabbed my car keys and headed outside to retrieve the perfume from my car. I didn't even grab my coat although it was thirty degrees outside. I figured I'd only be two minutes, so it wouldn't matter much.

Outside, it was pretty dark and colder than I anticipated. February was in the air, without a doubt. The street lamps outside Leidy Hall were unusually dim. Near the bushes in front of the dorm, I heard muffled voices—a male and a female. They were voices I didn't recognize. I walked up to the curb and conscientiously glimpsed over my shoulder as I waited for an opportunity to cross the street.

Without warning, I heard: "There she is! Grab that bitch!" I felt somebody sneak up on me from behind. The man placed a gloved hand over my mouth. Meanwhile, a big, burly broad, after smacking me in the face, grabbed me by both wrists, pulled my fourteen-inch ponytail, and dragged me off the curb behind a parked car. I fell to the ground and was unable to see.

All I felt were kicks and punches. My head banged against the fender of the parked car and gave me the biggest headache. I felt a knot forming, as well as the sting of the wintry air hitting open scratches and wounds on my face. I heard the chick say, "You made it easy for us by coming outside, 'cause we were gonna roll right up to room 201 and beat dat ass!" I was defenseless as I laid there not knowing where I was.

I shut my eyes tightly, thinking this was all a bad dream and wondering when I would wake up. A rubber-soled boot kicked my side and I couldn't tell who was beating me. I was punched in my face and literally saw stars. The girl didn't have on gloves because when she punched me, I felt the stab and imprint of a jeweled ring. I cried in pain and screamed for help. They said nothing to me except right before they ran off into a car that apparently was driven by a third accomplice who was double-parked and waiting to pick them up. They were wearing black jackets, jeans, and ski masks, so I couldn't see their faces.

The female kneeled down to me, "Yeah, Jasmyn! You think you can mess around on my cousin Damon and not get caught! Well think again, you sneaky bitch! Yeah, we know all about your so-called boyfriends Kyle and Maurice . . . you think we didn't? Oh, and don't forget how you had sex with Damon's roommate, you nasty smut! The whole time you were running around with your men, we were right behind you . . . following your every move! In your dorm, the lobby, the cafeteria. Everywhere you went, someone was watching your trick-ass. You think you're slick, but you're not! We let you lay low for a couple months, but we had to teach you one last lesson! I advise you if you want to keep the glass in your car windows this semester and protect the rest of that pretty little face of yours, you give Damon an explanation and make up with him!" With that, they jumped in their getaway car and sped off. It was so dark that I couldn't see what kind of car it was, but I thought it was a navy blue four-door sedan.

Finally, campus police pulled up with sirens blaring.

"Did someone call in an assault-in-progress?"

the officer said as he got out of his car to approach me.

With a swollen lip and bloody nose, I looked up at him as if to say "What do you think?"

He came closer and tried to get me to stand, but I sat frozen. Speaking into the walkie-talkie on his shoulder, he requested another patrol car and an ambulance.

A few minutes later, I was being helped up by a few EMTs and into the back of an ambulance. One of my eyes was swollen shut, but I saw Kyle walking down the street, slowing down because of the small crowd gathered at the foot of Leidy's stairs. I was shocked I could get beaten so severely. More importantly, those who'd witnessed it actually stood by passively as if they were watching a fight on pay-per-view. The person who called campus police must have been looking out their window. No one came to my rescue. I was so embarrassed and felt like the biggest idiot in the world. I knew my face was jacked up. My cheek was bleeding profusely. I couldn't believe Damon would have someone do this to me. All these months, he had me followed. I wanted to cry, but I was too shocked and outraged. When I did manage one tear, it slid down my cheek slowly, burning my scrapes and open wounds. At that moment, I realized I was no longer untouchable and not as tough as I pretended to be.

My attackers watched and waited for me to leave the dorm and banked me just like that. I suppose they assumed I was going out on Valentine's Day and decided to lay in wait for me like a predator does for its prey.

I knew from now on I'd better watch my back. *As soon as this is over, I'm buying mace and pepper spray to keep on my key chain. On top of that, I'm keeping a razor in every pocketbook. There won't be a next time.* If somebody ever stepped to me like this again, I'd take that razor out to their throat and say, "I wish you would—"

I wish this ambulance drove faster.

_____*Kyle*

"Excuse me, ma'am, where can I find the emergency room?"

The female security guard directed me towards the waiting area. "Over there to the right is the waiting room." She suspiciously looked me up and down. "You have to be a family member to go inside."

"Okay. Thanks," I replied ignoring the rent-a-cop. She probably dropped out the police academy and couldn't get a better gig. I spotted the Triage Emergency admissions desk and asked for Jasmyn Simmons.

"Simmons . . . hmmm . . . ." she looked at her computer screen, scrolling her mouse down until she landed on her name. "She's in Triage Room Eight. Are you a relative?"

"Yes," I lied. "She's my sister." It's not like Jazz had any family members to come visit her.

I headed back to room eight and peeked

through the curtain. Crystal was seated in a chair by the wall, reading a magazine. She looked up, spotted me, and gave me a hug. "I told them she was my cousin," she laughed.

"It's cool. I said she was my sister," I smiled. I hugged her back and asked how Jazz was doing. From the looks of it, she wasn't doing so well. She was asleep with an IV in her hand. Two small scratches were under her left eye, which was purple and swollen. She had bruises on her upper arm and I peeked under her blanket and hospital gown to see that her thighs were even black and blue.

"I can't believe this, can you? On Valentine's Day at that," Crystal stated. "She told me she planned a special evening for the two of you. We even went shopping last weekend and she bought lingerie and a pair of stilettos to wear for you."

I was inclined to believe Jasmyn didn't buy that sexy stuff for me. When I thought of how much she'd been sweating me and how I knew she and Moe were a done deal, I reconsidered that thought. Maybe Jazz was digging me again, and maybe, for once, she realized you don't miss what you have until it's gone.

The attending doctor came in and checked on her. He told us she would be fine in a few weeks. Luckily, she only needed three stitches on her face. With some ointment, ice, and hot and cold compresses, her face and bruises would heal in a few days. The following week, she would get her stitches taken out and there would be a small, but visible scar.

Crystal and I sat and talked for about an hour

until Jazz woke up. It was nearly two in the morning. Jazz painfully turned her head. "Hey, y'all," she whispered.

I grabbed Jasmyn's hand and held it gently but firmly. "How you doing, Miss Lady?" I asked.

"I'm okay," she said, touching her scars and the gauze on her face. "I guess it'll be a while till my face is back to normal."

I gazed at Jasmyn and all the negative emotions I harbored inside slowly released and transformed into feelings of sympathy and pity. Even though she was sneaky and conniving, no woman deserved to be beaten like this.

"Kyle, I need to level with you. I knew I was wrong to mess with Moe behind your back, but also because I've had a boyfriend named Damon since last year. He's on the football team and when this school year began and I met you and Moe, I cut him off."

"So Damon was the guy knocking on the door that night?" I asked.

She nodded. "And, he's the one responsible for the broken car window and for me getting beat up tonight."

My face fell. I wished there was something I could do for her. "It's in the past now and I can't do nothing about it. So just forget about it for now."

"I am so sorry." Jazz then sat up a bit and looked at us. "Yo," she shook her head intensely. "I think it's time my cousins came to handle some business." She then leaned forward and looked in the mirror on the side wall, touched the bruises on her face, and began crying again.

I left after talking to Jazz for another half-hour. I wasn't sure how things would be with her from that day on, but I hoped this experience taught her a lesson about being with one too many guys.

_____*Jasmyn*

Two months had passed since I was attacked.
The whole thing still had me somewhat shook. Just
the thought of knowing someone was watching
me—and still could be watching me—was enough
to keep me looking over my shoulder. I carried
mace and razor blades whenever I left my room,
even if it was just to go downstairs to get a candy
bar out the machine. My face healed up for the
most part, with the exception of a very pale line on
my cheek from the stitches. I was still pretty and
the mark was nothing a little concealer couldn't
hide.

I was so happy Kyle didn't get mad at me. I knew
he probably felt some type of way when I told him
about Damon, especially after he found out about
Maurice and me before winter break. The whole
situation was fucked up. My life was turning into a
ghetto soap opera. My whole concern that year
had been men, and I couldn't even begin to tell
you why. Maybe it had something to do with miss-

ing my dad and brother and needing men around me, I don't know. All I know is Kyle and I have been seeing each other again. Not as much as before, but I was glad he at least still paid attention to me.

It was a bright, sunny Saturday morning and Crystal was going to Smyrna Hill with me to visit Jerome. I needed to put money on his books. I hated asking my uncle and grandmom for money, so I figured that it was time to get a job. It would keep some money in my pocket and I would stay busy and hopefully out of trouble. A week after I was jumped, I thought of ways to stay on the go, figuring I could dodge any potential stalkers. I went to the local Pathmark and applied to be a cashier. I'd been working there ever since. It definitely helped. I worked twenty hours a week, making about two hundred dollars every two weeks, which was enough for me to help Jerome with his commissary and for me to pay a little bit on my Visa, Macy's, and Lord and Taylor charge cards.

"Hey Jazz, you ready?" Crystal arrived at my door at eight-thirty sharp. She was truly a good friend, waking up early on a Saturday morning to ride with me.

"Yeah, I guess," I replied, looking in my closet for a jacket. "It's a little cool outside. The weatherman said it was fifty-eight degrees. I should've worn long sleeves." I found my navy blue Gap jacket and put it on, grabbed my keys and my purse, and headed out the door.

We began the hour-and-a-half drive by stopping off at the McDonald's drive-through to grab breakfast. The visit was scheduled for eleven o'clock, but you have to arrive fifteen to thirty minutes early or else you'd be unable to have the visit.

Once we arrived at the prison, we signed in and sat by the wall. I whispered to Crystal, "Girl, I can't wait 'til these visitations go to open and I don't have to talk to him on that nasty-ass phone. The windows are so dirty and you can hardly hear your conversation with all those people around. I can't stand that place!"

Crystal smiled and hugged me. "It's almost over. He'll be out by the end of the year, right?"

"Yeah girl, December—a little less than eight months."

I was happy Crystal reminded me that Jerome's sentence would be ending soon. I couldn't wait to have my big brother back home again. Maybe if he was around all of this drama in my life might not be happening. I knew for a fact if my brother had been home when I got beat up, he would have come to Marshall with like ten of his friends and our cousins and they would've turned it out! I remember a few visits ago when I told him I was attacked, he was so mad he looked like he wanted to punch the wall.

My brother always guarded four women in his life: his mother, sister, grandmother, and son's mother, Michelle. Even though Michelle had a fiancé, my brother was still protective of her. My nephew J.J. (Jerome, Jr.) is so adorable. He is the spitting image of Jerome. Since he's only five years old, Michelle doesn't bring him to visit. Hell, she barely visited, save maybe once every three or four months. As far as I was concerned, I was all Jerome had. With my mother away and Daddy gone,

Jerome was all I had too. I knew my uncles, aunts, cousins, and grandmother were around, but it wasn't the same. We felt the same pain and were so much alike. We planned on spending more time with JJ so he could get to know our side of his family when Jerome got out.

At the visit, Jerome and I talked a while and Crystal said a few words to him too. She met Jerome through bars since Crystal and I became friends freshman year. Jerome liked Crystal and was happy I had found a good, honest girlfriend. He knew all through high school I mostly stayed to myself or talked to a few of his boys.

When the visit was over, I left teary-eyed as usual and dropped Crystal off at the dorm. I had to be to work by three-thirty. I was working until eleven, which was just as well. I knew that I'd get a good night sleep tonight.

Kyle

Jasmyn and I had been together for a while ever since her beatdown. I think there was a soft spot in my heart for her because she went all out to impress me on Valentine's Day, and I still felt bad for her being attacked the way she was. We were intimate several times, but not nearly as often as we used to be. I was glad she eventually chose not to seek retaliation by having her cousins come down to beat Damon up. God only knows what else may have occurred.

Even though two more months went by, I still wasn't ready to put a title on our relationship, and she seemed cool with that. I sensed there was some distance with her and that Damon probably had something to do with it. I finally figured out who he was. I saw him here and there across campus, but never stepped to him. I didn't want a confrontation and knew any dude who would get a chick beat down the way he did was the type of cat I didn't want to mess with.

But I started thinking more about Tiana. We talked once every other week and when we did, she always managed to talk about her man. It was always "Chauncey-this" and "Chauncey-that" and "Guess what he bought me? Guess where we went? Oh, that sounds like something Chauncey did." I was fed up with hearing about the guy.

I finally told Tiana I had a female friend, but I never told her everything that went down with us—all of the drama and everything else. I assumed with spring and romance in the air, things must have been going well with Tiana and her new boyfriend. I could tell she was really falling for this dude.

One Friday night, I gave her a call to see how she was doing. After a few minutes of niceties and small talk, Tiana went into serious mode.

"Kyle, can I trust you?"

Can she trust me? "Of course you can, baby girl," I wanted to say. I wish there was a way I could convey my true feelings to her, but as they say, timing is everything. She had her man now and I had— well, I don't know what you want to call what me and Jasmyn had. The bottom line was telling Tiana how I felt would not be a smart thing to do at this time.

"This is your boy Kyle. You know we go way back like MC Hammer and polka-dot pants!"

Tiana giggled and added, "I'm three months pregnant."

What the—? You could've knocked me down with a feather. I couldn't believe it. Even though I never slept with her, I couldn't imagine another dude sleeping with her, and, even worse, knocking her up! In a strange way, I felt betrayed. Needless to say, I congratulated her and quickly made up an excuse to get off the phone.

"That's nice, Tee. I know you are excited. Congratulations, baby girl. I'm happy for you. Let me get off this phone. I think I hear someone knocking on my door."

We said our goodbyes and I called Moe to tell him I was coming over. We patched things up and he swore he would never do anything foul like that again. I believed him and we went back to hanging out like normal. The four of us, Shawn, Raheem, Moe, and I made a pact: if we ever started digging the same female, we wouldn't fight over her; we would let the female choose who she wanted to be with. It was kind of stupid, I know, but at least it protected our friendship. I guess you could say that Jazz had "picked" me over Moe. Moe pulled many chicks on the account of all those Philly girls who like New Yorkers, so losing Jasmyn was really no big deal to him. After I called Moe, I called Shawn on his cell phone to tell him to meet me over Moe's in a half. Shawn had left out earlier to go take his young girl to the store. I needed to be around my boys and get my mind on something else besides Tiana.

"Y'all think he did it?" I nodded towards Moe's Kobe Bryant poster. I was reclined on the floor, playing *Mortal Kombat* with Raheem on his PS2. Moe, who was cutting Shawn's hair, looked up and stated, "Hell no! Kobe might've smashed, but that white girl damn sure was with it."

Shawn added, "Yo, that's what he gets for cheating on his wife. Now, they're gonna pin rape charges on him." I couldn't believe Shawn, out of all people, was advocating monogamy.

I looked at Shawn and said, "You of all people—talking about *cheating*?" I cracked up. "This coming from the same man who is messing with two chicks on campus right now and one of those chicks has a man!" I stated, referring to Crystal and his new "young babe."

"Look dog, I'm not married. Just like Crystal and her girls be saying: 'No ring? No thing!!' " Shawn flashed his palm back and forth like a female. We fell out laughing.

Moe looked at Shawn as though he couldn't believe what he just said. "Shawn, get the hell outta here! Kobe didn't rape that chick, she was wit' it. He probably didn't give her no money so she saw an opportunity to get paid! You know how these females are with NBA and NFL players; it's all about getting paid. Why you think so many of them got paternity suits? These athletes get caught up and sleep with groupies and pay the price for it later."

We spent the rest of the night philosophizing on all sorts of topics: celebrities, sports, and rappers. It was a Friday night and there were no parties on campus. Heem made a liquor store run, we ordered pizza and hot wings, played some PS2 and spades, watched part of a Lakers game, and continued talking about Kobe. While watching a bootleg DVD, we sparked up for the third time.

Between the alcohol and chief, I was in another zone. I needed to be outside my normal self after the bomb Tiana dropped on me. I couldn't even sleep. Raheem fell asleep on his bed. Shawn was knocked out on the floor. Moe and I stayed up to blow some more. It was around one-thirty in the morning when he asked me the craziest question, and now I know it must have been the weed and Henny talking

"Yo kid, lets call Jasmyn and see what that ho is doing," Moe suggested. I didn't pay attention to the fact he'd said "let's" as in the both of us calling her. But I was high and, like a dummy, I pulled out my cell phone and called her. Of course, she picked up.

"Yo Jazz, it's me and Moe. We both about to come downstairs to see you, aiight?"

Jasmyn mumbled, "Look, I'm going back to sleep. Y'all are bugging!"

Moe snatched the phone from my hand. "Ay Jazz, this is Moe. Yo ass betta be up!" Moe hung up on her. We laughed and went downstairs.

Jasmyn

Moe and Kyle had a lot of nerve calling me at one-thirty in the morning. I was so tired, being that I didn't get home from work until eleven-thirty. When I got in, I threw my clothes off and piled them next to the bathroom door and scrambled into the bed, half-dead to the world. I was pissed the phone rang when I had only been asleep for two hours. Nevertheless, I got up and dug out my red negligee and robe. Kyle said he was coming. As for Moe, he was probably playing on the phone. Moe knew I didn't so much as speak to him much anymore, because I was feeling Kyle. I told Moe, "Look, I made a mistake and I'm really trying to see your boy Kyle like that, so I'll still speak to you, but there can't be anything else between us." Moe said he was cool with that and for the past few months, things have been straight. So, if he knew like I knew, he'd keep his behind upstairs.

I heard a few faint knocks at my door. I looked

through the peephole and saw both Kyle and Moe standing there. *What's Moe here for? I'm not inviting both of those niggas in!*

I slowly opened the door, careful not to reveal my outfit to them. "What do y'all want?" I smirked.

Moe stuck his hand out and pushed the door open. "We came here to kick it with you." Kyle entered behind him and didn't say much. I rolled my eyes as they walked past me. I caught a whiff of their liquor and marijuana-scented trail. I never saw the two of them together, much less high and drunk. They sat down and made themselves comfortable like it was the middle of the afternoon. Moe was the worse of the two; he was totally chiefed-up and drunk as a skunk.

I tugged on Moe's arm. "Come on, Maurice. You gotta go, baby. Go back upstairs and get some sleep." I needed for Kyle and me to be alone.

Moe overpowered me and pulled me down on his lap. He began touching and hugging me. Kyle, half-asleep, didn't try to stop him. I couldn't believe it!

I pulled away. "Boy, get off me, you stink," I insisted in a half-serious, half-flirtatious manner. I did manage a slight giggle. Moe was still attractive, even when high. When he kissed my neck, I stopped resisting as much.

It didn't take a genius to realize that they set me up. Moe was going to try to get it and then pass me off to Kyle. I became nervous and afraid as Moe began running his hands underneath my gown and feeling on my breasts. I kept my eyes open as Moe kissed me. I looked over at Kyle helplessly. Kyle became more alert, grabbed me off of Moe's lap and pulled me down on the bed with him.

Moe's kisses felt good, but Kyle was my heart. If anybody was going to get some tonight in room 201, it was going to be him. I gave Kyle a kiss and told him, "Tell your boy to leave, so we can be alone."

Moe stood up and pulled down his pants, ignoring the fact that Kyle and I were on the bed. He then looked at Kyle, "Yo homey, you want to go first?"

Oh snap. These mutha-fathers are trying to pull a train on me? Oh, helllllll no! There isn't going to be a ménage-a-trois jumping off tonight!

Before I knew it and before Kyle had a chance to respond, Moe grabbed me and positioned me doggy-style in front of him. I had to admit the thought of letting them toss it up intrigued me for a hot second but I realized as cute as they were, I couldn't go out like that. I knew Kyle was somewhat of a punk and probably too afraid to stand up to Moe, who was taking charge of this entire situation.

I tried to stand up as Moe forcefully snatched my weave by its ends with one hand and held me down with his other hand. I felt him lift my gown up and before I could protest, he had entered me. My body took over and common sense began to fly out the window with each thrust.

Kyle must have become jealous because after a few minutes he snatched me away from Moe and had his way with me on the bed. I couldn't believe any of this was happening. I was scared, yet still excited and caught up in all of this steamy passion. But then I realized I was playing myself and that I was putting myself in a dangerous predicament.

Suddenly, tears began to stream down my face. I was really into Kyle and knew even though he was high, he was well aware of what was going on and from this day forward would lose all respect for me.

Thirty minutes later, they were knocked out, but I was still awake. Moe was in the chair and Kyle was in the bed. I took a shower, came out, looked and saw the two of them, and got scared.

I just let two guys come down here in the middle of the night and run a train on me. I didn't even try to fight them off, so it wasn't like I could really say I was raped. In a sick way, part of me enjoyed it. What the hell is my problem?

I put on the least sexy thing I could find—a pair of raggedy Joe Boxer shorts and a faded Old Navy tee-shirt to sleep in. Lying next to Kyle, I silently cried myself to sleep, feeling the scar on my face courtesy of Damon's beatdown crew.

Maybe I should try to work things out with Damon. I did apologize for cheating on him and he apologized for having me beat up and my car damaged. He even gave me three hundred dollars as a peace offering and said he moved on and I was free to be with other guys. I knew I wanted to be with Kyle, but after tonight, it was definitely a wrap. I resolved that both Kyle and Moe were officially out of my life. *They better be glad I'm on the birth control patch, otherwise, we'd be on the Ricki Lake show taking paternity tests.*

For the first time in my life I was truly ashamed of myself. I was spinning out of control, letting my desires rule everything. I felt like a true whore; but I think the right label for me was "a misunderstood ho." I just didn't know what I wanted. Finally, I said to myself, *enough is enough. I think it's time for me to really be alone.*

I wished the Chinese store was open. I wanted to order an egg roll and shrimp fried rice. Food was the only thing those days that didn't disappoint me.

_____*Kyle*

The next day, I woke up around one o'clock in the afternoon. I'm not sure when I left Jazz's room, but somehow I made it back to my room. Everything was a blur. My head was achy and I reeked of marijuana, cognac, beer, and feminine juices. I got up and gazed at myself in the mirror. I was wearing a wife-beater and a pair of boxers. I tried to get a sense of reality and figure out what I did during the past twelve hours.

Did me and Moe run a train on Jazz? What was I thinking? Did we set her up? What if she gets us arrested on rape charges? Then again, she didn't even scream from what I could remember. Moe hit it and passed it off to me. So, she better not even cry rape. This is fucked up.

I never thought in a million years that I would do something foul like that. I just didn't want something like that getting out, but on a campus like this one, where a lot of the black people were really close, the news was bound to spread soon. *Damn, Jazz is a real smut.* You expect guys to be triflin' as hell; but when chicks get down like that—letting two friends do it to them—that mess is just nasty.

I relaxed my thoughts. Maybe it was a dream, but it wasn't. I knew I'd slept with Jazz because there were passion marks on my collarbone and chest. I ran my hand along the nape of my neck and felt indentations from where her nails dug into me. I knew Jazz had some nails on her. She almost scratched me down to the white meat! I turned and looked over my shoulder in the mirror and noticed three scratches on my shoulder blade. I felt strangely tired—like a cross between being in a fight and finishing a wildly passionate lovemaking session.

It was Sunday and I knew I should at least acknowledge God. Mom, Dad, Ty, and Jamir were probably at church, and if I were home I would be too. I whispered a quick prayer to confess my sins and to ease some of my guilt.

Heavenly Father, I ask you to forgive me for any sins I committed last night. Forgive me for drinking, smoking, and having sex with Jasmyn. Lord, please forgive us for what we did and forgive all my boys for all the mess we get into. Make us better men and more able to resist temptation. Amen.

It was time to pack for summer and I couldn't wait. It was a long time coming. Jazz and I were officially over. Moe and I never spoke on what happened. We pulled a train on Jazz and I felt horrible about it. Even though Jasmyn still called me and I stopped by to see her from time to time, we were never intimate again—not even a kiss. I apologized for what happened and she forgave me. It never would have happened had I not overreacted to Tiana being pregnant. That triggered my smoking and drinking and took me totally out of character.

I felt remorse since the incident and began reading my Bible and praying more often. I asked God for forgiveness and it was as though a huge weight was lifted off me. I was glad God said He would remove our sins "as far as the east is from the west." When I reflected on my junior year, I saw it as a life-altering experience. But it was time to go back to Philly and focus on making some money this summer. I needed to gear up for my senior year and landing a job after graduation. Soon, I would be getting my "grown man on" and the childish days would end.

Back in Philly things were normal. I was home several times during the semester, so it wasn't as though my family had time to miss me. Jamir and Ty looked as if they'd matured some. And of course, my mom and pops were glad to see me.

During the previous school year, I lost my desire to attend church. The weekends I came home during the semester, I tended to sleep late and miss church. I believe Jazz, Moe, Shawn, and Raheem drained something out of me, each one in their own little way. Whatever it was, it affected my attitude when I returned home.

But it was summer and my family was together again. I had a desire to draw closer to God. That Sunday we went to church and Pastor Green preached on the Prodigal Son. Now if that wasn't a direct sign from God intended just for me, I don't know what was. His message was "you can always return home." I went up at the end of the sermon during the altar call, asking for prayer because I backslid so much by fornicating, drinking, and smoking weed. Granted, it wasn't anywhere as excessive as my boys, but in God's eyes, sin is sin. I wasn't a bigger or smaller sinner than the next guy.

As interesting as the sermon was, I was more excited to have a chance to see the now-expectant mother, Tiana. I wanted to hug, see, and talk to her. I missed that girl so much and really needed to be around her. I vibed so much off her and missed the good feelings I used to get from spending time with her.

After service, I told my family I was going to say hi to some people and that Shawn would give me a ride, so I would see them at home." Yes, even crazy-borderline-heathen-at-college Shawn took his butt to church too. Shawn was busy hollering at the young girls who were now seniors in high school. He was amazed how grown and adult looking they had become. He liked to flex his "I'm-a-college-man" bravado around them. I let him get his church game on while I tracked Tiana down. I noticed her outside near the front steps standing next to a tall dark-skinned guy. Her stomach was plump and she had that motherly glow. At closer observation, I realized her male companion was the same Chauncey that Shawn and I reminisced about. Shawn came outside and joined me as I approached Tiana and her man.

"Ooooh, look who came to church. Oh my God, Mount Zion just lets anybody up in here nowadays, don't they?" Tiana laughed. She still had that teasing sisterly sense of humor I loved.

"What's up, ma?" I smiled as I ignored Chauncey and gave her a hug.

Shawn added his two cents, also giving Tiana a hug and rubbing her belly. "What's up, shorty? Or should I say 'fat mamaaaa?'" I didn't want to be nearly as intrusive as Shawn by touching her stomach, but I broke down and stroked it gently.

"Man shut up, I'm about six months pregnant!" Tiana smiled and then patted Shawn's gut. "Now what's your excuse, Biggie?"

We fell out laughing. Another thing I dug about her was she always had jokes and could keep a brother cracking up. I stepped back and acknowledged Chauncey.

"What's up, brother?" I shook his hand.

"Yo man, ain't your name Chauncey?" Shawn asked. "You used to live on Fifty-Ninth Street, right?" Chauncey released my hand and shook Shawn's.

"Yeah, that's right," Chauncey responded. "Hold up, y'all both do look familiar—oh snap, aren't y'all the ones they used to call 'Keenan and Kel?'" He laughed and Tiana started laughing too. "What's up?" He gave us both dap. "Shawn and um—Lyle, right?"

"Kyle," I corrected him and redirected my attention towards Tiana. Looking at her, I wanted to step to her so badly. I wanted her to know I was officially single and that, even though she had a baby's-daddy, I still wanted to holla. She looked angelic in a sheer floral dress that skimmed her ankles, which were still slim and not swollen as you might expect. Her hair was longer than I remembered. It was blown straight and curled under slightly at the ends, a few inches below her shoulder. Pregnancy definitely looked good on her. *God, I know this ain't right, but I wish her baby was mine!*

Tiana made it a point to let us know Chauncey was her man, and if I wasn't mistaken, she was wearing a ring. It didn't look like a friendship ring either.

"Congrats, man," Shawn extended his hand to Chauncey. I looked at Shawn in disbelief.

"Thanks man," Chauncey replied. "This is my first one, so you know I'm hoping it's a boy," he patted Tiana's belly like a proud father.

I looked down and acted as if I were text-messaging on my cell phone to avoid looking at the seemingly happy parents. I wished I'd stepped to Tiana a long time ago and come fall, that would be *my* baby popping out of her.

_____Jasmyn

The summer breeze felt cool against my face as I rolled down I-95 on my way to Smyrna to visit Jerome. The school year finally ended and I managed to earn a 2.5 grade point average and risked being put on academic probation. That whole year was fucked up and I decided to spend the summer focusing on me and my family. _Fuck men!_ They were full of shit and nothing but trouble. I needed a break from all of them just for a few months, at least.

I neglected my mother and Jerome, the two most important people in my life, because I was consumed with having a man. In the end, what did it get me? A low GPA, a broken car window, fifteen damaged CDs, four stitches on my face, black and blue marks, and overall embarrassment. Worst of all was the humiliation of knowing that by the time I returned to Marshall this fall, half of the black population on campus would, no doubt, know all of my business. From the reason behind me getting my ass kicked, to the fact that I let two guys double-bang me; I would no doubt be labeled the campus slut.

None of that was important right now. I had a long heart-to-heart talk with Crystal before I left and was so glad we were best friends. She gave me sound advice telling me to "stop chasing water-falls" or in other words, stop living on the edge when it came to men and sex. She always talked in clichés, but it was cool; it was her way of getting a point across. I finally opened up to her about Damon, Brandon, Moe, and Kyle. I even had my eyes on Raheem too—it was some sort of sick con-quest thing with me. She told me how I was going to continue getting hurt if I didn't slow down, I de-served so much better, and yadda yadda yadda. I agreed with her and decided not to let any of those events shake me. Even after the "train" inci-dent, I kept my head up.

My mom was supposed to ride down with me today to visit Jerome. For the past few months, she had been acting normal. Meadowpines had success-fully transitioned her from living in its institution-style setting to living back at home and working in a regular career. I was proud of her. She had a job in the banking field again; she was a bank teller at Wachovia. It would be a while before she worked her way up to Loan Officer or Branch Manager, but I had faith in her. She was looking good too. I made sure she kept regular hair and nail appoint-ments. On that particular Saturday, she attended a mandatory training session for her new job, so she couldn't go with me to see Jerome.

Uncle Jeff and Aunt Tammy continued to stay with us to help with the bills because the Jerome-stash was getting low. Uncle Jeff used a lot of it on household repairs, or so he said. I knew one thing: he better not be running to Atlantic City and giving all of Jerome's money to Trump Plaza and Caesars! Although he was a nice guy, he loved to gamble. I would never approach him about it because he looked out for us by keeping the house payments up and everything else functional bill-wise. I was glad there was money left and I qualified for student loans. Plus, my dad's will left part of his pension to us. My mom cashed a portion of it in and gave some to Jerome and me in drips and drabs. She was scared we would blow it on a shopping spree. I quit my job at Pathmark when the semester ended, but lucked up getting a job at Target.

When I arrived in Smyrna, I checked in and paced back and forth anxiously. Because he was approaching the end of his term, Jerome moved to open visitation. This meant we could talk face-to-face in a large open multi-purpose room which housed cafeteria-style tables. I brought him a turkey hoagie, French fries, and a bag of Doritos. He was excited to see me and even more excited to see the food

"Heyyy, little sis!" Jerome yelled and gave me a long hug. We held the embrace for five minutes and I dampened his shoulder with tears. He stepped back and gave me the once-over. "Girl, let me look at you! It was hard to see you through those dirty windows before, but check you out! You're getting kinda thick! You'd better start working out!" Jerome expressed amusingly.

I wiped away my tears and huffed amusingly. "Boy, shut the hell up! I am still a dime. You just mad 'cause I got all this ba-dunk-a-dunk," I laughed, turned sideways, and did a little booty-shaking dance like I was on *Soul Train*.

"Yeah aiight," Jerome continued. "Ain't nobody ready for all that jelly! Keep it up, you ain't gonna be a dime, you gonna be the whole damn quarter!" Then he playfully punched my arm. "Sike, girl, you know I'm just playin'!"

I teasingly smacked him upside the head and warned him, "Keep talking, hear? I'mma take all my food back home!"

I'd packed on about fifteen pounds since the fall. Now that Jerome, my brother and closest of closest friends, had mentioned it, I knew it was time to do something about it. Starting Monday, I'm pulling out the Tae-Bo videos. *As soon as I get home, I'm running to the store to get a six-pack of Slim-Fast.*

My hour with Jerome flew by. I confided in him that I was going to be single for a while. Jerome almost hit the roof when I told him this guy I was talking to had set me up and ran a train on me with his boy. If he wasn't locked already, he sure would've been coming to campus and seeking revenge. I left it alone, but Jerome said he wasn't going to let it die. He told me that this fall, since he'd be out, he would be around to protect me. I told him his first priority should be to get a j-o-b and help hold it down at home. There is nothing worse than a recently released ex-felon who can't get a job and gets back into the same trouble that got him locked up in the first place.

"Yo, Rome, you gonna have to keep your nose clean when you get out, all right?" I wanted Jerome to know how serious I was.

"Jazz, you just worry about keeping those grades

up and graduating in May. Leave those clowns
alone at your school 'cause I'm gonna be up there
to check on you!"

I was glad to have Jerome watching over me and
I almost wanted the summer to hasten, so it would
be fall and I could have my big brother back again.
Maybe then, I'd feel all the love and protection I
so desperately sought in Damon, Moe, and Kyle.

_____*Kyle*

June, July, and August had to be the shortest months on the calendar. I was glad to have made a couple thousand dollars working at the car dealership. Despite all the "excitement" in my life, I maintained decent grades, enough for Marshall to hook me up with a paid internship at a BMW/Audi dealer right outside Philadelphia. I helped keep track of inventory, analyzed their weekly sales, profits, and assisted with payroll.

Senior year was upon me and aside from Tiana getting ready to drop that sorry mutha-you-know-what's baby, I didn't have anything to look forward to this fall. I secured an on-campus apartment with Shawn. I needed the privacy and figured, by not being in the mix so much, I would avoid unnecessary drama. Most importantly, I wanted to avoid Jasmyn-drama and not attract more negative energy from Moe or Raheem. Now Shawn, I could deal with one-on-one, but paired with them, it was a deadly ghetto combination. Smoking, drinking, and careless talk and behavior were sure to follow. I wanted my newfound peace and maturity to rub off on Shawn, but I wasn't so sure it had.

The apartment was about a half-mile from the dorms. Shawn and I had separate rooms, finally, after three years. Our parents still sent us money, so we were able to pay the electric and cable bills. The school provided free local phone service and we ate in the dining hall.

The reality of my fast-approaching adulthood was enough to make me buckle down on my academics. I was determined to graduate with above a 3.0 grade point average. One of the most important things I did, however, was cut ties with Jazz.

I remember reading the Bible over the summer and something stuck out to me, which reminded me of her. In the book of Proverbs, Solomon warns his son to avoid the wicked woman, that she is a seductress who will lead you on the path to Hell. Jasmyn Simmons was my wicked woman. She had scheming ways about her. Just the fact she allowed Moe and me to take advantage of her the way we did that night made me believe, deep down inside, she enjoyed it. I may have been high, but I was still aware of what was going on. Not one time did she scream, yell, cry, or do any of the things a girl who was being sexually assaulted would do. She willingly let us pass her back and forth—a couple of times, I might add.

That night I had an "I-don't-even-care-about-this-ho" mentality and let my body take control over my mind. So for that reason alone, Jasmyn Boulevard was one street I couldn't afford to walk down again. I was surprised she didn't give me some nasty STD. As long as it didn't hurt when I went to the bathroom and my seed never made it to her womb, I was straight. As a matter of fact, I was overjoyed to cut all dealings with her. The most she would get from me would be a "hi" and "bye."

I spent the first two months of the semester virtually drama-free. Classes were going well, my grades were up, and Jasmyn had not tried to work things out and re-establish a love connection. Even Shawn became more serious about his studies. We still saw Moe and Raheem around campus, and they started coming over to our apartment instead of us trekking down to the dorms to visit them. It was the end of October and I knew Tiana was due to deliver any day now. Just as I expected, on the fifteenth, which was her due date, she called me with the good news.

"Kyle, guess what? It's a girl! Jayda Sade Anderson. Seven pounds, twelve ounces. She was born four hours ago." She sounded rested and calm. Motherhood seemed to suit her well. It was as though she'd transformed into a more mature woman.

I was happy for her. I congratulated Tiana and told her to tell Chauncey the same. Even though I faked being glad for them, my insides were seething with resentment. I knew it was wrong and I should've been asking myself "What would Jesus do?" but I couldn't stand Chauncey.

"Yeah, well I'll tell him you said congratulations— whenever I see him," Tiana said sarcastically. Her tone changed from enthusiastic to somber. Obviously, the whole hormonal thing was still in effect.

I perked up when I heard her actually say something negative about the guy. "What do you mean, 'whenever you see him?' Where is he?" *Don't tell me he skated on her!*

"Kyle," she continued. "I can't even begin to tell you . . ." Tiana's voice started to fade. I heard her sniffle, and knew she was about to cry. My insides burned, hearing her so upset on what should've been the happiest day of her life. "I'm having second thoughts about Chauncey. He's just . . ." She paused and sucked her teeth. ". . . so irresponsible and unreliable. My whole last month he was hardly around. Do you know I had to call my cousin to get a damn ride to the hospital? It's a mess!" She sighed heavily and I wanted to jump through the phone to be with her.

I could've told you that, baby girl. Not wanting to upset her any further, I told her she didn't have to talk about him anymore and all I wanted to hear about was the baby. Then I heard Chauncey in the background acting like the Notorious B.I.G. singing, "I love it when you call me big pop-pa! Where's my baby girl?"

"Oh, here he comes," she whispered. "Let me call you back." Tiana hung up quickly. With no one around to talk to, I decided to go make moves.

Feeling somewhat envious of Chauncey, I thought about which one of my female associates I could call to take my mind off Tiana. I knew I was trying to turn over a new leaf this semester and all by not messing with any more drama-filled chicks, but it wasn't easy to let go of my physical needs. A young man like myself was full of desire and energy that had to be released. The problem was I didn't have many female friends—and certainly no chicks on reserve waiting for a booty call. Aside from Aliya and Jasmyn, my two so-called 'girlfriends' at Marshall, the other females I associated with were nothing more than classmates and acquaintances.

That semester, only a few women stepped to me on campus. Out of those few, I'd only called one. She was this half-Puerto Rican, half-Cuban mami named Damaris Cruz. I called her Mari or Mah-ree for short. She was in my American Studies class and worked out in the fitness center. I would catch her there a few times a week. I figured since I was on my self-improvement kick, I'd might as well add about ten more pounds of muscle to this five-foot eleven, one hundred seventy pound frame of mine.

I only went into this whole other mode of having to be with another woman physically whenever I became jealous and started catching feelings for Tiana real hard. Nothing happened with Damaris right away. Whenever I saw her at the gym, she always looked damn good walking on the treadmill. I was a sucker for thick, pretty legs just like Jazz's. Damaris was very cute and curvy and she was sweating a brother. Being I remained single all summer, I needed female attention or else I was going to explode.

_____Jasmyn

The fall was flying by and I was glad. That only meant graduation was soon approaching. Without a man in my life, I was able to concentrate on my classes. I had to get a 2.5 this semester if I wanted to student teach this spring. There were a lot of Elementary Education majors competing for placement in the best suburban schools. The higher your GPA was, the more likely you were to be placed in your first or second choice school. I just wanted to be placed, even if it was in an inner city school; it didn't matter to me. I knew I may have made some poor decisions in life, but selecting my major wasn't one of them. I knew that education was a good career move because schools would always be in business. I felt pretty confident I would be able to hold down a steady job once I graduated and was employed by a school district. I was going to make sure I became certified in both Pennsylvania and New Jersey in order to increase my marketability.

Jerome was getting out right before Christmas. I knew that with he and Adrienne, along with my sometimes-I-spend-my-entire-paycheck-on-the-lotto Uncle Jeff, there would need to be more money in the house. When I started teaching, there would be a steady consistent flow of income. Although Uncle Jeff and Aunt Tammy kept up the bills, I was no dummy. The earnings from my uncle's gambling supplemented his income, along with the Jerome stash. I was glad Jerome was getting out and I'd be turning twenty-one in February. We could withdraw the funds Daddy saved for us.

Early in September, I hooked up with two guys, Hassan and Antoine, mainly out of boredom. They hollered at me when I needed someone to take notice since Kyle, Moe, and Damon no longer seemed interested. I met Hassan at the bookstore and Antoine in town at the dry cleaner. It was easy for me to juggle since Antoine didn't go to Marshall. After a month, I got bored and dropped them, but they had it going on in the bedroom.

I didn't want to have to worry about either guy hanging around me during holiday time. So, slowly I stopped returning their calls. I must admit I got jealous watching Crystal and Shawn sometimes. *Maybe Kyle will come to his senses and try to get with me this year.* Life was getting kind of boring without a man.

_____Kyle

Flirting with Damaris was getting played out, and after about two weeks, I walked over to her while she was bent over at the water fountain, refilling her bottle.

"How you doing, Mari?" I asked as she rose up and gently shook her hair out of her face.

"Aw, damn," she giggled. "You scared the hell outta me! You know you shouldn't sneak up on people like that."

My eyes were focused on her bronze-colored legs and her firm, yet curvaceous, shape. She saw my wandering eyes and smirked. "Take a picture, it'll last longer."

"My bad." I smiled and lowered my head. _I need to step my game up._ "But I've been seeing you for a couple of weeks, and I told you my name already. So, I'm not a stranger. And I know you've been watching me."

"And?" _All right, I see she's got a smart mouth. It's cool, she's still sexy._

"And you know you want to give me your number, so stop playing with me, girl!"

Damaris smiled and eventually wrote her number down on the inside of my arm.

"Don't wash it off," she said with a flirtatious grin and went back to lifting weights. I didn't want to sweat her, so I left before she'd call me a stalker.

After a few days of contemplation, I finally called Damaris and asked her to come over. I told her that I would fix dinner. She was with it and within two hours, Damaris was at my door sporting a short jean skirt and a tight baby blue zip-up jersey hoodie with a pair of fresh white Nikes. Now I knew that Spanish people were known for dressing outrageously, and although her outfit was fly, she definitely was dressed like it was the middle of July rather than the end of October. I didn't care. She was still fine. And fashion tips weren't exactly what I was looking to get from her.

Shawn was gone somewhere with Crystal, and I knew I had the apartment to myself for a while. The two of them were starting to get serious; so serious, that Crystal supposedly had broken up with her man back home during the summer. I had just lowered the heat on the spaghetti sauce when Damaris showed up at my door, ringing the bell. I tucked my button-up striped shirt inside my khakis and went to the door to greet her.

"Hey, Ky-yuhl," she smiled. Her Nuyorican accent was thick; her people were straight off the island, but she was born and raised in the Bronx. Whenever she spoke, every syllable was exaggerated.

As I hugged her, I got turned on feeling her ample chest press against mine. She smelled good, too. Plus, that long, silky curly hair was a brother's dream. No disrespect to the sisters, but with an Asian, Caucasian, or Hispanic woman, you didn't have to worry about messing somebody's do up, and you damn sure didn't have to wake up to an ugly scarf tied around their head like Aunt Jemima.

"What's up, mami?" I loved to flex my little Spanish papi-chulo phrases on her.

"Not much, what's up with you, pa?" she said while planting a kiss on my cheek. "Ooh, it smells good in here," she noted. "Spaghetti? Mmm, one day you gon' 'ave to let me fix you some pastelillos like my ti-ti Benita makes." She was referring to a traditional dish that her aunt makes. Pastelillos were like little meat patties.

After all of the small talk and a little bit of my dinner of spaghetti and Caesar salad, we relaxed on the couch. I had prepared a medley of classic contemporary romantic films for us to view: *Love and Basketball, Save the Last Dance,* and *The Best Man.*

"Oooh, me gusta a él!" she exclaimed picking up the cover to *The Best Man.* "Taye Diggs ees mee baby! Ay, qué chulo!" She fanned herself, shaking her head. Then she laughed and handed the DVD case back to me.

"Oh, so you like those chocolate brothers, huhn?" I teased. "I guess I'm not 'black' enough!" I joked, stroking my face.

"Oh deja eso Ky-yuhl!" She grabbed my face. "You know I think you're a cutie, my little morenito." She planted a kiss on my lips and the rest was history. The stereotype of the Latin Lover was true for the women as well because I'd be lying if I didn't say this babe put it on me. If she wasn't screaming and moaning, it was "Ay papi!" this and "Ay papi!" that. I closed my eyes at one point and imagined I was making love to Tiana. I was so into it, I even went bareback. You know how it is when you're in the heat of passion and the female tells you she's on the pill. Consequently, I just went with the flow.

When we finished our business, she thanked me and left. "I 'ave to go, pero call me later, okay?"

I assured her I'd definitely call her, lying through my teeth. "All right ma, I'll call you."

Damaris was tight and all, but I didn't need another semester of dealing with a crazy chick and her issues, especially during my senior year. Not to say she had issues, but I couldn't take chances. Therefore, I wasn't going to guarantee I'd be calling her more often. At one time, I thought Jasmyn was cool and drama-free, and you see how that situation turned out. The reality was I had an itch that needed to be scratched. Damaris scratched it. That was all there was to it.

Over the next few weeks, Damaris and I continued to see each other. We both knew that our relationship was strictly physical—no strings attached. I felt spiritually convicted after every time we were intimate, but I gradually became more and more accustomed to the fornication. And I figured as long as I prayed for forgiveness both before and after doing the deed, and even read a Psalm or two, then me and God would be cool. Hey, I had come a long way since last year when I was drinking, smoking a little bit, and having sex almost every day. At least I wasn't doing anything illegal.

I had been home to Philly once, but when I tried calling Tiana to find out what was up with her and Chauncey, she was putting the baby to sleep and couldn't talk. So even though I was a bit vexed, I decided to wait and let her call me. As for Jasmyn, I saw her on campus here and there. We spoke casually, sometimes exchanging a friendly hug, but that was about it. She always seemed to be in a hurry and looking over her shoulder, talking to me really fast, as though she was afraid someone might see her. Her appearance was frazzled, and she definitely lost the fly, fashionable style I was used to seeing. I didn't know what was up with her, but she was no longer my concern since she was no longer my girl. So, I didn't worry much about it.

It was a few weeks before Thanksgiving, nearly one year after all my Jasmyn drama began. I think God really has a sense of humor, because before too long more drama started. This time, it was a new year, a new female, and a new set of problems.

Damaris called me, as she usually did every couple of days, just to see how I was doing. I was in my bedroom studying and feeling lonely. I asked her to come by and keep me company. She agreed. "I'm glad you asked, 'cause I need to talk to you." The tone of her voice was serious and I knew that she wasn't coming over for a lovemaking session. "I'll be over in an hour."

As I waited all sorts of thoughts ran through my

head. What if she had a boyfriend? Or maybe she's flunking out of school. Or what if her mom was sick? I had no idea, but I decided not to worry. I flipped into my spiritual mode, knelt down next to my bed, and whispered a prayer asking God to calm my nerves and not allow the news to be anything larger than I could handle.

I got off my knees and threw on my Kanye West CD, figuring he was a 'safe' rapper to listen to and I wouldn't appear hypocritical by listening to him right after praying. As I was scanning the CD for a song, Shawn came in. I heard him say "Shhh!" to two female voices that followed him. I knew one of the voices belonged to Jasmyn.

I walked into the living room to see Crystal and Jasmyn dressed like twins with matching white sneakers, gray sweatpants, gray sweatshirts, and lavender scarves tied around their heads. They wore braids pulled back into ponytails and looked tired and worn out—just totally busted. "Hey boo!" Jasmyn smiled, as she plopped down on the sofa with Crystal. They were a little out of breath as if having just finished running five miles.

I gave them a slight nod of the chin. "What's up?" I asked with raised eyebrows.

Jasmyn smiled back, looking like she wanted to get up and hug me, but didn't have the energy to do so.

I didn't appreciate Shawn springing my ex-girlfriend on me unannounced like this. What if Damaris and I were having sex? I mean, I knew that he saw Jasmyn often from the mere fact Crystal was his girl, but there were some things you just didn't do to your boy! All I knew was Damaris would be there in about forty-five minutes, so I had to think of a way not to look stupid. But even more than that, I wanted to know why Jazz and Crystal were in my crib half-asleep looking like Aunt Esther and Celie.

_____*Jasmyn*

For our senior year, Crystal and I had decided to become roommates. One night we were sitting around in our room just talking. We thought about it being our final year in college and the things we had yet to accomplish. The one thing we had not done yet was explore Greek life and pledging. There were a few sororities on campus. Some of them, either the girls were busted and ugly, they were conceited, or they were just straight-up bitches. But one sorority got our interest. Gamma Upsilon Theta. I had been peeping them since sophomore year, and Crystal and I both found them to be mad cool. So, since it was senior year and I was trying to avoid drama, I figured one way to avoid men was to focus on solidifying some positive female relationships. What better way to do that than to join a sorority? Crystal was more geeked about it than I was. At first I was hesitant because I didn't think females could be trusted, but we both went for it. And then, the Gamma girls were taking up every ounce of free time I had.

"G-UUUUU! Gamma Up-si-lon The-ta! Greet!" ordered Big Sister Brittany "Diva-tude" White.

"Greetings, most illustrious big sisters of Gamma-Upsilon-Theta Sorority, Innnn-corporated! Always imitated, never duplicated! Brains *and* beauty—every man's dream! Lavender and silver reign supreme! Most high and divine, beautiful, and fine! There can only be few. Oh one day, someday, we want to be just-like-you!"

My pledge sisters and I—the "Rosebuds"—were lined up in a row inside Big Sister Asia "Cleopatra" Brown's apartment reciting that tired-ass greeting for the millionth time. It had to be perfectly uttered, each syllable clear and distinct. It took exactly twelve seconds to recite.

Not only was I getting tired of yelling that greeting, I was fed up with wearing these sweatpants. Tired of the entire outfit, for that matter. I was sick of ducking corners and laying low. It had been like this for going on five weeks now.

"Little Sister number three, we're gonna call you 'Unbeweaveable.' I remember seeing you around campus flinging them fake ponytails. Uh huh!" All the big sisters laughed. Big Sister and Dean of Pledges Cleopatra once again singled me out of all eight on line as the one to pick on tonight. Asia was a true hater.

Another big sister, Kelly a.k.a. "Untouchable," joined in on the insults. "Yeah, Asia. I heard she used to mess with quite a few guys on campus. Remember, she's the one who got her butt kicked for cheating on that fine chocolate brother Damon." She walked right up to me, as I focused my attention straight ahead, and added, "We don't want no hoes in Gamma."

Now these bitches were getting personal. I tried not to break my stare. We were to always keep our head up and look straight ahead or at whoever was addressing us. It was hard as hell not to shed a single tear as they continued hurling insults at me. I didn't know how much more of this mental hazing I could take. I promised Crystal we'd stick it out, even though I wasn't crazy about doing this whole pledge thing at first. She begged me almost two months ago to pledge Gamma with her. Now, I was starting to regret it.

"Come on Jazz, it'll be fun. Go to this Gamma rush with me tonight. You know they're gonna want you. You're my best friend; don't leave me hanging."

"Girl, I'm not worried about them broads. A room full of females ain't nothing but hate waiting to happen. It's always one bitch that will have something smart to say."

Whatever my reservations were, Crystal talked me out of them and I began seeing the positive side of pledging. We went to the rush, were accepted, and had been Gamma Rosebuds ever since.

Our pledge session ended after an hour of yelling insults. I knew it was said a strong sisterly bond would form after this experience, and maybe that would be true with my line sisters. As for forming a sisterly bond with these Big Sisters who were like Hater Phi Hater, it was hard for me to imagine. I had to admit my mental fortitude and patience had strengthened immensely.

Crystal and I were going to hang out at Shawn and Kyle's apartment. I hadn't been there yet and I was anxious to see it. I was glad that Shawn and Crystal were officially dating now. At least one of my friends could be in a decent relationship after my dating fiascos last year.

We left Big Sister Cleopatra's apartment and ran to the parking lot, sneaking into Shawn's car like we just robbed a bank and he was driving the getaway car. Pledges were not allowed to be seen socializing, so that was why we had to sneak.

When we arrived at the apartment, I was a little tense because I hadn't really had a chance to talk to Kyle much this semester. We spoke here and there around campus, but pretty much kept our distance. I didn't call him and he didn't call me. Since I still lived in the dorms, I didn't see him as often. I knew I looked busted, but I didn't really care.

Kyle must've been expecting some company because he looked all edgy when I said, "What's up, boo?" It was as though he wanted to say, "What the hell are you doing in my apartment?"

I wanted to give him a hug because he looked so fine in his khaki pants and his green and white striped button-up shirt. I was too tired to get up off the couch, though. He wouldn't have been responsive anyway. I couldn't blame him as bad as I looked with all this pledge gear on. Last year, Kyle was used to seeing me look sharp all the time.

We weren't there a half-hour before some Spanish chick showed up. I fell asleep watching an old episode of *Girlfriends,* but when Kyle opened the door to let her in, I woke up. She was cute, but had nothing on me except maybe a smaller waist and a bigger chest. When she came in, Kyle hugged her like he was nervous and didn't want me to see him touch her. I was glad to know my presence in the room still had an effect on him. The girl didn't seem too happy to see him, however. She gave Kyle a real stern look and in a real thick accent stated, "Ky-yuhl, we need to talk." She scanned the room, eying us. "In private, puh-lease!"

I started to say, "Bitch, what? Don't get that head rocked 'cause of your smart mouth! I will slap the shit out of you!!"

Pledging not only made me more patient, but I was also fiercer. I definitely was not for the nonsense, especially not from some non-dressing seven-dollar-store-outfit-wearing, beans-and-rice-eating-wanna-be-Selena chick.

We left as soon as his little enchilada arrived. I had a feeling they were going to need their privacy because they immediately went into his room, shut the door, and blasted the music. Besides, I wasn't completely over Kyle, so being in the same room with him and his new girlfriend made me a little upset. I wished Thanksgiving break would hurry up and get there so the pledging process could be over and I would get my Gamma letters. Most of all, I missed my family. I wanted to see Adrienne and prepare a big welcome-home party for Jerome, who was due to get out in three weeks.

_____Kyle

I felt uncomfortable with my ex and new lady friend in the same room at the same time. I focused on Damaris, who looked pretty heated about something. We went into my room and I shut the door behind us. Then I turned up the stereo volume really high in case Shawn, Jazz, and Crystal decided to eavesdrop.

"Ky-yuhl," Damaris looked at me with widened eyes and spoke in a soft voice. "I'm two weeks late!"

Late? As in late-on-your-period late? My jaw literally fell open. I was shocked and in disbelief.

"Yes," she continued, not giving me a chance to respond.

"What?! Aren't you on the pill?" Unless she was lying. Why do chicks do that? Tell a brother she's on the pill when she really isn't.

This was horrible. The chick that me and my boy tossed it up with was sitting in my living room. The woman of my dreams just gave birth to another man's baby. Now, my new Latina babe was telling me she might be pregnant!

She was going to have to get an abortion. That's all there was to it.

"Well, look Mari, you know I'm trying to graduate . . ." My voice began to fade.

"So what 'chu saying?" she asked.

"I'm saying 'do you' and I'mma 'do me.' I mean, I ain't tryna be nobody's daddy!"

I had never thought I would be telling a woman to get rid of a baby that I helped create. But the truth was, I was getting ready to graduate and I wasn't about to be tied down with some chick and a baby, unless that chick was Tiana.

"Kyle, *estas loco?* Are you crazy? You telling me to get an abortion?" She began to swell up and start crying and muttering *"Ay Dios mio"* over and over.

"Look, Mari, don't get upset. I mean, look—I can't tell you what to do. All I'm saying is that I ain't ready to be no father. I just wish you'd think about it, that's all."

"Think?! Think about what?" Then she started rattling off in Spanglish. "If you think that I'mma have this baby—*y tu no vas a hacer nada . . . bueno, te lo juro, tu no te vas a ir*—I'm about to let you know, it's not going down like that, *cabron!*" With that, she reached out and smacked me in the face! I flinched because she caught me off guard. I balled my fist up. *Don't hit this girl. This campus will lock you up.* I was ready to go upside her head. Finally, Mari ran out the apartment in a rage.

I tried to ease the situation, rubbing my stinging cheek and yelling behind her. "I mean, it's still kinda early, Mari! Just wait till you go to the doctor and get tested!" I doubted she heard one word I said. I was glad Shawn, Jazz, and Crystal left. I didn't feel like explaining none of what just went down.

I lowered my head in desperation, heeding the voice that whispered deep inside, prompting me to pray and seek God.

Dear Lord, I'm sorry for coming to you only when I'm in trouble, but if I never needed you before, I need you now! God, please don't let Mari be pregnant. I know children are a blessing, but I can't be a father right now. Lord, just work this out somehow, as only you can. Amen.

I knew God was getting sick of me and my mess. I didn't know what I had gotten myself into, but I knew I needed a way out.

_____*Jasmyn*

The next day, our Rosebud line went into Hell Night. In Greek terms, that signified the beginning of the end. It was the last night of pledging—the hardest and longest night. You had to prove you could make it to the end and then the moment you had been waiting for: you'd get your letters.

The Big Sisters kidnapped us from our dorms, so to speak. They called at seven o'clock sharp and told us to be outside and dressed in our sweats in exactly ten minutes. They were all lined up in a car brigade and directed us to get in their cars, about two or three Rosebuds per car; none of us rode with a Big Sister alone. We were blindfolded and driven far away from campus to a big field. There we ran, marched, and chanted various pledge songs we learned and recited Gamma history.

After what felt like hours, we were driven back to campus and directed to go inside of Big Sister Cleopatra's apartment. All the lights were off, which was pretty scary. The next thing we knew, Big Sister Brittany a.k.a. "Teena Marie," the only white girl in the chapter, entered the room followed by Gamma sisters from other campuses holding lavender candles and singing the sorority hymn. The lights were turned on and, to our surprise, gifts and personalized paraphernalia were all around. We made it! They presented us with sorority jackets and t-shirts, along with paddles and other gifts. I cried tears of joy because for once in my life, I made a commitment to something serious and didn't blow it in the process. I hugged my line sisters and new sorors and felt relieved that the whole thing was over.

About a week later, Thanksgiving break arrived. I went home, sporting new Gamma gear with a fresh silver and lavender license plate on my car. Amidst all the pledging excitement, I almost forgot Jerome was due to be released in a little over two weeks. I spent the entire break planning a huge welcome-home bash to be held the Saturday after his arrival. I called some of Jerome's friends whose numbers I could remember.

I wound up going out with Omar, one of his cutest friends. I hadn't had any since I was on line and wasn't used to going over a month without it. He always liked me, but didn't get too close when Jerome was home. Now that Jerome was locked up, every time I came home from college he would come around to see me. We had an only-when-I'm-home-in-Jersey type of relationship. We hung out at his house and messed around a bit. I knew Jerome was cool with me spending time with his boy. Omar contacted his boys and the party was all set. "Hello, Michelle? What's up? It's Jasmyn. How's my nephew doing?"

"Hey Jasmyn, what's up, girl? I haven't talked to you in a minute! How you doing?" She could be real fake sometimes. I wanted to really tell her about herself, but for the sake of Jerome and JJ I kept my mouth shut.

"Oh, I'm good," I pleasantly responded. Pledging also told me how to force a smile even when I was pissed. "You know Jerome is coming home soon, right?"

"Oh, for real? When?" How could Michelle be so blasé? She doesn't care one bit about her baby's daddy. That was a damn shame 'cause JJ didn't even know his own father.

"December sixth. I'm throwing a party for him at our house on the eleventh, the following Saturday. I wanted to invite you and JJ."

"Oh okayyy," she sang, as though she had to think about whether or not she would grace our house with her presence. "I'm sure we can make it." You'd better make it your business to be there Michelle. My brother has been locked up for too long to come out and have to put up with your shit.

I knew Michelle wouldn't try to get shady because even though Rome was locked up, he made sure that part of his stash went to them. Plus, Uncle Jeff still sent her a few dollars here and there. I also made sure to send JJ a birthday and Christmas card every year with money. I'd only seen JJ about once a year, but she managed to send pictures of him that I'd share with Jerome. She was really torn up when Jerome was locked up because they were together for two years beforehand and talked of marriage. She was so devastated, she rarely wrote to Jerome or answered his phone calls and letters.

I talked to Michelle for a few more minutes about JJ. According to her, he was learning to write his name and tie his shoes. I was happy to hear he was doing well. I was thankful Michelle wasn't a chickenhead. She had a good job at State Farm and bought herself a small house in Moorestown, a town located about fifteen minutes away from Willingboro. The word was her so-called fiancé was some broke, non-job-keeping dude who was only with her because of her money.

The rest of the break flew by, and before I knew it, I was back at Marshall. All I could do was count the final few days until my big brother was a free man.

_____*Kyle*

The news of Damaris' possible pregnancy stayed
in the back of my mind as I packed my bags to go
home for Thanksgiving. It had been a week since
I'd seen or spoken to Damaris, and that was when
she had hurried out of my apartment in a rage.
She hadn't been in the gym or our American
Studies class. Every time I called her room, her
roommate Monica would say, "she's not here" or
"she's lying down." Finally, I decided to walk to her
dorm and knock on her door.

Damaris lived in McKennan with the rest of the
athletes. I knew Jazz's nut ex-boyfriend Damon
used to live there. He graduated since he was a senior last year. After the beat down he plotted on
Jazz last year, if I were him, I wouldn't hang
around too long, if he knew what I knew. Underneath her suburban Jersey girl exterior, Jasmyn
was ghetto and her people were gangsta. When I
learned her brother was incarcerated and due to

get out this year, I got scared for Moe, Damon, myself, and every other guy who did wrong by her. Based on all the attention and smiles Jasmyn threw my way when she was at the apartment a few weeks ago, I felt confident she wouldn't seek retaliation on me.

I called Damaris from my cell phone as I approached McKennan. This time, she picked up.

"Hello?"

"Oh so you don't have Monica screening your calls now?" I questioned sarcastically.

"Who is this?" Damaris asked. *I know she's bugging now. How's she going to forget me that quick?*

"It's your more-nito." I knew my Spanish accent was jacked up, but I didn't care.

"Ky-yuhl? Hey, what's been up with you? You all ready for Thanksgiving?" She sounded sleepy and her voice began to drift.

"I was trying to see you before I went home since you haven't returned my calls. What's your room number?"

She yawned and replied, "110."

"All right, I'll be down there soon."

Within minutes, I was at Mc Kennan flashing my ID at the front desk security and heading down the hall to her room.

When Damaris opened the door, I gave her a hug and kissed her softly. I began caressing her hair and stroking her face and chin with my fingers. She looked as though she hadn't got a good night's sleep in days. She seemed to have been crying a lot, as evidenced by the empty tissue box in her waste basket.

"Look Mari, I'm sorry about our argument and

I want you to know whatever decision you make, it's your body and I understand."

"It's gone."

"What's gone?" I knew she couldn't be talking about the baby.

"Look Kyle, when I told you my period was late, the next day I went to the doctor like you suggested. The GYN there examined me and confirmed I was four weeks pregnant."

"Well, she gave me a full exam. She was feeling, pressing, grabbing, and poking while looking for the heartbeat. She found the baby, but there was no heartbeat. She did an ultrasound, but the baby already detached itself from the uterus."

I was stunned. I couldn't say a word. I let Mari know I didn't want a baby, but now that she told me the baby had actually died, my heart sunk into my shoes. Seeing the pain in her eyes made me wish I never told her that I was against her being pregnant.

"So," she continued, "the doctor told me I had two choices. I could wait and abort the baby naturally—basically walk around with a dead fetus inside me and wait to miscarry or I could have a D and E. So, I chose the D and E." Damaris sounded like a pre-med student with all the medical lingo she was saying.

All this gynecological female talk was gross. It's funny how, as a man, you can be so into a woman and all the feminine physical attributes could turn you on. As soon as it came to menstrual cycles, childbirth, and female reproductive stuff, it was disgusting. I think we enjoy visualizing the female privacy as a place for pleasure—not surgery and disfigurement.

"What is that?" I knew I was going to regret knowing the answer to this question.

"A dilation and evacuation. Basically, they dilate you and remove the baby," she responded. "It's kind of like an abortion." Her voice lowered on the word "abortion" as she bore her eyes into me, as if to say *"Isn't that what you wanted in the first place?"*

I sat there in silence. For a moment, I looked at Damaris and got a mental picture of what our child would have looked like. I imagined a little boy with a tan complexion and black curly hair. He would've had a tight Spanish name like Yamil or Felix. My paternal desire ignited for about sixty seconds and then came the image of messy diapers, foul-smelling formula, bitter visitation battles, dragging the infant between New York and Philly, and the worst image of all: being pulled into court to pay child support.

Abortion. The word resounded in my ear. I always said I never believed in abortions until it involved me. I used to think it was wrong to kill a human life, but when thrown into the situation, I understood why a lot of women ended their pregnancies. As the saying goes, 'timing is everything.' And it just wasn't the time.

"I didn't really know how to tell you," Damaris said with gentleness in her voice.

"Well, I am glad you told me. I wish there was something I could say." I approached her and smoothed her hair with my palm, rubbing her ever so delicately. "How are you feeling?" I asked sympathetically.

"Well, I'm feeling better. I cry every so often." Damaris sat up from where she was lying in bed.

She reached behind her to the bookshelf that was built into the headboard and retrieved a small white Bible. She opened it to the middle, pulled out two folded pieces of paper, and handed one to me.

"Here. I had asked the nurse to print me out two copies, so I could give one to the father."

I opened it and it was an ultrasound printout. I had never seen one, but all the black and gray fuzzy spots gave it away. At the bottom of the ultrasound picture, was printed:

Baby Cruz 10:02 a.m. Approx. age: 4 wks.

A heaviness came upon my heart. The brief time I was awarded fatherhood was cut abruptly by the news of Mari's miscarriage. Actually seeing the image of the baby let me know pregnancy was no joke. I spent the rest of the night in her room. Although her roommate Monica returned to the room, we silently made love beneath the covers. Afterwards, Damaris sat up and whispered, "*Mira*, where do we go from here?" The look in her eyes conveyed uncertainty and doubt, as though she thought I was going to knock her off and then leave.

"We're cool boo. I mean, it's almost Thanksgiving break. Let's kick it like we've already been doing. Is that all right with you?" I was hoping she didn't want some type of relationship because I didn't dig her all like that. No female had ever measured to the caliber of Tiana.

"It's cool," she lowered her eyes and laid her head back on the pillow. She turned her back to me and went back to the sloop. "Good night, morenito." I knew that "morenito" meant "little brown one." At least I knew she wasn't totally mad at me.

My cell phone rang. It was after midnight in the middle of the week. I glanced over at Damaris who had fallen asleep quickly, or at least was pretending to be asleep. I looked at the screen which read "Call from TIANA." I started to press "Ignore" but deciding to take the chance Mari was sound asleep, I pressed "Answer" as I climbed out of the bed and went to the bathroom.

Cupping my hand over the mouthpiece, I spoke in my Barry White voice. "Hey. Wassup, girl?" I turned the water on to drown out our conversation.

"Hey, Kyle," Tiana said. "Are you busy? I'm sorry to call you so late."

"It's no problem. I wasn't doing anything. So, what's up with you? You don't usually call this late. How's little Jayda?"

"Kyle, I am so sick of this mess with Chauncey. I'm up here in the house by myself with Jayda. It's cold as I don't know what and the baby's got a little temperature. All I wanted him to do is to go by the twenty-four hour CVS and pick up some Infant Tylenol and drop it off. My mom is working late at the hospital." Her mom was a nurse at Jefferson Hospital which inspired Tiana to study nursing. "I have called his cell phone all night and his damn voice mail keeps coming on. I mean, hell, I could go my damn self, but why should I bundle my baby up and take her out in this forty degree weather?"

"Well Tee, if I was there, you know I'd go to the store for you in minute." It seemed that, in the month since the baby was born, whenever Tiana called me it was to vent about Chauncey. Maybe she did it to let me know she wouldn't mind me pushing up on her.

I turned the water off and heard Mari talking in her sleep. Monica had gotten up and was banging on the bathroom door. "What are you doing, taking a dump?! Hurry up, Kyle!" I pressed the mute button on my phone so Tiana wouldn't hear the knocking.

I pressed the mute button again, so she could hear my end. "Yo, Tee, my phone is breaking up," I lied. "Let me call you back in a little while."

"Hmm, well you seem busy Kyle. Just call me tomorrow. I'm gonna call Sheila or Karen." Those were two of her friends. Karen was her sorority sister, and if I am not mistaken, Sheila was Jayda's godmother. "Sheila lives close to the CVS downtown. I'll talk to you later." With that, she banged on me. I couldn't believe it. Tiana never hung up on me like that!

I opened the bathroom door and frowned at Monica. "Here. The bathroom's all yours."

"It's about time you got off the phone." Monica rolled her eyes at me and shut the door behind her.

"Yo, Mon, mind your business," I shot back.

I climbed back into the bed with Mari. She rolled over and placed her arm around me. As she snored softly I shook my head and smiled to myself. That woman could sleep through an earthquake. I grabbed my cell phone, turned the ringer off, and made a mental reminder to myself to call Tiana in a day or so when I got home, just to make sure she wasn't mad at me.

* * *

Thanksgiving break began the next day. The Friday after the holiday I called Tiana to find out how the baby was doing and to let her know I wasn't trying to rush her off the phone the other night.

"How you doing, sweetheart?" *Please don't let her be mad at me.* I knew Tiana wasn't my girl yet, but I wanted to stay in her good graces. All in case she decided to cut that Chauncey cat; I left the door open for me to make my move. That's another reason why I couldn't be bogged down in some jive-ass on-campus relationship with Damaris.

Tiana sounded like she was in a good mood. "Oh, I'm fine. I'm surprised you called me, seeing as how the other night, you were uh . . ." she cleared her throat. ". . . a little busy, I should say?" she teased.

"What?!" I tried to play it off. "Girl, I was just tired and my phone was acting up. You know how it is when you're in a building and you can't get a signal."

She giggled a bit. "Yeah, right!" Tiana was good. She had woman's intuition like a mug! "Don't even try it! I heard some Spanish-sounding babe banging on the door telling you to get out the bathroom! And you with that running water I was like, 'Kyle thinks he's slick. Ain't that much hand-washing in the world!' " Tiana was good-natured about it. I was glad she didn't try to blast me out for lying to her.

"All right, all right! You got me. I surrender. I was in a friend's room." I thought maybe by letting Tiana know I had female friends I visited overnight, she may become more interested in me. People who are involved with someone always seem more attractive; it makes them more desirable—trying to get a person who is off-limits.

"Oh, so you have a new friend? What'd you do? Go south of the border and get a Spanish chick?" If I wasn't mistaken, I heard a twinge of jealousy in her voice. That was music to my ears.

I decided to lay my mack game down and flip the script on her. "Well, seeing as how you got that Chauncey cat and had his baby . . . I mean, what you want a man to do?"

Tiana had no reply.

After a few seconds, she came back with "You didn't have to sleep with somebody!" Now she was getting feisty and I was turned on by her new-found interest in me.

"Since when are you interested in my love-life, Tiana?" *And furthermore, how is she going to try to sit up here and be mad when she not only slept with some-one, she had a baby!*

"Who said I was interested?" she came back at me, sounding annoyed.

"All right. Then, what's up with the twenty questions?" I snapped back.

The way I was throwing all of her questions back at her must have caught her off guard.

"Well look, my bad. I guess I'm having Postpartum Stress or something," she laughed. "Plus, you know Chauncey has been fucking up, right? He only comes by to see Jayda once a week, and when he does come, he only stays like a half-hour. He never offers to watch her and whenever I need him to take her for a while, just so I can get some rest or go to the store or something, he never answers his cell phone. And to top it off, he hasn't bought her shit!" I'd never heard Tiana go off and start cursing like that. I knew she had to be really angry.

"So why are you still with him, Tee?"

Tiana hesitated for a moment. "Chauncey is just a baby's daddy. We have not been together, together in a long time. I mean," she switched her tone from angry to serious, "I'm ready for new people in my life, you know?" I decided to take this door that she'd opened.

I breathed heavily for a second and carefully considered my next words. She had been the object of my affection for the past five years. I didn't want to sound like a nut, but I didn't want to miss my chance to get at her either.

"Tiana, I don't know how to say it, but I've been feeling you for a long time now. I always felt you were out of my league. We've always been cool and I never wanted to ruin our friendship by kicking it to you." I felt myself rambling.

I felt a smile on Tiana's face as she said, "What are you trying to say?"

"Come on now, you know what I'm trying to say." Her other line beeped in.

"Wait a minute" she abruptly cut me off. "Hold that thought. It's my other line."

Now, of all times, her other line would ring, wouldn't it?

She clicked back over. "All right, I'm back. That was Chauncey. So, what were you saying?"

Now she was playing dumb. Tiana knew exactly

what I was getting at. "What? Are you trying to put your bid in, Kyle?"

"Yeah, I guess you could say that."

"Well, what about that female friend of yours?" she asked, emphasizing the word 'friend.' "You know I'm not a home wrecker."

"Home wrecker? Girl, come on now. I ain't got no 'home' with anybody you could wreck! Look, me and that female had a physical thing. It's hard to stay celibate, especially at college, you know?"

Tiana sucked her teeth. "You're telling me! Look at me, I have a baby! At least you don't!" She paused and took the humor out of her voice for a split second. "Or do you?"

Not trying to go there with the Damaris pregnancy thing, I swiftly responded, "Of course not, girl! What I look like, being somebody's daddy? You know I'm trying to get up out this piece in May." We laughed and I sighed a quick breath of relief that she didn't proceed with any more fatherhood type of questions.

We continued to talk for about another hour about what we liked about each other. We decided to just take things slow and not put a title on our new relationship. With the luck I'd been having with women, I wanted to be careful not to jinx myself.

During break, Tiana had her friend Sheila watch Jayda for her while and we went to the movies and dinner. We chose the King of Prussia Mall because we enjoyed the IMAX-style theaters with stadium seating. Afterwards, we dined at The Cheesecake

Factory, a very popular restaurant in the mall where the wait is never less than an hour. It was worth it because the food was excellent and they always give you big portions. We spent the wait strolling the mall, window-shopping, and people-watching.

Our date ended respectfully. Our pastor would've been proud. I resisted the urge to grab her and shove my tongue down her throat. I thought by playing hard to get, it would to be easier for me to lure her in close enough to make her forget about Chauncey. I had to make sure she wanted me and no one else. In fact, when she asked me for a kiss, I kept it short, but passionate—just enough to whet her appetite and leave her wanting more, like I did with Aliya, Jasmyn, and Damaris. My ability to let a female know I was interested without sweating her was why I never had to chase women like Shawn and my other boys did. I'd never had a problem attracting women, and now that I'd attracted the one I had been wanting for so long, all I'd have to do was reel her in.

I showed interest in everything she did, from what new things Jayda was doing, to her Gamma sorority. I even went with her to the hairdresser the weekend after Thanksgiving. I told her she would look cute with short hair, and she went and got it razor cut in a fly shoulder-length style.

After the break, I went home every weekend. My family was happy to see me but little did they know, my reasons for going home were to see Tiana and get a break from Damaris.

I didn't know how long I was going to have to continue this balancing act. As soon as we felt it

was time to commit, I would drop Damaris. Until
then, a brother had needs and itches that needed
scratching. Tiana had my mind and soul, and she
was slowly getting my heart. Damaris, for the time
being, had everything else.

_____Jasmyn

Jerome's party was off the hook. I didn't go to class the day he came home, even though final exams were right around the corner. Spending time with him was more important. My uncle and mother came to pick me up and we drove down to Smyrna. We took him a Rocawear sweater and jeans, along with a pair of new sneakers to come home in. I took off again on Friday to prepare for the welcome-back party.

Michelle's somtimey ass ending up bringing JJ to the party. Jerome was excited to see both of them, and I watched how he interacted with Michelle, complimenting her and telling her how good she looked. He was as smooth as me and if Michelle wasn't careful, she'd be breaking up with her fiancé soon and trying to reunite with Jerome.

JJ, surprisingly, took pretty well to Jerome. It was as if he knew that was his dad. JJ let Jerome pick him up and ride him around the house on his shoulders.

Jerome's friends and our family gave him money and other gifts. He smiled and laughed the entire time. It felt good seeing my brother happy again. I was so glad to have him back home.

On his second day home, I drove Jerome around to put in job applications. We hit various stores in the mall, the post office, New Jersey Transit, and a few hospitals. The most promising seemed to be in the dietary department at Lourdes Medical Center of Burlington County. He was turned down at the post office because of his felonies and he didn't have a CDL license to drive a bus, so food service was the easiest position to get. I knew it wasn't much, but at least it would pay the bills. In due time, I'd make sure Jerome would get registered for classes, maybe at the Willingboro campus of Burlington County College. It would take some effort, but my big brother would be back on his feet in no time.

A week after Jerome came home, I participated in my first Gamma community service project. All the local Gamma chapters—Marshall, West Chester, Temple, and the University of Pennsylvania—were doing volunteer gift wrapping at area malls and collecting toys to donate to the children of incarcerated parents.

Crystal and I signed up to work Wednesday night at the Exton Mall wrapping presents, along with Brittany, Asia, and my line sister Jamilah. It was my first opportunity to represent the sorority in public, so I was psyched.

The mall was jam-packed with Christmas shoppers. People were lined up waiting to get their packages wrapped. The wrapping was free, but we accepted donations. We had a large sign that read, "Complimentary Gift Wrapping courtesy of the Ladies of Gamma Upsilon Theta—Donations accepted—Proceeds benefit Gamma Youth Development Activities." Our donation jar was full of fives, tens, and twenties, which told me people out there in Chester County were high rollers. Never would I pay ten dollars to get a shirt wrapped.

The five of us were decked out in Gamma gear. We formed an assembly line, dividing the tasks of cutting, wrapping, and decorating the gifts with ribbon. Since I considered myself a people person, I was assigned to be a greeter.

Sorors from other local chapters in Chester County, West Chester, and Lincoln University mainly, came out to support us. Some of them stopped by and helped for a few minutes, allowing us to take short breaks. They put in about an hour of work, but we did the majority of it since we were sponsoring the table. We wrapped for two solid hours, rotating the work between all of the sorors who were there.

A few Temple sorors who were shopping spotted our sign and came over to show us some love. I knew they were from Temple because one of them had on a sorority jacket with the symbol representing Temple's chapter on her sleeve. I recognized a few of them from when we were on line and received visits from Big Sisters at other campuses. Even though a couple of them graduated, just like Asia and one or two other Gammas still active at Marshall, they were still involved. The Temple Gammas were cool as hell though. They were all dressed fly, had nice hairstyles, and stylish coats, purses, and shoes.

I noticed one soror pushing a baby stroller. She was light-skinned, petite, and had dark brown wavy hair styled loosely in a cute bob that stopped right above her shoulders. She had to be all of a size four. Her skin was flawless, and I noticed she wore the same shade of lipstick as me. The little girl was adorable, wearing a pink snowsuit and an infant cap with the flaps wrapped around her chubby little cheeks and chin.

"Hey y'all! G-UUUU!" A few of the Temple Gammas walked up to and hugged Brittany, Asia, and a few of the older sorors from West Chester and Lincoln.

After exchanging small talk, one of the Temple girls who wore a wooden Gamma pin on her navy blue pea coat, introduced herself to the rest of us.

"Hey sorors, I'm Tosh, spring 0-1," she said, announcing spring 2001 as the semester she "crossed," or in other words, became an official member of Gamma Upsilon Theta.

Tosh looked at Brittany. "So these are the neos?" She smiled. "What's up, sorors? Welcome to Gamma!" She hugged us with the secret Gamma hug and handshake. She narrowed her eyes at Crystal, Jamilah, and me. "Check y'all out with the fresh paraphernalia on!" she commented on our embroidered Gamma caps and sweatshirts. "I love neophytes! Y'all are soo cu-ute!" Tosh spoke as though she was one of the Gamma founders from way back in the 1930's. It was cool though. I didn't think she meant any harm by it.

Brittany looked at us. "Yeah," she stated. "These are some of the new Gammas representing for Marshall State. They're mad cool. This is Jasmyn, Crystal, and Jamilah."

"Nice to meet all of you," Tosh replied. She turned to the girls she was with. "This is Karen and the one over there—" she motioned towards the soror with the stroller, ". . . that's Tiana." She was in front of the stroller, playing with the baby and talking on her cell phone at the same time.

"Hey, Miss Mama! You're not gonna wave to your sorors?" Tosh yelled jokingly. She looked up and waved, but didn't hang up the phone.

"She doesn't look like she just had that baby, does she?" mentioned Karen.

"I know, right?! Jayda is two months old!" said Tosh. "She makes me sick with her skinny self! We always tease her, telling her she looked like she popped that baby out and shrunk the next day!" Tosh added.

It sounded like a small part of Tosh was hating on Tiana, just like a small part of me was. I didn't even know her. I guess I was guilty of the stereotypical 'big-girl-hating-on-skinny-women' playful kind of jealousy. Tosh was a little bigger than me. I was a little embarrassed because I had let myself go from a tight eight to a perfect-fitting twelve.

I looked over at Tiana, who looked like she just finished cursing somebody out on the phone. "Oooh, I can't stand him!" Tiana yelled, as she rolled her eyes, slammed her phone shut and headed over towards us.

"I'm sorry, sorors, for being so rude. I was talking to my no-good 'baby-daaaa-dddy,'" she said as she changed her voice into a Southern-like ghetto-girl when she said "baby-daddy."

We all laughed. "Girl, don't even worry about it," Crystal offered.

"I'm digging that lip gloss you've got on," I complimented. "Is that MAC?"

"Oh, yeah. You know it. Viva Glam." Tiana said.

"Oh okay," I replied. "I thought it was a different shade. I'm going to have to check that one out."

"Yeah. I like it 'cause they donate the proceeds from this shade to AIDS research. I'm a nursing major; I'm into anything supporting cures for cancer, AIDS, all of that kind of stuff. Plus they've had Mary J. Blige, Missy, and a few other celebrities support them, so it must be all right, you know?" I noticed Tiana was wearing a pink ribbon lapel pin on her coat collar. I was impressed by how proactive and aware she was.

"I heard that." I agreed with her even though I never thought about donating to AIDS research. The word AIDS disgusted me. I thought of faggots, bisexual men in jail, dirty crackheads, and nasty hookers. I didn't fit into any of those categories, and neither did anybody I knew; therefore, AIDS did not affect me.

After talking make-up, clothes, and school, we shut down our gift-wrapping table for the night. We decided to go to Applebee's to hang out for a little while.

"Can the little mama hang?" Tosh asked Tiana, looking at the baby who fell asleep in her stroller.

"Oh yeah, she'll probably stay asleep since that's what she does most of the time anyway. It's not too cold out tonight. Besides, I need some girlfriend time." Tiana went on to say she hadn't been out since the baby was born and missed hanging out with the girls since she dropped out of school for the semester.

I admired the baby as she slept so soundly and peacefully. "Girl, your baby is so beautiful. She's got a head full of hair!" I commented.

"Thanks girl," Tiana smiled. "Too bad her dad is a pain in the you-know-what, but it's all good. Little does he know, I've already got somebody else lined up to take his place," she added with a sneaky grin.

"I heard that! O-kay?!" we all gave each other girlfriend-style high fives and dap in agreement.

At Applebee's, we ordered appetizers and drinks. It was amazing how you could have an instant connection with women you hardly knew, solely on the fact that you shared a sisterly bond established by three Greek letters. *A year ago, I would've said there was no way you could take eight chicks out together to have a good time and there would be no argument.* But that night proved otherwise.

My Temple sorors were friendly and chilling with them felt natural. We promised to stay in touch, exchanging cell phone numbers and e-mail addresses. I knew I'd probably never call Tosh, Karen, or Tiana, but then again, never say never. Maybe there'd be an event going on sometime in the future in Philly I could invite them to. Who knew? When I got back to the dorm, I copied their information in my monogrammed lavender address book with silver-lined pages reserved especially for sorors.

Two weeks later, I was home for Christmas break. I bought a Coach pocketbook for Adrienne and a Burberry cologne gift set for Jerome. They both needed a little hip, upscale fashion makeover. All

Adrienne knew when it came to pocketbooks was Liz Claiborne and the only cologne Jerome knew before he went in was Calvin Klein Eternity.

When I arrived home and turned the corner that led onto my block, the first thing I noticed were sirens blaring and the unusual presence of police, fire, and emergency vehicles. The street was partially blocked off by two parked county patrol cars. As soon as I made an attempt to drive onto my street, a cop put his hand up to stop me. I rolled my window down and asked him, "Excuse me, can you tell me what's going on?"

The cop, who was wearing sunglasses even though it was a cloudy day, bent over and peered at me. "Um, ma'am. This street is being temporarily closed to thru-traffic. Are you a resident?"

"Yes, I am."

"I need to see some ID before I can allow your vehicle to come through." As he said that, I noticed the activity was centered around my house. I saw police dogs sniffing our lawn and my family was outside talking to detectives.

I screamed, "Sir! That is my house! What happened?" I flashed my driver's license in his face. I didn't have time for the bullshit. I started to panic, hoping everything was okay. I didn't know if there was a fire or we got robbed or what.

I saw shattered glass and a firefighter exiting our front door. I cried hysterically, "Oh my God! What is going on?!"

Kyle

Damaris was probably sensing my growing disinterest in her. Whenever we were together, I didn't talk to her like I used to. I didn't want her to think it had anything to do with the miscarriage, but you can't control a female's mind. She was going to think whatever she wanted to think. I was enjoying going home every weekend and being with Tiana. It got to the point where I was using Damaris for physical pleasure and to basically tide my hormones over during the week. I didn't feel the need to sleep with Tiana when I was around her because there was enough emotional attraction between us. I couldn't say the same thing about Damaris; with her, it was strictly physical.

It was a week before final exams and I decided to let Damaris know I thought we should give our relationship a break. She came by the apartment and I prepared a little dinner for her just like I did on our first date. The layers of lasagna and tomato sauce bubbled in the oven, blending with three different Italian cheeses, and releasing a fragrant, delicious aroma in the air.

"So, what's up with all of this food?"

"Oh, I can't be a gentleman?"

"You know what I mean." She grinned. Her smile was enthralling and it was one of the things that attracted me to her in the first place.

"Mari, look . . . ." I pulled her chair out and sat her down at the place setting I prepared. I poured her something to drink and then pushed her chair in to the table after she was seated.

She looked up at me with her big, gorgeous brown eyes. I swallowed hard and breathed nervously. "Si, mi'jo?"

Damn. She would start spitting that sexy Spanish right now, wouldn't she?

"I think you're cool and everything, but I think we're moving a little too fast. When you got pregnant, I ain't gonna lie, I was scared as I don't know what. I just don't want us to get too close too fast."

I waited in worried anticipation for the tongue-lashing in Spanglish. But it never came.

"Look baby, it's okay." Damaris stood up and placed a gentle peck on my cheek. "I can tell you aren't into me like you used to be. It's obvious by the way you keep checking your cell phone and staring off into space when I try to get your attention."

I didn't realize I was coming off as bad as she was making it sound.

"But it's okay," she continued. She stood up from the table, walked over to the couch, and flopped down. She picked up and began thumbing through a copy of *The Source* magazine lying on the table.

"We don't have a title right? So, if you want to talk to other women, go 'head."

The only time a woman tells you it's okay to talk to someone else is when she has already started talking to someone else. Damaris was playing like she was "Little Señorita Innocent," but she probably had her other male friends the whole time! What was I going to say to her? I couldn't get mad. She wasn't my girl. I would look like a straight-up clown if I started throwing a bunch of questions at her. So I chilled.

"You're right. We don't have a title." I sat down on the couch next to her, leaned over and gave her a quick kiss on the lips. "We're still cool though." I smiled at her flirtatiously to keep my window of opportunity open with her in case things with Tiana didn't quite work out.

That year, Christmas in Philly was better than any I remembered in recent years. I spent a lot of time with Tiana and Jayda. At least twice a week, I went over to her house to keep her company; we'd watch DVD's and order pizza or Chinese food. It gave her some time to relax and unwind without having to worry about finding a babysitter. I found out that she wasn't lying when it came to talking about how inactive Chauncey was with his kid. Not once did he call any of the times we were together, and you would think a man would call every night to check on his newborn baby. Not Chauncey.

As I spent more time with Tiana, going over her house and sitting with her at church on Sundays, I realized how serious she was when it came to God.

When I asked her about it, she said, "Kyle, ever since I became a mother, I've realized how important it is for me to be grounded in the Lord."

She still slipped up and showed anger once in a while, especially when it came to talking about Chauncey, but nobody's perfect. I was impressed by her commitment to the Lord. That commitment is what kept her from pursuing another sexual relationship. She didn't act like a nun; she was cool, laid-back, and still fine. I guess she found a way to be fly and sexy, but remain respectful to God.

"Kyle, I really want to get to know you better. I'm not just saying that. I want to get to know you. I think part of my problem with men in the past, including Jayda's dad, is I never took the chance to get to know them. I would be so excited to have somebody show me attention, I'd rush into a relationship, get my emotions tangled up, and give them that precious part of me, even when they didn't deserve it. I mean, I love Jayda with all my heart; I would never call her a mistake. But, I told God the next time he sent me somebody, I would do my best to not get myself sexually involved with him. Kyle, you and I have been friends for so long, and I don't want either one of us to get hurt. I see you and Shawn like the brothers I never had. I always thought you were a smart, nice-looking guy, but I didn't want those nosy church folks in my business, so I said I'd never get involved with a guy from church. Now I think God has sent you to me at just the right time."

When she said that, she totally messed my whole head up. I mean, if I had it like that I would've grabbed her, put her in my car, and driven her to

Zales and planted a five carat platinum diamond ring on her finger. She had me right then. I knew I couldn't mess that up.

Speaking of temptation, I'd been neglecting my boy Shawn for a while. He was turning twenty-one on January ninth and wanted to hit a strip club. We were on our way down to South Philly to hit Geno's for an authentic cheesesteak. They didn't make them like that in Exton where we went to school.

"Yo, Kyle, what's up with hitting the boom-boom room, man? You know your boy is about to turn twenty-one." Shawn was beaming with excitement. I understood because I had just turned twenty-one the week before Christmas and celebrated with some E&J and Bacardi with my boys.

"Man, I ain't trying to go see those nasty broads," I protested. The real deal was I didn't want to get aroused and have no way to satisfy myself. Tiana wasn't having it. She was serious about her faith, and didn't want to compromise herself, even though I could tell when we were alone she had a look that said she wanted me to touch her and hold her close.

"Come on, nigga" Shawn pleaded. "I just wanna go see some booties shake, drink a little Henny— maybe some Hypnotic—and spark a few L's with my boys," he added. He had obviously planned the whole evening in his head already, and of course, I couldn't turn my best friend down.

Shawn took a Newport from behind his ear and lit it. "I know you all up Tiana's ass now that you're home for break." He laughed and shook his head as he drove.

I wasn't amused. I shot him a dirty look and

flipped him the finger. "Man, you just stop worrying about my business and worry about how long it's going to take until you get sick from puffing on them emphysema sticks."

Shawn ignored my last comment and continued smoking. "You know your little Spanish babe wouldn't like to see you spending all your time with some other woman and her baby. Yo, if I didn't know any better, I would say you were trying to make a little family, player! You wanna make Tiana your wifey, don't you?" he gave me a sly grin.

"First of all," I waved his smoke from in front of my face. "Yo, can you put that out?" I asked. Shawn put the cigarette out in the ashtray. I had to set him straight. "Me and Mari are a done deal. I wasn't into her like that. We cut it right before break—right around my birthday, matter of fact."

"Word?" Shawn replied, almost sounding apologetic. "Damn, I know you're missing that. She was fine, man."

I sighed and agreed with him. "Yeah family. I am gonna miss it a little bit."

"I bet you she'll still be open if you tried to get at her again before the end of the school year. You know you always get those babes hooked."

I didn't know my boy thought so highly of me. He was right, though. Ever since high school I found myself with females who were really on me. I usually was the first one to break things off.

"Tiana is good people, but yo man, we're in our sexual prime. Don't let that pregnancy stuff keep you from slaying Damaris or Jazz one last time before graduation this spring," Shawn continued. "You're a man, Kyle. Do you, dog," he slapped my back and nodded. "Do you!"

For a split second, I considered his suggestion. One last time couldn't hurt, could it? The more I began to think about how sweet and Christ-like Tiana was, I felt ashamed for having such thoughts. She wasn't officially my woman, but straying into the arms of another would be deemed cheating as far as I was concerned.

"Man, you must be crazy!" I said to Shawn, giving him a strange look. "I'm not thinking about getting with Jasmyn, Mari, or any of those other Marshall broads again. I'm not messing up what I have going on with Tiana. You must've bumped your head, son!"

Shawn snickered. "Don't let me tell Crystal that. 'Cause you know her girl still talks about you."

"Jazz? Her chunky self needs to go 'head."

"Yo man, you ain't right. Jazz is still pretty. She ain't fat! She's just thick, like my girl."

I eyed Shawn up and down and smiled. "Look who's talking! You like them big girls, man." I patted Shawn's gut and laughed.

"Yo, man," he rubbed his belly like Santa Claus. "Don't hate on this overweight lover. We back in style, aiight? Luther, Gerald Levert, Fat Joe—even the young boy on American Idol, Ruben. Y'all skinny brothers are played out! Ya heard?!"

I fell out laughing. We arrived at Geno's on Passyunk Avenue, ordered some steaks and cheese fries, and went back to my house to chill.

On Shawn's birthday, we got up with a few of our boys from around the way: Cedric, Trey, and Darrell. The five of us went to a place called Club Temptations. It was a so-called "gentlemen's club," as opposed to your run-of-the-mill topless bar on the corner.

Once inside, before I got a chance to look at the scantily clad women, I looked across the room and spotted Chauncey up in some dancer's face, tucking dollars in her G-string.

"Gentlemen, give it up for Am-berrr!" the host announced, stressing every letter in the dancer's name. "Next, coming to the stage, is Miss Diamooooond Jaaaade!"

Chauncey clapped wildly. I shook my head in disbelief, tapped Shawn, and pointed out Chauncey across the room, standing up and clutching a fistful of money.

The cheesy host gave Chauncey a shout-out. "I see a lot of our favorite faces in the crowd tonight. We want to say goooood evening to Mr. Chauncey Davis and the rest of our VIP members."

V-I-P? I couldn't believe this guy got shout-outs at the strip club. He won't buy things for his baby, but he's here throwing away fives and tens—diapers and formula money? I drowned out the music and clenched my jaw tight as I thought of how my girl has to borrow money from her mom and drop out of school to work full-time just to keep Jayda taken care of. Shawn and the guys had ordered drinks by now, but I got up from the table and went over to Chauncey.

Nervousness was brewing inside me when I tapped on Chauncey's shoulder. I was unaware of what kind of response I would get. I was usually non-confrontational, but if there was going to be a confrontation, so be it.

"Yo, excuse me, is your name Chauncey? I need to speak to you outside for a minute."

I regretted my decision because the longer I stood there, the more I smelled alcohol from his breath. *What is this drunk dude going to do?*

_____*Jasmyn*

I turned my car off and jumped out. I tried to walk up the street to my house, but an officer grabbed my arm and said, "Excuse me, miss. My name is Officer Freely. I'm going to have to ask you not go up there right now. We need to question all of the individuals who were inside the home at the time of the incident."

"What incident? Somebody please tell me what the hell is going on!" I looked around at the other officers who were standing around keeping the curious neighbors at bay.

"Well, it seems that an unidentified explosive was thrown into your front living room window," Officer Freely informed me.

"A fire bomb?!" *Where are my cigarettes? Damn!* I had done pretty well with cutting back on smoking, but with the news he was about to lay on me, a nice cigarette was what I needed.

"Yes, ma'am. Usually, acts of this nature are conducted by gang members or individuals seeking retaliation. It's customary procedure to investigate if there is a history of domestic violence or drug-related offenses by any members of the household."

As soon as he said "drug-related" my thoughts went to Jerome. I hoped he hadn't been messing around with Fats and all the other guys that he used to sell drugs with before he got locked up. I looked over at him still being questioned by an officer.

"Ma'am," Officer Freely continued talking looking at some notes he had made on a note pad, "I take it that you are related to this, uh, Mr. Jerome Latrell Simmons?"

I nodded. "Yeah, that's my brother. Why? Is he in trouble?" As soon as Jerome got out, leave it to him to start messing up again.

"Oh no, not at all. He's not in any trouble. Officer Savage is over there, just asking him a few routine questions. I understand he very recently served some time on some drug and fraud charges. Is that correct?"

Aren't y'all the damn cops? Don't you already know this? I found a cigarette at the bottom of my pocketbook, took it out and lit it. Otherwise, there would have been no way I would have bitten my tongue.

With the cigarette pursed between my fingers, I replied, "Yes. My brother was incarcerated, but he paid his debt to society and served his time. What does that have to do with somebody throwing a bomb through our window?"

"Well, ma'am, it seems that one of your neighbors witnessed a brown four-door late-model vehicle fleeing the scene approximately one hour ago. We now have an APB out for all vehicles that match that description. We are not yet sure, but our records have a similar vehicle description on file of one which is known to belong to a Mr. Wendell 'Fats' Thomas. Mr. Thomas is a notorious drug dealer who has been involved in a lot of criminal activity in recent months."

I remember Jerome's boy Omar telling me that Fats had gotten locked up about a year after Jerome went in to Smyrna. But apparently, Fats had his own attorney on retainer who was able to get his charges reduced to misdemeanors, and for the past year and a half, Fats had been out and serving five years of probation. But, a brown four-door late-model sedan? I remembered the last time I saw Fats driving, he was in a black Dodge Durango—an SUV, nothing even remotely close to a brown sedan. Fats was smart enough to keep switching up his cars a few times a year. So as for this so-called brown sedan that may belong to Fats, I doubted Fats even still had that car. I didn't want to make too many assumptions, so I went along with the cops and their suspicion of Fats.

"So, you all are trying to state that Fats, I mean, uh, Wendell, might be implicated in this incident?" I asked, trying to appear somewhat educated. I hated when police officers assumed young black females were ghetto and ignorant. *Don't get it twisted, pig. Your girl will be graduating from college soon!*

Officer Freely hesitated, evidently stunned by my word usage and proper articulation. "Yes, that's correct," he stated.

I tilted my head to one side as if to say "Is there anything else?"

Officer Freeley must've read my mind because

he then questioned me again. "Now, miss, do you mind if I have your name?"

I took out my license again and handed it to him.

"Jasmyn," he began writing on his notepad, "Chantel. Simmons. Okay. Date of birth: February twenty-seventh nineteen eighty-two." He sounded out every word as though he were retarded.

I eyed him with contempt. He should've known that by now, I was getting a little tired of conversing. "Yes? That's me. Do you need to speak to me too, even though I wasn't here when the incident occurred?"

"Well, as far as you are aware, does your brother have any dealings with Mr. 'Fats' Thomas, or any of Mr. Thomas's cohorts?"

"Are you asking me if my brother is out and selling drugs again?"

He looked back at me. "Yes, are you aware of any illegal activity that your brother may have been recently involved in?"

The truth was I really didn't know whether or not Jerome had started selling again. Fats was a very influential brother with a whole lot of dinero. I knew Fats was crazy, just from all the stories around about him. On top of everything else, he was half-Haitian, half-Jamaican. People called him "Jamaitian," and he definitely personified every fiery, violent, short-tempered stereotype that existed about West Indies. With Jerome trying to go legit by working at the hospital, I wouldn't be surprised if he had gotten up with Fats and them and started pushing some weight for him. Nevertheless, I still wanted to defend my brother. The cops should have known that there was no way I was going to snitch on him.

"No, sir. Jerome hasn't been involved in any illegal activity. In fact, he just got a job in food service over at the hospital. You can check over there if you want to."

"That won't be necessary." He looked over and noticed that the small crowd of investigating officers had dissipated. Jerome and the rest of the family had started going back inside the house as the cops made their way back to their vehicles.

"Yooooo, Jazz! What-up, girl?!" Jerome yelled down the street, spotting me on my way back to go park my car.

I spun around, "Hey, y'all! I'm on my way in the house. Let me go move my car!"

I couldn't wait to get inside the house and to find out the truth about what really went down and find out if this whole thing had anything to do with Fats. Fats had been known to do some pretty ill stuff when somebody crossed him: everything from shooting somebody's tires out to even kidnapping some dude's girlfriend and holding her hostage for a couple of hours. He was like Nino Brown from New Jack City.

If Jerome had gotten back into the same shit that got his ass locked up in the first place, even though he was my brother and all, I was going to be mad as hell. The last thing we needed around here was to be tangled up in some old ghetto-behind fiasco that came along with the drug game.

After seeing what damage the fire bomb did, I was glad that we still had our house standing. Our couch and piano suffered some damage, but Jerome apparently had put out the fire. We all gathered in the kitchen for a family meeting.

"What was up with all that?" I was seated inside of our kitchen with Jerome, Adrienne, Aunt Tammy, and Uncle Jeff. "I mean, I come home for Christmas vacation and I find out we got people throwing bombs in our house. I mean, damn! What the hell?" I took a long look at Jerome. "And don't tell me it was the Al-Qaeda or some shit like that. I don't wanna hear it. Tell me the truth, Rome. Are you running with Fats and them niggas again?"

"Jasmyn, don't talk to your brother like that," Adrienne ordered.

I sucked my teeth. "Look, I need to know. Am I going to have to sleep with one eye open during my entire vacation?"

"Jazz, it ain't even like that. I'm not even fucking with Fats and them. I'm trying to stay clean and take care of my son, 'nah mean? Come on now. Why would I want to go back to wearing them whack-ass orange jumpsuits again?"

We laughed in agreement. "Yeah, your thing was getting a little young on you!"

Jerome exclaimed, "Whaaat? Snacks?! I know you ain't trying to go on nobody!" I knew Jerome was about to go hard and talk about my weight gain. It was all in good fun.

I gave him the finger. "Forget you, nukka!"

"Now you know you wrong for that, nephew," said Uncle Jeff. Aunt Tammy was just smiling and shaking her head back and forth.

"Excuse me, everyone," Tammy said. "I'm going to go lay down." She left the kitchen hugging me and saying, "Jazz, honey, don't worry about them.

Ain't nothing wrong with being a big girl!" *Of course you would say that, Aunt Tammy. You ain't never been skinny as long as I've known you.*

Adrienne walked over and gave me a hug as well. "Y'all leave my baby alone. She's fine just the way she is. Besides, men like a little meat on their bones." My mom was slim and attractive. Her metabolism was the shit. She never gained any weight.

"Thank you, Mom. And we're not talking about me. We're talking about you, Jerome, and that bomb that Fats threw in our living room."

Jerome looked around the kitchen. All eyes were on him and he knew we all wanted an explanation. Adrienne, Jeff, and Tammy just didn't have the guts to be so direct with him, but he was a lot like me. So he could say anything to me and I could say anything to him.

"All right," Jerome sighed. "When I got out the other week, I did holla at Wendell and all them other cats. At first, Wendell—well Fats—he was trying to get me to go move a little weight for him from Jersey up to Connecticut. It was gonna be an easy twelve hundred. I told him I wasn't wit' it though. But, word on everything, I don't think Fats did it."

The sincerity in Jerome's voice told me he wasn't lying.

Jerome went on to plead Fats' case. "I don't know who did it. For real for real. And I didn't tell the cops this, but Fats ain't even gonna be down here for the next couple of weeks. Shiiiiit, that nigga done took his girl to Jamaica! When I saw him, he was even like, 'Yo family, I'm getting the hell up outta this piece for awhile. It's hot all up and down Willingboro, Camden, everywhere. I'm taking Nicky to the islands for a little while.' I knew he was even trying to go legit 'cause he asked me if I could put a word in at the hospital for him so he could start having a verifiable income and the cops could stop sweating him. I told him, 'Man I just started working there myself, but I'll see what I can do.' So to answer your question, no I'm not selling drugs, I'm not doing no runs, I'm not doing nothing but walking the straight and narrow."

I walked over and hugged Jerome. A tear landed on my cheek and the saltiness ran down and tickled my tongue. "Awww! That's my big brother. I knew you were serious. I knew you were going to do right by us."

Adrienne smiled. "Son, you know I'm happy, but if Fats didn't do it, then who did?"

Jerome shrugged his shoulders. "I don't know, Mom, just let the cops find out. That's all I can say."

All this time I observed my Uncle Jeff, who had made himself a sandwich and was leaning against the counter eating. He didn't have much to contribute to the conversation. At last he spoke up. "Well, I say let's call the insurance company and see how much we can get for it."

That evening, we took his advice. Now that I was twenty-one, I decided to step up as a family representative and call the insurance company.

"Ma'am, before we can agree to pay for any repairs or loss suffered, we must have a police report. We'll arrange for one of our adjustors to come out and examine the damages."

I agreed, and two days later an adjustor came out. Everyone was at work so I had to take care of business.

The adjustor observed the damage and walked around the entire house and yard. In the back yard, he noticed a pile of firewood and a few cans of gasoline sitting in the carport.

"Ma'am, do you have a fireplace?"

I was puzzled by the adjustor's question but answered him anyway. "No, why?"

He pointed to the wood and gasoline. "Well, when investigating cases that involve fire and explosives, we have to know these things. I'm sorry to say this ma'am, but, uh," He picked up the firewood and said, "it looks like we might have a case of arson."

"Arson? Nahh, I don't think so. This is a pretty nice neighborhood."

"Well, Ms. Simmons," he glanced down at his clipboard. "The police have investigated this matter further and they have surmised a few ideas. One idea is that it was an intentional bombing as a result of retaliation by area drug dealers. But their other suspicion is that it is was a work of arson. Do you know a Mr. Sonny Roberts from Philadelphia?"

"Mr. Sonny? Oh yeah, that's one of my Uncle Jeff's best friends." I had a hunch that the adjustor was about to tell me some bad news.

"Well, it seems that Mr. Roberts has a history of conducting insurance fraud. He has even served a bit of time for it. Well, apparently the police located the vehicle that fled the fire-bombing scene. After pulling over a few cars, one of the cars they pulled over was being driven by Mr. Roberts."

"Well, how come this is the first I am hearing of it?" I knew Uncle Jeff wouldn't be stupid enough to let Mr. Sonny lure him into some stupid insurance scam.

"I spoke with Township police yesterday and they told me that they shared the news with a Mr. Jeffrey Lawson. I presume that's your uncle?"

It was all starting to come together. The gambling, the fact that Uncle Jeff was always concerned with getting more and more money. So that's why he was so quiet when we were all sitting around the kitchen giving Jerome the third degree!

My silence was enough to prompt the adjustor to continue filling in the blanks of this mystery for me. "As evidenced by these kerosene and gasoline canisters, the firewood, and other obvious flammable material, and the fact that you just told me that your uncle is well-acquainted with Mr. Roberts—"

I cut him off. "So in other words, y'all are trying to say that Uncle Jeff and Mr. Sonny set up a plan to scam y'all for insurance money?"

"It hasn't been formally investigated, but I would venture to say so."

For the rest of the time that the insurance adjustor was at our house, he asked me a thousand questions about Uncle Jeff, his finances, his wife's finances, his employment history, and everything else he could think of. I terminated our conversation after about twenty minutes, telling him that he would have to make arrangements to come out and talk to Uncle Jeff face-to-face later.

Needless to say, Uncle Jeff and Mr. Sonny were implicated in the fire bombing. The insurance company dropped our policy and charged them both with insurance fraud. Luckily, they didn't have to go to jail. They received a hefty fine, five g's a piece, and they were sentenced to a year of probation.

I couldn't believe how greedy my uncle was. I

wanted so bad to kick him out, but it wasn't my house. It was Adrienne's house and that was her only brother and "he's the only one who has been there for us ever since Wayne died." Well, I wished Wayne, my daddy, was still around. If he were, all of our lives—Jerome's, Adrienne's, and mine— would be a whole lot better.

_____Kyle

"Yo man, do I know you?" he scowled. I clenched
my fist in case Chauncey decided to get crazy and
raise his hand. Instead, he broke his icy stare.
Clearly, he had to have recognized me.

Before I could respond, he broke into a wide
grin, snatched my hand, and gave me a bunch of
dap like we were long lost best friends.

"You know Tiana, don't 'chu? Yeah, okay. I remember you and your boy." He looked across the
club and saw Shawn seated at the table. "Yeah, that
cat over there! Yeah, yeah, yeah. . . ." he went on,
obviously intoxicated. "What's up, man? How you
been? You trying to get up in the VIP lounge
tonight? " He elbowed me and whispered, "Ain't
nuttin' yo. I got 'chu! I'mma hook you up. I know
everybody up in 'dis piece!" Chauncey's speech
was as slow and ghetto as he was.

I was relieved that he didn't wild out or snap in
any way. In fact, he was trying to hook up me and
my boys to go into the back with him and some of

the strippers later on to get private dances. I wasn't interested in any of that. I just wanted to get up out of there. My insides felt uneasy and my whole vibe was just uncomfortable. Tiana must have been rubbing off on me, because I had started feeling guilty.

"Yo, man, I just need to holla at you a quick minute. Can you step outside?" I leaned into him so he could hear me over the loud music that was drowning out our conversation. I glanced briefly at the stage and Diamond Jade was finishing up her pole dance and was now straddling a chair doing what hoes do.

"Oh aiigght. Cool, cool. No doubt no doubt." He shook my hand and slapped me five like six or seven times. Yeah he was definitely drunk. He had to be if he was saying everything twice.

I exchanged dap with Chauncey but remained unmoved. I still intended on letting him know what was on my mind. Somebody had to tell him about himself and it might as well be me.

"Look yo, my name is Kyle, man. And, look, I ain't tryna start no beef or nothing like that, family. I just thought you should know that I've been spending a lot of time with your little baby girl's mother, and I'm sayin'—"

"Which one?" Chauncey interrupted, half-way paying attention to me, but still looking at the X-rated entertainment that was bopping across the stage.

"Which one? I'm talking about Tiana, of course! You know, the one who just gave birth to your daughter Jayda?" I was beginning to dislike this dude the more I looked at him.

"Oh. I'm saying, I got like three of them jawns

you know?! I do have four kids, 'nah mean?" He reached out for me to slap five, but I didn't return it.

I shook my head. I wasn't worried about any other baby mamas he had. In fact, I wondered if Tiana even knew that he had these other baby mamas.

"Look man, I know it ain't my business, but don't you feel some type of way for being out here spending all that money on these smuts down here, when you got a little girl at home?"

That's when Chauncey snapped. "What the fuck you got to do with that? That ain't none of your business. Do you know who I am? Didn't you hear that announcer, nigga? Whaaat? I am Chauncey Davis, nigga! Whatchu, Tiana's new little boyfriend or something?" He eyed me up and down.

"Yeah, something like that." *Damn. Why did I just get rowdy with this drunk nigga?*

Chuancey snickered. "Yo man, I ain't even hitting that no more, so I ain't mad at 'chu. But, yo, just stay up out of my business, aiight? And don't worry about how I take care of mine. I sees all my kids, ya feel me? So just go 'bout your business, dog, aiight?" He turned his back on me. I decided to let it go. It wasn't worth arguing over.

I spent the next two hours in Temptations with my boys, resolving to call Tiana first thing tomorrow.

I called Tiana the next afternoon.

"Tiana? What's up, girl? What you doing? You want some company?"

I knew she was planning to go down to Temple

later that day to get the books for her class. I was proud of her; she decided against taking an entire year off, and instead, registered for this spring semester. With the baby, she could only take half the course load that she was used to taking, meaning that she would be graduating next spring instead of that May, when I was walking.

"Of course. You know I do. Do you feel like helping me wash bottles?" she laughed.

"I guess I can do that." She always kept me in high spirits. I hung up the phone and told my people that I was going by to see Tiana for a while and that I'd be back in a few hours.

"Oooohhh, Kyle got a girlfriend!" my little brother Ty teased.

My moms joined in on the teasing, pinching my cheek as I went to go put on my coat. "Now Ty, you know better than to get in your big brother's business." She shot me a pensive look. "So, what is up with you and Miss Tiana? Huh, Kyle?" Mom smirked playfully.

"Mom," I gave her a peck on the cheek. "you know all of us go way back at Mount Zion. I mean, Shawn, Tiana—all of us—we go way back to Miss Sherman's primary Sunday School class! Tiana is like a little sister!"

"I'm not saying anything. I think Tiana is a lovely girl. But, she is a mother now, Kyle. And you have been away at school for a few years. Even though you've only brought home Aliya, I'm sure you've had a few little girlfriends at Marshall. Am I right?"

That woman's intuition was no joke. Moms had my number. She was on point with hers, I'd give her that.

"Yeah, so what are you saying Mom?" I didn't feel like a lecture, I wanted to go see my baby.

"All I'm saying, Kyle, is to be careful. Watch Tiana's heart, and more importantly, watch your own heart. I know you're grown and everything. . . ."

I wanted to tell her desperately, *"Yeah, Moms, I am a grown-ass man now. I think I know what I'm doing. But I allowed her to continue treating me like her baby boy."*

"Relax, Mom. I got this." I hugged my mother and playfully shadow-boxed with Ty before I left. It felt good to know that Moms was concerned about my heart. As soon as I made Tiana my exclusive woman officially, I could start thinking about how serious things were getting. For now, we were just kicking it and getting closer as the days went by.

When I got to Tiana's her mother answered the door. I greeted Ms. Anderson with a hug and a kiss on the cheek. She was as fine as Tiana was. I had never seen Tiana's dad, but it was clear where Tiana had gotten her looks from. Ms. Anderson looked to be in her early thirties, but I knew she was around forty-three or so. Her figure was slim and petite like Tiana's. She had a fly short haircut that made her look like Halle Berry. *If I were ten years older or she were ten years younger. . . .*

My crazy older-woman-fantasy abruptly ended when Tiana came downstairs holding Jayda against her hip and swinging a diaper cloth in her hand. She was dressed in a pair of black leggings and a lavender Gamma t-shirt. She had the sleeves rolled up, revealing her shapely arms. "Hey, Kyle. Mom, ain't Kyle sweet? He came over to help me wash bottles tonight!"

"Is that right?" Ms. Anderson looked at me. If I didn't know any better, I'd say it was a flirtatious glance. "How nice!" The two Anderson women giggled like girlfriends.

"Sike, Kyle. Come on," Tiana said. I followed her into the kitchen. As she held Jayda out for me to take, her sleeve inched up a bit, revealing what looked to be some cursive writing paired with a red heart. "Here, can you hold her for a little bit?"

Jayda cried as her mother passed her to me. I bounced Jayda up and down in my arms and took in her freshly-powdered-baby scent. Yeah, fatherhood was something I could get used to. I looked at Jayda lovingly, but kept fixating my eyes on what looked like a tattoo on Tiana's arm.

"Yo, Tee. Is that a tat on your arm?" I asked.

Tiana looked down at her arm and tugged on her sleeve to lift it up. "Oh. This?" she sucked her teeth and rolled her eyes as she went over to the sink to begin washing baby bottles.

"Yeah. That."

Tiana sucked her teeth and flagged her hand. "Man, I got that done when I was like three months pregnant and thought I was in love. He came around with some old so-called promise ring and then he took me down to South Street and paid for me to get it done. It just has his name and a heart. He promised that he was going to get my name on him for his birthday in August. Do you think he did? Of course not. That's when I knew we were growing apart. I stopped wearing that little fake cubic zirconia ring of his and I vowed to wear sleeves as much as possible. Now, you will never catch me in a tank top. And if I go to the beach this year, I'm wearing a cover-up."

"So, you knew before Jayda was born that you and him weren't going to work out?"

"Yep. Plus, I don't know if I ever told you this, but Chauncey has other kids. When he told the nurse that at our first visit, I wanted to smack the crap out of him."

"So, then you won't be shocked if I told you that I ran into him the other night?"

"Oh, really? Where?"

"All right, don't get mad at me, but I was at Temptations. It was me and Shawn and some of our boys down there for Shawn's birthday."

"Mmmhmmm, sure. Tell me anything!" Tiana smirked. "So did y'all speak?"

"Yeah, and I told him about himself. He was all up in that place, throwing his cash at those hoes like it was nothing. So I told him I thought it was kinda ill for him to be doing that when he could be home with his child." I noticed Tiana's eyes glisten as she listen attentively.

"So," I continued. "I'm sorry to get in your business. My bad, you know? I just don't like seeing you working so hard with just you and your mom taking care of the baby and his butt is giving away the same money he should be giving to you and his daughter."

"Don't worry about it." She turned the water off and stopped washing the bottles for a minute. "Let me tell you something. When God brings people in your life, it is for a reason. Chauncey was brought to me so that I would know the joy of motherhood. And then God brought you back into my life so that I would see how good a friendship with a man can be and to help me get over the pain of breaking up with Chauncey."

I didn't know what to say. I was getting that love-sick feeling you get when you start feeling all those lovey-dovey emotions. I would be a fool to let a woman like Tiana get by. She had, so far, laid all of her cards on the table. I think she was waiting on me to make the move to bring our friendship into "relationship-mode."

"Tiana, let me ask you a question."

"Yes?"

"I know it's been only a few months since you and Chauncey sort of ended things, and I know that you've just had a baby and all. But, I really want you to be in my life. I want you to be more than a friend. I know we said we would take things slow, but these past weeks have been the best weeks of my life. I can't stop thinking about you. When I go back to school next week, I want to go back telling all my boys that I've settled down."

"Are you asking me to be your woman, Kyle?" she smiled.

"Come on, girl. You know I am. What you want me to do? Hand you a note that reads 'Will you go with me Tiana? Check Yes or No.' Come on now, we both are grown folks! So what's up?"

Tiana let out a heavy sigh and walked over to me with her sudsy hands. She wiped some of the foamy lather in my hair jokingly. "Yes, Kyle. Yes!"

_____*Jasmyn*

I was still pretty shook up about Uncle Jeff's betrayal. I hardly spoke to him during the rest of winter break. The rest of the family was a bit more forgiving than I was. I didn't see how they could be, seeing how he risked everyone's life by instigating a fire.

When I arrived back at school for the spring semester, it was time to begin preparing for graduation. I devoted my time to studying, teaching, and dieting. I got a student teaching job at Gompers Elementary School, located in Wynnefield, in the outskirts of West Philadelphia. It was almost an hour's drive from campus, but I didn't mind because Gompers was one of the milder schools in the school district of Philadelphia.

My student teaching experience was positive. My students liked me and I learned how to appreciate the little things in life. It amazed me how innocent children could be. The simplest things made their day—like tying their own shoes, blow-ing bubbles in bubble gum, and writing their name in cursive by themselves. I taught third graders, but I walked through the halls and observed every age there at the school, from the kindergartners up to the fourth graders. True, some of them were smart asses, but the majority of them were sweet.

As May approached, my social life dwindled. In an effort to spark up my social and my sex life, I decided to give a few of my former jump-offs one last call. I had dropped twelve pounds by simply staying busy and cutting back on junk food. I was thrilled to be back into a size ten. About ten more pounds and I'd be in an eight again. I really wanted to get with Kyle, but Crystal told me that Shawn said that Kyle was dating some girl they grew up with named Tiana. I thought of the soror I met from Temple named Tiana and panicked for a minute.

Hold up, slow your roll, Jazz. Don't you know Philadelphia is a huge city? There are probably hundreds of Tianas.

I didn't bother to question Crystal or Shawn about the girl Kyle was seeing, because, frankly, I didn't like the idea of Kyle being with other women. Just seeing him with the Spanish girl last semester was enough to stir up some jealousy. I was guilty of often comparing myself to others and I had become very self-conscious of my appearance, especially since I gained a few pounds. So it was better for my own self-esteem that I didn't know what Tiana looked like or anything else about her.

I wound up hooking up with some African guy named Al that I met at a Gamma party. I noticed that Kyle didn't go to parties anymore. To tell you the truth, I didn't care if any of my other exes saw me at a party flirting. I was only worried about Kyle. He was the good catch who I let get away. I really messed things up with him. Moe had even tried to get back with me, but I gave him a flat-out "no." I just chalked up my relationship with Kyle to another love lesson learned.

I was unsatisfied emotionally and physically. After Al, out of sheer loneliness, I filled that void for male companionship with a series of insignificant dudes who meant very little to me. I went out with them here and there. And despite how busy Gamma and student teaching kept me, I managed to be intimate in one way or another with all of them. Crystal thought I was being a slut, but she had a man, so she had no room to talk. It was a long winter ahead, and I didn't have any plans of spending it alone.

As springtime eased in, I took a look back at my time at Marshall. I had gone through a lot, trying to earn a college degree without my mother and brother being there. I hadn't really had any solid relationships with anyone. True, I did join a fabulous sorority, but even Gamma had some issues. There were girls who were petty and two-faced, so it wasn't like you could totally trust everyone in the sorority. I had worries at home with wondering how we were going to make it with my mother's income and the little bit of funds that Jerome brought in from his job. There was always the worry of Adrienne having a relapse or Jerome getting sucked back into the game. And, of course, ever since Uncle Jeff tried to burn the house down, he couldn't be trusted. I really believe that the real reason Adrienne let him continue to stay at the house was for financial reasons.

It was April and I was in a daze with all of the end-of-school preparations. I had final exams to take soon and papers to write, not to mention my little darlings at the school that I had grown so close to. I now had to start preparing them for Miss Simmons's departure. I swear, if it weren't for them, I probably would have lost my mind after the arson incident. But the kids gave me a sense of purpose. I started feeling better about myself. I did as much as I could to present fun, interesting, and interactive lessons to them. Every Friday, I even brought them candy. I used my discount from Target to buy a few end-of-the-year gifts for my supervising teacher and for the principal. They always kept me motivated.

The principal, Mrs. Harvey, told me, "Miss Simmons, you are doing a wonderful job with these children. It's like you were born to teach. These kids just really seem to take to you so well. You are going to be an excellent teacher. If I can ever write a recommendation for you, don't hesitate to ask."

I took Mrs. Harvey up on her offer and she wrote a glowing recommendation for me. She also told me that she was aware of a few vacancies coming up in a couple of schools, and that she would talk to one of her friends at the district about holding one of those spots for me. I hadn't thought about working in Philadelphia after graduation, but if the opportunity presented itself, I was going to go for it. It was the first time in my life that I felt truly respected and appreciated for my skills and abilities. I felt valued just for being Jasmyn Chantel Simmons.

"I advise you to start getting the health check-ups and criminal background checks that Pennsylvania requires," advised Mrs. Harvey. "If you already have your preliminary requirements done when you go down to apply, you will be a few steps ahead of the other applicants. Most people don't start getting that kind of stuff done until after a position is offered to them. But you always want to stay one step ahead of the competition because there are a lot of young people like yourself embarking on this profession. Just a little advice." Mrs. Harvey was really down-to-earth and I was glad that she was hipping me to all that I needed to do. I thought by just having my resume and a little portfolio, I was doing something.

"Yo, little sis. What are you doing?" Jerome called me one night as I was writing my final paper for my Methods for Exceptional Children class.

"Writing a paper, what you think, dummy?" I teased. "Sike, what are y'all up to?"

"Jasmyn, look. I know you're all into your classes and everything right now. So I don't want you worrying, but me and Uncle Jeff got into it last night."

"What do you mean y'all 'got into it' last night?" I rolled my eyes. "What did that fool do now?"

"Yo, now you know I wasn't real cool with him staying here after that whole fire-bomb shit, but you know how Adrienne was all crying and everything. That's her only brother or whatever. But look, how 'bout him and Sonny tried to do that shit again?"

I couldn't believe what I was hearing.

"Yo, Jazz, let me tell you. They had a whole 'nother scam set up. This time, they were going to flood the basement out. You know how it's been raining a lot this week?"

"Yeah."

"Well, I caught them downstairs in the basement with all these empty totes, filling them with water. I asked him what he was doing, and he was like 'Look, youngblood, this time, we can't lose. Now, you and Adrienne just go along with it and we can get paid and tell them how all the electronics and computer stuff got messed up. That's gotta be good for at least five grand.' I looked at him like he was crazy!"

"Are you serious? We just got another policy from that new company not that long ago."

"You know that and I know that. That nigga will mess our whole house up if we let him! And you know Adrienne is so twisted in the head, she don't even know what's gong on. She started slipping again, staying in her room acting all out of it and what-not. I had to drag her out of bed three days in a row so she could get ready for work."

I wasn't surprised about my mother. It was like she dealt with Uncle Jeff's betrayal in her own quiet little way, even if it meant withdrawing herself from the rest of the world.

"So, what'd you do?"

"Come on, girl. You know I don't play! I told him to get his shit and I wanted him out the house. I told him we didn't need him to do nothing for us and that he was too sneaky and conniving. Look, Jazz, we can't afford to keep getting new policies every time we turn around. I already got a record. The cops look at shit like that."

"You're right," I agreed. I was glad that my brother was being the man of the house. My dad wouldn't have put up with any mess like that.

"So, he'll be out within the next week."

"And what about the bills?" Although I knew that Uncle Jeff could not be trusted, I also knew that from a financial standpoint, we needed him to pay the bills. He paid the majority of the mortgage and took care of the electric, cable, and phone bills. As far as I knew, all Adrienne paid for were groceries. And that little chump change Jerome was making was only good enough for him to pay his child support. Lucky for me, I didn't have a car payment. My little Target job was just enough to pay for my car insurance and give me a little change in my pocket.

"Don't sweat it."

I knew that meant that he was cooking up some plan to get some money from some other source. "Jerome, I'm telling you now, don't borrow no money from any of your boys."

"Girl, didn't I tell you I got this? Just trust me. Now, I went down and put in a few applications yesterday at the cable company and a few other places."

I felt hopeful again. I knew Jerome would find a way to make it.

In the months that went by, as hard as it was, I had to leave my family problems back home in Willingboro. When May rolled around, I couldn't have been any happier. Jerome had gotten a night job in customer service at the Comcast cable company, and he was working on getting his record expunged. He had even gone back to New Jersey Transit to apply for a position; they told him that once he was employed consistently for a year, they would reconsider his application.

Two weeks before graduation, Marshall threw a Seniors Only Barbecue. I was reluctant to go, but Crystal insisted since half of our Gamma pledge sisters were seniors, as well as most of our friends. I didn't want to see any of my little one-night stand guys that I had hooked up with over the four years I was at Marshall. But it was all good. It'd be the last time that I'd see any of them, so whether or not they spoke to me would be unimportant.

I did, however, want to leave on good terms with Kyle. When I spotted him with Shawn at the picnic, I resisted the urge to play hard-to-get. I tapped over to him in my pink strappy high heels. I was looking ghetto-chic and I knew that I had the attention of every guy I sauntered past. Something about women in high heels made men notice, and I basked in all of the lusty stares I was getting. Several months before, when I was heavier, I had stopped wearing clothes that attracted attention. But, I had a newfound confidence. And even though I didn't crave the male attention I used to thrive on, it still felt good just to know that for a few seconds, I had the guys diverting their eyes away from whomever they were with and focusing on me.

As Kyle saw me approaching, his eyes widened. "So we're finally up out of here, huhn?" I smiled and gave him a hug.

Kyle paused, then glanced downwards, taking in

every inch of my newly-slimmed down body that slid easily into a pair of beige capris and a pink knit top. He slipped his arms around my waist and hugged me back. "You know?!" He smiled at me. "Girl, you're looking kind of good. I like that outfit."

Music was blaring and I tried to drown out the sounds of laughter, talking, and music. "I just wanted to get my last little hug in before graduation. I just wanted you to know that even though things went down kind of bad between us, I'm real happy I met you," I confessed.

"I know," Kyle shook his head apologetically. "Jazz, it's cool. I mean, I'm sorry for that mess with Moe and everything. I mean, we were dead wrong. I hope you can forgive us. I still got love for ya though."

My insides were tingling. I reached up and planted a soft closed-mouth kiss on his lips. "I'm sorry, I just had to do that. I heard you got a girlfriend now and everything."

Kyle shook his head. "Shawn, right?"

I laughed. "Come on now, you know that's my best friend's man! How else am I going to get the dirt on you?" I winked.

I could tell Kyle was digging my vibe. I still got it, I thought. I bet I could still get him if I wanted to. "Girl, you're still crazy!" said Kyle.

"So," I stepped in closer to him and whispered, "your girlfriend won't mind that I kissed you? You know I don't want to disrespect her or anything."

He slid his hand to the small of my back, leaned over, and kissed me back. "It's not a problem at all."

* * *

I was glad Kyle and I got a chance to reconcile at the senior barbecue. I really surprised myself. Usually I was the one making the first moves with men, but after that kiss, Kyle immediately began throwing me a lot of attention. I guess it's true what they say, "You don't miss what you have until it's gone." It just took Kyle over a year to realize it, though. I knew Kyle and I would never have a relationship again, but at least I knew that things weren't dead between us. That was enough to keep me happy.

Things had gotten so busy that I didn't get around to doing any of the things Mrs. Harvey had recommended that I do before applying for a teaching job. I made my appointment for a full physical and TB shots during final exam week.

Inside the exam room, after being asked a thousand questions and having everything checked out, the female physician asked, "When was the last time you had a gynecological exam?"

"I got one freshman year." I didn't see why it mattered. My coochie felt perfectly fine, thank you.

"Well, I would suggest that you get one while you're here, just to make sure you don't have anything to worry about. You don't want to be at risk for cervical cancer or anything serious like that."

I didn't have anything to lose. It had been a while since I had a Pap smear and STD tests. I guess since I had been with so many guys, I didn't want to get any bad news. But I went through with the exam, the poking and the prodding, and all of the other discomforts.

The doctor pulled her latex gloves off as I sat back up, relieved. "We're just going to screen you for any sexually transmitted infections. It's something we do here routinely. You can go ahead and put your clothes back on and I'll meet you back in my office."

"Okay," I replied. I got dressed and met her back in her office as she requested.

She shuffled some papers, sat down, and looked at me apologetically. "Jasmyn, I took a look at the culture I got and it seems that you have gonorrhea. Have you noticed any unusual discharge coming from that area?"

"No, nothing." *Gonorrhea?!!!!! Who the hell burned me?*

"Well, many times," she continued, "females are asymptomatic and never know they have it. But I would suggest that you go ahead and also get an HIV test, since you told me that you've had more than five partners in the past two years."

I looked at her in amazement. "HIV test? Um, no, I don't think so. I use protection. And I'm selective about who I'm intimate with." *For the most part.*

The nurse wrote out a prescription and handed it to me. "Well, all I can do is offer advice. You seem like an intelligent, otherwise healthy young woman. But it's my professional opinion that it's always better to know where you stand."

I snatched the prescription from her. "Thanks for the advice. But I'm very careful with mine."

"Well I would at least suggest that you contact your previous partners about the results of today's test." She stood up to walk me out.

I nodded, thanked her again, and left the office.

Is she crazy? I'm not about to go around to all those guys and say 'Excuse me, nigga, but did you burn me?' I

*had just gotten past that ho stereotype after that Moe and
Kyle incident went down. There is no way I was going to
play myself like that. Maybe when I get back home, I'll get
an HIV test, but not today.*

The following week, I graduated with a 2.5 GPA.
It wasn't exactly high, but in light of everything I
had been through, I was happy just to have made
it.

Now it was time to get serious. I had to get a job
and help at home with those bills that I knew had
to be piling up since Uncle Jeff left. My mom eventually saw why Jerome told him to leave, so she didn't
protest. I was just hoping that she would continue
going to work so she could set herself up for a pro-
motion soon. Maybe when I returned home, she
would feel like it was old times with just her,
Jerome, and me in the house. The stability was
bound to be good for her depression.

It was sad to leave college behind, because now I
knew for a fact that I had to be responsible. The
doctor's suggestion to get an HIV test kept echo-
ing in my head during the past week and I knew
that I really did need to go ahead and get that HIV
test. Deep inside, I really did want to know the result. If I could get gonorrhea and not know it,
there was no telling what else I might have had.

_____*Kyle*

"Yo, family, when's the last time you seen Jazz? She's looking kinda good now. Man, I don't know what came over me, but we started kissing at that barbecue yesterday."

Shawn and I were laid back in the apartment playing Madden for the last time.

"Yo, I saw that," Shawn snickered. "Don't let your girl Tee find out!"

I dismissed Shawn's warning. "Nah man, it was just a kiss. There was nothing to it. I think I just got thrown off guard because I didn't expect her to look the way she did. But, you know I love my girl."

"I hear you man." Shawn began smoking a Newport. He was trying to get clean and had been replacing sparking L's with smoking cigarettes. It was still a bad habit, but at least it was legal.

"I'm serious, man," I insisted. "By the end of the summer. Watch. I'mma propose to her."

Shawn dropped the controller. "Whaaaat?!" He paused the game, stood up, and grabbed me toward him in a brotherly embrace. "Yo man, that's what's up!"

"Thanks, yo." I gave him some dap. "You know I want you to be the best man, right?"

"No doubt, family. I got you."

Shawn had his issues, but he always had my back. I couldn't even begin to think about wedding plans right now. If I was going to propose by the end of the summer, I knew that I needed to make enough money to at least make a down payment on a ring. I wanted to be able to afford it and not be paying for it for the next five years.

Graduation came and went. It was like what took four long years to arrive, finally did arrive, and passed like it was almost nothing. Graduation was definitely overrated. All of those years studying, all of that just to hear your name called for a quick two seconds along with five thousand other people.

I spent the summer working hard, busting my butt at the same car dealership I worked at last summer. On the weekends, I had copped a job working at the deli at Acme. My parents and brothers rarely even saw me. I was always running in and out the house, either going to work, going to see Tee, or going to hang out with Shawn.

Around the end of July, I went out to Zales Jewelers at Granite Run Mall and spotted two nice iced-out one-and-a-half carat rings. One was a princess cut ring and the other was a solitaire with baguette diamonds on each side. I remember hearing Tiana oohing and aahing over some ring she saw on QVC that had baguettes, so I went with that one. I opened a line of credit, put five hundred towards it, and charged the other grand to the card.

All I had to do then was prepare the time and place that I would close the deal and propose to her. During the past year that we had been together, we hadn't had too many opportunities to be alone. She really wanted to honor her commitment to God, but there were a few moments of weakness when we had gotten into it, but it was always interrupted by Jayda crying or her mom coming home. And with all the people in my house, intimacy wasn't even a possibility over there. I had to put all of that energy into my academics and to working out. I had a six pack and my chest, back, and shoulders were cut tight as I don't know what.

We had never been off to a hotel together to be alone, but once I had found a way to romance her enough, I thought Tiana would succumb—giving in and giving all of herself to me. When that happened, then I'd pop the question.

I took a weekend off in late August and we made plans to go to Ocean City, Maryland for the weekend. Tiana had asked Jayda's godmother to watch her for the night since Chauncey was nowhere to be found. Every time she tried to call his cell phone, it was disconnected, and at his mom's house they were always saying Chauncey wasn't there. So she got tired of chasing him. "When he's ready to act like he got some sense and see his daughter, he knows how to reach me," she said. I agreed with her and it just made me that much more anxious to propose so I could just adopt Jayda and take care of her myself. I already had laced that little girl up, spending about a hundred dollars on toys and a coat for her at Christmas.

It was a mild August evening. We had driven down to Ocean City early and spent the day walking on the boardwalk and shopping at the outlets in nearby Rehoboth Beach. We ate crab cakes for dinner and got ice cream for dessert at this exclusive place where the cones were like four dollars each. After walking on the beach barefoot in the sand just like they do in the movies, I suggested we go back to our room. I had requested a room with separate beds like Tee suggested, but hoped that one of the beds would be used for suitcases, and not me.

I had packed a CD player and brought a few slow jam CDs. The sexual tension was getting so strong I felt like I was about to explode. I grabbed her hands and pulled her down to sit on the bed alongside of me.

"Tiana, I have to tell you something. This is turning out to be one of the most special evenings I've ever spent in my entire life."

Tiana smiled back at me and laid her head on my shoulder. She rubbed the back of my neck softly. "I know. The beach, everything is just so romantic." She eyed me with a "come-hither" look and I gave in to the temptations that were arising.

The beach sunset atmosphere was the perfect mood setter. We kissed awhile and, needless to say, we ended up making warm, passionate love. The surprising thing was that it was nothing carnal and freaky like it had been with Jazz, Mari, Aliya, and all of the other chicks I had messed with in the past. It was hard to explain; being with her was a strange, spiritually erotic feeling. Afterwards, I felt an extreme closeness I had never experienced before. Our bodies united and we simultaneously reached our highest points of euphoria. A tear rolled down my cheek and down onto her chest.

"I love you so much, Kyle," she whispered looking into my eyes.

"Tee, do you know how much I love you? I always have. I want to spend the rest of my life with you. I want to raise Jayda as my own daughter."

Tiana sat up in bed and listened tearfully yet attentively as I poured my heart out to her.

I was overcome with emotion as I continued. "We've been friends since we were twelve. You know everything about me. You're the closest person in the world to me."

"I feel the same way, Kyle. Everything I was missing in a man—it wasn't in Chauncey or none of my other boyfriends. I can't believe it, that all these years that we've been friends, it was in you all along."

I looked in her eyes. "Tiana Nicole Anderson, I want you to be my wife."

I leaned over and took the black velvet box out of the nightstand, where I had placed it, while she was in the bathroom earlier.

"Be my wife, Tiana, and make me the happiest brother on earth." I opened the box and revealed the ring to her.

Her eyes widened in amazement. "Are you for real?"

I smiled and nodded. "Word on everything."

"Yes, Kyle! Yes, baby!" Tee planted kisses all over me and fell into my arms.

That night we made more earth-moving, body-quaking love. I didn't know what lay ahead for us, but I knew that my young-boy days were over. Tiana was all I needed.

PART TWO:

AFTER COLLEGE
"Time to grow up"

I was lucky to get a job with the school district of Philadelphia at one of the premier public elementary schools in the city, Greenfield Elementary. The principal at Gompers, the school where I student taught, gave me a nice recommendation and was in tight with some people down at the district. The elementary positions were few and far-between. At first I was afraid that I was going to have to take a job as a substitute teacher, and I knew how badly kids treated them. I definitely didn't want to struggle through four years of college just to become a substitute teacher who earns money day by day and has to run all over the city to different schools. I knew I'd only finished with a 2.5 grade point average, but hell, I'd finished. And that's all that mattered.

Greenfield was situated at 22nd and Chestnut, right on the edge of Center City. I took 295 to the bridge and was downtown in about forty minutes, which wasn't a bad commute. I bought an E Z-Pass, which allowed me to go in faster lanes and kept me from digging out dollar bills for the toll every day.

I had a fourth grade class, which was around the level that I wanted. I knew that I didn't want first or second graders. I preferred the kids who were at least eight years old. That way I didn't have to spend so much time tying shoes and wiping noses.

It was June and I had been an official college graduate for exactly one year. I had settled easily into my new routine as Miss Simmons, the teacher in Room 104. I had a relatively manageable class size of twenty-six. The other teachers on staff were very helpful to me getting adjusted to my first year in the classroom. They shared materials and supplies and gave me a lot of ideas for lessons and ways to save time.

In spite of my success in my new career, there was still the reality of my mother's mental instability, a mortgage, and my need to get a new vehicle. My father's life insurance money, pension plans, and the little bit of savings I had was enough to keep us living comfortably. Now that we didn't have to pay Meadowpines for my mother's treatment, it was actually a good thing. So, Uncle Jeff's absence really didn't hit us as hard financially as I had thought it would originally. Apparently, even though Adrienne was going back and forth between nervous breakdowns and bouts of depression, she had cashed in part of my dad's life insurance, purchased some savings bonds, and stored them away in a safe in the back of her closet—to the tune of thirty thousand dollars' worth.

After she told us that she had a few dollars saved up and that her "baby boy" wouldn't have to keep riding the bus to work, she bought Jerome a used

Infiniti G35 and paid nine thousand dollars cash
for it. I couldn't believe that she would buy him a
car while she and I rode around in cars with over a
hundred thousand miles on them.

But even more important than the car was my
health. I had wrestled in my mind over and over
about getting an HIV test. *I'll go get one sometime before the summer is over.* I never *did* find out who gave
me gonorrhea, but I didn't stress over it. I just
tried to be extra-careful from then on whenever I
did have sex. I had only been with a few people
since college: Jerome's friend Omar and some
other guy I met at the Resorts Casino when Crystal
and I went to Atlantic City for my birthday weekend. Most recently there was this guy named
Marcus I met at the gym who claimed he played
for the Sixers, but was on the injured list. I had
never even heard of him. My thing was, if you
played for the Sixers, what were you doing on the
treadmill at Bally's? He claimed that since it was
the off-season they had a ton of free time. I admit I
fell for his game without even doing my research.
We had a little one-month fling. I let him take me
out and buy me expensive dinners. But then it occurred to me to go on the Internet and look up
the Sixers' roster. Sure enough, his name was
nowhere to be found. I was in a dry spell, so I let
him spend his money on the Four Seasons two or
three times. But I stopped calling him, so I assumed he got the hint that it was over.

It was a mild and breezy evening in June. The
school year was over and I was enjoying the bi-
weekly paychecks that were mailed to me, without

me having to get up and go work for it. But it was easy to become bored, as I was feeling tonight. Jerome was out on a date with some new babe Maya. Adrienne was out with her co-worker at some jazz festival going on down in Wilmington. It was at times like these that I kind of missed Uncle Jeff and Aunt Tammy. I wished Crystal lived closer; I didn't have too many other girlfriends. There were a few girls I was cool with, but that was back in high school and I never stayed in touch with them during college. I had female co-workers, but they were all over forty. I supposed that was why I spent so much time with the opposite sex. To combat my boredom, I hopped into my car, slid on some Jaheim, rolled the windows down, and soaked in all the summer air as I headed to the video store to make it a Blockbuster night.

While I was looking at the "New Releases" wall, I felt like the guy behind me was doing more than just staring at the titles.

"How you doin', love? I see you looking for something you and your man can watch this weekend." He grinned at me, waiting for a response.

Is that the best his tall, lanky ass can do? I rolled my eyes and gave him a brief hello.

He walked up and stood right next to me, "So I see you like Ice Cube, huhn?" he asked, eyeing the *Barbershop 2* DVD that was in my hand. I had picked up that and *Brown Sugar.* I loved comedies with a romantic twist.

"Why?" Up till then, I hadn't got a good look at him, but the curiosity got the best of me. When I looked up, I was pleasantly surprised at what I laid my eyes on. He looked so good. *Oh yes, he's official.*

"Well, I'm just making conversation," he continued as I took in every bit of him. "Ain't nothing wrong with that, is it, sis?" I looked up at him and his smile was intoxicating. He was tall and slim with very short neatly-done dreads. His face was clean-cut and his skin was smooth and the perfect shade of brown. He looked like he took care of his skin, too, because his face was blemish-free. A man who took care of his skin was a definite plus. He got like ten bonus points for that one. *Oh yeah, he can get it.*

"No, I can't be mad at you for that," I smiled coyly. "So, I see you like those ghetto movies, huh?" I reached my hands for his DVDs. *"Juice? Menace to Society?"*

"What can I say? I felt like watching some old-school hood flicks."

I spotted *Titanic* in his hand and reached for it. "Mmm. Then what do you call this, then?" He was just about to lose like fifty points for being a corn-ball.

"Oh, this? Girl, *Titanic* is the shit. You know you like them romances."

I raised one eyebrow. "Uhn."

"Anyway, I might be trying to watch this movie with some pretty brown cutie," he smiled and looked me up and down. "Some brown cutie with a pair of tight jeans and a yellow shirt. . . ." Then he reached his hand out to touch the edge of my bucket hat. "And a cute little hat too."

Please. No he didn't. I was looking a hot mess. I placed both hands on top of my head. I only had a hat on because I needed a perm, and in the summer-time it was too hot to be wearing fourteen-inch ponytails and I didn't feel like getting micro-braids either. And he must've bumped his head thinking

I was about to watch that boring, long ass movie with him.

"How do you know this cutie don't have a man?" I asked.

"Well does she?" He didn't take his eyes off me one minute during our entire conversation. *Hmm. He seems pretty confident. Okay, he scored a few more points for that.*

"Well, I can answer that question if you put that corny ass *Titanic* back," I nodded towards his hand.

"All right, all right. I'll put it back," he said as he set it on the shelf out of place among the newly re-leased videos. "Now can I get an answer?"

"It depends. Do you have a girl? Where is she at this Friday night?

The dude rolled his eyes and shook his head like he couldn't believe I was trying to play so cute. "Now you see I'm up in the video store just like you. So stop playing games. I'm saying, what's good, ma? I'm digging your style."

I was feeling him too. But I knew that if I let this guy just come over my house, I would be so stupid. What kind of message would that send? I mean, yes, I have slept with guys on the first night, but the older I got, the more I learned that a female couldn't play herself and look real easy right off the bat. She couldn't be a sucker for the slick-behind game that these guys were always talking.

"Well, let me see if my brother is home. You might be a rapist or some kind of stalker. I don't even know you, so I might need some back-up." Jerome was always my protector when it came to men. My boyfriends always knew I had a crazy brother and a bunch of psycho cousins.

"Girl, please. I'm not a stalker or a rapist. I'm a

good brother. But you know, do what you gotta do. I understand."

"Good," I said, closing my phone when Jerome didn't pick up.

"Look, check this out. What you like to eat? 'Cause I've never seen *Brown Sugar*. So I'm trying to see that with you."

"Well, I like Chinese food. Shrimp fried rice and spring rolls."

"All right, Shorty-rock. That's what's up. I'll get us some dinner and follow you back to your house to come keep you some company."

Eww. Shorty-rock? Who still says that?

I raised my eyebrows. The thought of a stranger following me home, even though he was a dime, still wasn't sitting right with me. He must've seen the uncertain expression on my face.

"I promise." He threw both arms in the air and said, "I won't touch you. Word is bond."

Now it's 'word is bond'? Okay, this guy is cute, but please somebody tell him we are in the new millennium. I figured I would ignore his potential corniness for now, 'cause cute ones like him didn't come around often.

"Let me go pick up one more movie." I went down the drama aisle and picked up *Enough* with Jennifer Lopez just in case he needed a reality check to see a man get his ass kicked by his woman.

I went to the register with him following close behind. "So you never told me your name."

"My bad," he smiled. "Tarik." He tilted his head to one side and extended his hand.

"How you doin'? I'm Jasmyn."

I shook his hand. He took my hand with one of his, and put the other hand on top of it. "Jassssmyn," he repeated sexily. "Like the flower. That's a beautiful name. It fits you."

Aww sukie-sukie. I remember my mom used to have me, Jerome, and my dad cracking up every time she said that.

"Nice to meet you, Tarik." Just then, Jerome called me back on the cell phone. I told him I was at Blockbuster and to come home soon because I was having company.

"Jazz, are you crazy?!" Jerome yelled through the phone. I turned away from Tarik and cupped my hand over the phone so he couldn't hear Jerome snapping on me. "You don't even know that nigga! How the hell are you gonna be picking up muthafuckas in Blockbuster and bringing them to the crib? Dude might be a serial killer. You need to wake up, Jazz! Sometimes, I just don't know about you. That was a real chickenhead move."

I sighed heavily and patiently listened, while rolling my eyes heavenward. Jerome swore he was my dad. Despite his fury with me, he agreed to bring his date back to the house in a half hour.

Tarik and I went to the register and got rung up. I got into my car and watched him in my side-view mirror as he walked to his white Chevy Blazer. *Nice car.* I was always partial to SUVs.

By the time Tarik and I pulled up to my house, Jerome's Infiniti was already in the driveway. We went inside where I met Jerome's new little girlfriend. They were both in the kitchen. I saw two tall brown paper bags. Obviously, they had been to the liquor store. Jerome had plugged up the blender and was getting ready to make some frozen drinks.

"What's up, y'all?" Jerome said as he gave Tarik a once-over and then glanced back at me with a nod of approval. I smiled and gave Maya a "Don't-even-think-of-looking-at-my-man" stare.

Jerome introduced Maya to us and I introduced Tarik to them. Jerome blended us some piña coladas with Bacardi. We took our large red plastic cups, along with our Chinese food, downstairs to the family room in the basement where there was a large-screen television.

We kicked it for a few hours and watched all of *Brown Sugar* and half of *Juice.* Tarik was a perfect gentleman, so I didn't make him watch the movie where Jennifer Lopez kicked her ex-husband's butt. He was really sincere and polite; he sort of reminded me of Kyle, only a bit more street—the way I liked my men. Kyle was more of a good guy, pretty boy type.

Tarik was a contractor and did a lot of remodeling projects for various businesses in Southern New Jersey. His schedule was flexible and he made lots of time available to spend with me. I was happy for the first time in a very long time.

Kyle

Tiana and I moved in together that summer right after we got engaged. It was against our parents' better judgment, but they knew that it would be a great help having a man in the house. Tiana went back to school and had two semesters left before she went to do her senior practicum at Temple University Hospital, shadowing a nurse and actually doing real on-the-job nursing duties.

"Babe, did you get your suit out the cleaners for the Ladies in Lavender gala? Don't forget, it's Saturday night."

Ladies in Lavender was some annual gala event that the Gammas did to raise money for scholarships.

"I'm going to go by the cleaners after work tonight, unless you want to go."

"Like I got time. You know I have to go by Lori's and pick my dress up. I hope she's finished." Lori was a dressmaker one of her sorors referred her to. My fiancée wasn't about to be caught dead in the same gown as another woman. So she opted for the custom made look. Plus, I had insisted on her getting a dress that covered her arms and that tattoo of hers. We were going to schedule surgery with a dermatologist to get it removed before the wedding, so she could let her arms show at our wedding next year.

At the ball, it was a sea of lavender and silver gowns. I had to admit Gamma had some beautiful women. I didn't know too much about Greek life, but I remembered the Gammas on our yard at Marshall. I even recalled the time Jasmyn and Crystal were up in our apartment looking all tore up with those lavender scarves tied around their heads, and how a few days later I saw them all around campus doing that silly catcall with their sorority gear on. I would never knock Greek life though; they did positive things in the Black community and have been around for years and years.

It's funny how I should think of Jasmyn at a time like this when I am at this event with my girl. I'm glad this was a Philly event and that Jazz lived in Jersey. Not that I was thinking of her like that. She did look good at that Senior Barbecue. *All right, Kyle, wake up brother! Stop thinking about your ex. Your girl is a dime, she is mad cute and Jazz or any other broad can hold a candle to her. You're here to enjoy the time with her. Not look for other women.*

Tiana was excited to be there, saying she didn't have many formal events to look forward to and she thought that we needed to be seen out in public more as a couple.

A group of three women headed over to our

table. Tiana shrieked in excitement upon seeing them!

"Tooooosssh! What's up *sororrrrr*?"

"Hey, Tiana! How you doing, boo?" the plump, but attractive one replied.

"So, is this your man?" another one chimed in.

"Yeah, girl. I'm gettin' married." Tiana stuck her left hand out and waved her rock in front of her sorors.

"Oh my damn! Girl, that ring is big as I don't know what!" She looked at me and asked, "Okay, um what is your name and do you have any brothers?"

I smiled sheepishly, somewhat embarrassed by the attention. "Yeah I do, but uh, they're only fifteen and eighteen years old." It was hard to believe Jamir was starting his first semester at Penn State. My parents didn't get a moment's rest; as soon as one son finished school, another one was beginning. And after Jamir, they still had Ty.

"Fifteen and eighteen? Nah, that's okay. I'm twenty-six. I don't wanna R Kelly him, you know?"

We laughed and Tiana realized she hadn't introduced us.

"Oh baby, I'm sorry. My bad. Kyle, these are some of my Temple sorors: Tosh, Karen, and Dannette. Y'all, this is my fiancé, Kyle."

"Ooh okay, we like the sound of that," another added. "So that's why you disappeared on us, huhn?"

"Girl, no. I'm just finishing up school. I've been incognegro the past semester. I'm trying to finish this nursing program and start this practicum in the spring. I plan to graduate next fall. So you know a sister got love for y'all, but I gotta do me for a minute!"

"I know that's right!" the others agreed.

"You see the West Chester and Marshall Gammas here, right? Remember the ones we met out at that Christmas thing at the mall last year?"

"Oh yeah, and we all went to Applebee's afterwards? Yeah. I remember them. Where they at? I don't see them."

"They're over there near the bar. You want to go over there?"

"Well girl, you know I don't really drink that much, but let me see if he wants something. Maybe I can get me a nice little daiquiri or something— nothing too strong."

Tiana finally turned to me. "I'm sorry babe. I've been ignoring you. You want something from the bar?"

"Oh I can go get it. I can walk y'all over there," I stood back teasingly. "Unless it's just a *Gamma thing?*"

Tiana shoved me playfully. "Boy, stop playing and come on. Besides, I don't want you sitting over here all lonely looking like I abandoned you or something."

"Girl, I know that's right. I knew these are sorors but um, shiiiiiit, bitches are single, honey. They will snatch your man up if you don't watch!"

Even though the girl was joking, Tiana smiled nervously, knowing that what she said was indeed true. Some women are so desperate that they will take anybody's man.

Over at the bar, I asked Tiana and her three sorors what they would like to drink. I didn't care what anyone said. Those women could drink. I was thinking they were just going to get fuzzy navels and here they were getting these mixed drinks with two and three kinds of alcohol in them. I ordered a daiquiri for Tiana, and a chocolate martini, mai tai, and Long Island iced tea for her sorors. I wondered where all these women's husbands and boyfriends were. I guess I was one of the suckers who got pulled into going to this event. As I looked around, the only women who appeared to be with dates were the older, forty and over set.

"Where'd they go? I just saw them." I heard one of Tiana's friends say.

"There they go," replied Tiana.

That's when I saw her. Jasmyn, my ex-drama queen, ghetto princess, was walking over with two other ladies. They all had smiles on their faces, with the exception of Jasmyn, who shot me a very flirtatious, interested glare. I looked down and immediately began drinking my rum and coke.

"Hey, Britt! What's up y'all?" Tosh said. Tosh appeared to always be the spokesperson.

"Hey, y'all remember Asia and Jasmyn, right?" the tall, caramel-brown complexioned one said.

Jasmyn looked exquisite. She appeared to have slimmed down some more and was sporting a perfectly styled wrap. I liked that she was wearing her own hair, which now touched her shoulder. *I bet she is still a stone cold freak.* I started picturing myself alone with her, with her face in the pillow, moaning.

"Babe! Hey!" Tiana interrupted my daydreaming and smacked me twice on the chest with the back of her hand. "What's wrong with you? You look like you've seen a ghost!"

Just then, Jasmyn lowered her eyelids and turned around to start walking away. *Good Jazz. Keep walking.*

But of course Tiana tried to get Jasmyn's attention. That damn girl and her hospitality. "Hey Jasmyn, hold up. You remember me? I'm Tiana." Tiana smiled like she was actually happy to see Jazz.

Jasmyn avoided eye contact with me and played it off, grinning all up in my wifey's face. "Oh yeah, you had a little baby with you, right?

"Yeah that's right—Jayda. Well that baby is going on one and a half years old! Can you believe it?"

What the hell was this? Why are they acting like they are all buddy buddy? And since when did Tiana and Jasmyn know each other? I mean, I knew they were both Gammas but shit, I thought there were like twenty thousand of them in the country. You mean to tell me all these Gammas were that close from one school to another? What was next? Crystal and Shawn gonna pop up around the corner, serving drinks and whatnot?

All right, Kyle. Play it off, dog. Don't smile. Don't look at her face. And for God's sake, don't look at her body. That's the kiss of death: letting your woman seeing you eye another woman!

Jasmyn, Tiana, and the group of women all started talking Gamma talk and catching up with each other.

I decided to make my move and gracefully exit. I slowly inched my way out of the throng of silver and lavender gowns and tapped Tiana, "Hey Tee, I'm going back to sit down for a while. I thought I heard them say they had a comedian coming out."

"Oh, okay. Hold up babe. These are some of my sorors from Marshall State and West Chester. This is Asia, Brittany, Simone, Jasmyn, and Jamilah. This is my fiancé, Kyle. Kyle, you don't know any of them from school?"

I waved quickly. "Hi, um, I don't think we had any classes together. But it was nice meeting you ladies." I nodded and turned away quickly before Jasmyn and I could look at each other. But it was too late. She opened her big mouth.

"Kyle? Kyle Clayton? " Jasmyn asked. "Yes, we went to school together. How've you been, Kyle?" Jasmyn gave me a look that said, *if you know like I know, you better just play along*.

I squinted my eyes as though I barely recognized her. "Oh yeah, you do look familiar." I switched the focus to Shawn. "Your friend Crystal dates my best friend Shawn."

Tee smiled and looked at Jasmyn. "Oh, so your girlfriend is the one who finally got that player Shawn's nose open? Girl, he swore he was all that back in the day!"

They both laughed. "Oh, see? Y'all wrong for talking about my boy. I'mma let you slide though! Good seeing you again, Jasmyn. Babe, I'm going back over to the table."

I heard them continue talking. Jasmyn told Tiana that Crystal was a Gamma but that she didn't come because she claimed she couldn't find a dress to wear. I continued to glance over at them nonchalantly. God please don't let that girl open up her mouth about us to Tiana. Jazz might still have those psychotic tendencies. When she wanted a man she let him know. She did kiss me at the picnic. But that was over a year ago. I was now a man, an *en-*

gaged one at that. Jazz was history and there was no way I was going to let her mess my thing up with Tee.

God must've heard my prayer because Tiana and Tosh broke away from the group over by the bar and headed back over toward us.

Tosh leaned over as Tiana sat down. I stood up to let Tee in her chair and pushed it in. "It was a pleasure meeting you, Kyle." She shook my hand and then turned to face Tiana and grabbed her hand to look at her ring again. "Congratulations again, soror. I'm digging that ring, girl. I see you, girl, all iced out. I see you blinging!" She and Tiana laughed.

"Kyle, they were nice, weren't they, baby? I didn't know you knew the sorors at Marshall? That Jasmyn girl is real cool. We hung out last year a little bit."

"What?" I shot back. "So y'all are best friends or something?"

"No, we're not best friends. Why'd you ask that like you got an attitude or something?"

"No reason."

"Well this daiquiri is talking, boo. I'm going to the ladies room. I'll be back in a few minutes."

When Tiana left to go to the bathroom, it was like Jasmyn appeared out of nowhere. She strolled over to my table, wearing a clingy spaghetti-strap silver gown, a sexy smile, and if I wasn't mistaken, no bra.

"So, that's your wife-to-be?" she asked. "Huhn. Well congratulations, boo. At least you picked a Gamma woman. You must got a thing for us."

"Don't flatter yourself, Jazz. Remember, me and you messed around way before you got involved with all this Gamma stuff."

"And if my memory serves me correctly, you kissed me after it. Um, at the senior barbecue, or have you forgotten?" I looked the other way and tried not to let her get to me. She was looking really sexy and I didn't want to start walking down memory lane with her all over again.

"Kyle, I'm not here to mess anything up with you and Tiana. I just wanted to wish you congratulations." She stroked my shoulder and added, "Just remember my cell number hasn't changed." She reached into her purse, retrieved a small beige business card, and flicked it at me. *"Adrienne L. Simmons Wachovia Bank, Loans Officer."* The name Adrienne was scratched out and Jasmyn's name was written above it and her cell number was in the corner.

I looked at the card and looked back up at her. How tacky could she possibly get, carrying her mother's business cards around with her name scratched out?

"Just a little something something. I know. It's ghetto, right? That's really my mom's card, but I don't have a sheet of paper on me."

It figured. I glanced at it. Surprisingly, I had remembered her number. She was right. It hadn't changed. I pushed the card back at her.

Jasmyn looked across the room, "No Kyle, you keep that card," she gently glided her fingers on the card and pushed it under my folded linen napkin. "Well, hey, look. Tiana is on her way back over. It was *real* good seeing you, Kyle. Let me go back over here with my girls." She winked goodbye to me and disappeared.

"See you." I peeked under my napkin, snatched up the card, and stuffed it in my pocket.

Tiana came back and sat down. She must have seen Jasmyn leaving the table.

"What did Jasmyn want, baby? Oh hold up, don't tell me. Did y'all have a little *thing*, Kyle? Because if you did, I wouldn't be mad. The past is the past as far as I'm concerned."

I didn't want to lie to Tiana. So, if she had her suspicions, I might as well tell her the truth. "Well Tee—"

Tiana cut me off. "So my instincts were right! I did sense something back there at the bar between you two. I said to myself, those two must know each other from Marshall because they are the only ones avoiding eye contact."

I didn't say anything. My girl had the deepest intuition of any woman I'd ever met.

"Kyle," she said with narrowed eyes. "Did you sleep with that girl?"

I looked away from Tiana and up at the stage. The hostess came out and greeted the audience.

I leaned over and whispered, "Let's talk about it later, all right? You see the show is about to start."

Tiana shook her head. She must be incredibly self-confident. She gave me a sneer and replied, "It's cool. As long as it's a done deal and you don't have any feelings for her, why would I get mad?

"Trust me baby, it's nothing. Jazz—I mean Jasmyn—was just a friend. We dated a little bit back then, but it didn't work out too well. You know how things go."

Tiana grabbed my hand. "It's cool, boo." She squeezed my thigh under the table. "Because I know who you really want."

I looked over at Tiana, who had a smoldering look on her face. Despite that, the image of Jazz's curves in that tight gown popped in my head. I hadn't had any wild sex in a long time. Jazz was definitely a beast and she did some things to make a brother's head spin.

I felt Tiana's eyes bore into my soul like she could read my mind. I really loved my fiancée, but I started feeling the same attraction I had for Jasmyn when I first laid eyes on her at that Kappa party a few years ago. It was like we had so much drama that our relationship back at Marshall felt like unfinished business.

The show began and we watched in silence. I put my arm around Tiana and leaned over to kiss her on the cheek every so often. I slid my other hand that rested on my lap into my pocket and slowly retrieved Jasmyn's card when Tiana wasn't looking. I glanced at it, with a devilish grin. It felt good to know that I still had it. And that if I wanted, I could have the best of both worlds. I had never been one to cheat, but now that Jasmyn was leaving the door open to do so, I knew that I definitely was going to give her a call later. Plus, a small, really small, part of me, missed her and still wondered what would have happened if we had actually stayed together.

_____Jasmyn

I can't believe I ran into Kyle like that at the Gamma event last weekend. A whole year later and he still looks good. Damn, if he wasn't with my soror, I would've slid him more than my number. I would've sat down, talked, and even stolen a kiss.

I could tell by the way he kept trying to avoid looking in my eyes that he was still feeling me. I wondered if his cell number was still the same. Even though I met Tarik and was digging him too, I always liked keeping my options open in case one of these men started acting a fool.

I was back in my old South Philly neighborhood circling around the block looking for a space. I went there to go to the clinic. I didn't even want to do it anywhere near my house. I found a parking space, went in, and signed in with the receptionist.

Moments later, a middle-aged woman in a lab coat with a clipboard came up to me.

"Miss Simmons?

"Yes, that's me.

"You can come back now."

"It says here you are here today for an HIV test. Correct?"

I nodded. "Yes," I said in a low voice.

"Oh honey, you don't have to be scared. It's quick and painless."

She walked me back to a semi-private lab area. I sat down in a chair. "We don't even need to take blood." She pulled out a swab and prepared to take a saliva sample from the insides of my mouth.

"Say ahhh."

I opened my mouth and she scraped the insides with a cotton-tipped stick.

"We do our own lab work here, Miss Simmons. So, if you have the time to wait, we can give you the results in about thirty minutes."

You damn right. I wasn't even about to leave this place with my destiny unknown somewhere up under a microscope.

"I'll wait," I said. I pulled my cell phone out and began playing blackjack and text-messaging Crystal. I told her where I was.

A half hour later, she came back to where I had been sitting.

"Come with me, please," she motioned for me to follow her.

I reluctantly followed her back to the lab room that she took my sample in. "I'm sorry to have to tell you this. But, it looks like you have the HIV virus present in the sample we took." She said it so matter-of-factly. She might as well have told me that it was sixty-eight degrees and partly cloudy outside.

"Well take another sample!"

"Miss Simmons, this brand of test is ninety-eight

percent accurate. Just calm down and have a seat in our waiting room. I'll have someone see you in a minute."

Over the next three hours, I talked to more people in white lab coats and even some social worker named Nina Calderon. At first, I was reluctant, but then when she told me that she was HIV positive *and* happily married, I felt like I could trust her. I spilled my guts out to her about college and how triflin' and promiscuous I was back then. I let her know all the nasty shit I did. I felt relieved. It was therapeutic in a way. I think I never had sat down and really thought about my times back at Marshall.

How could I face any of those guys again? I didn't even know where most of them were. I just gave the clinic the old phone numbers that I could remember off the top of my head. For the ones whose numbers I couldn't remember, I just gave them the guys' last names and the city they lived in. Let the health department find them.

Millions of thoughts ran through my head as I drove back home to Willingboro. Kyle seemed to be doing well for himself. I had to admit, he and Tiana *did* make a cute couple. I was sorry that now I may have fucked up his life. Shit, all those niggas on that list were in danger. *If only I knew who gave it to me and when. I don't know if I got it back in high school, in college, or just this year some time.* Most of those dudes on that list, I didn't give a damn about anymore. My whole attitude was "Fuck it". *It's all about Jasmyn now.* I was so pissed and my eyes were so dried up from crying so much, all I could do was walk around pissed off at the world. I knew it was wrong to feel this way. I just needed to get home and talk to Jerome or Crystal. Then again, I thought Jerome would probably be mad at me because I may have burned his boy Omar. At that point, I didn't really care anymore. I had half a mind to go track down some of those mutha-fathers and do something devious—like giving their cars a new paint job with a bottle of acetone and some bleach.

A few days went by and all I could do was get out of the house so as not to sit around and be upset. I found places to go: the movies, the park, the mall, anywhere was good. I found myself taking daily trips to Philly. There was no place like Philly in the summertime. I drove down South Street, went to Penn's Landing, and just walked around downtown a lot. I did this every day for about a week. One day on my way back home as I stewed in my anger and sped through the toll booth E-Z pass lane, my cell phone rang. *Who the hell is this, calling me on a Thursday afternoon in July?* Everybody I knew worked. My cell phone hardly ever rang before seven o'clock in the evening. My family, my male associates, and Crystal were the only people who did call me, and they knew with me, it was all about free night and weekend minutes. But because I saw an unfamiliar Philadelphia number on the screen, I decided to pick up.

"Hello?" I asked sternly. I was emotionless and couldn't muster up any enthusiasm to greet a caller right about now.

"What's up, Miss Lady?" *Oh yes! It's my baby Kyle. He's the only one who called me "Miss Lady" but didn't sound like a cornball when he did.*

"Hey, how you doin'?" I adjusted my voice to sound more upbeat.

"You know me, I'm just chillin', working hard. I

just wanted to give you a little call, you know, since you slipped me that card."

"Oh, yeah. I sure did, didn't I? That was a couple of weekends ago. So what took you so long to call?" I smiled, making sure he sensed every ounce of flirtatiousness I was throwing through the phone. I knew Tiana was a soror and all, but fuck it. I need love too. And if I can have two men, then why not? That's why I got this death sentence on me now! From messing around with these trifling ass men.

"Well, I *am* engaged. To *your* sorority sister, I might add. I don't want to disrespect her. I just really wanted to see how you were doing. I meant to tell you, you looked real nice that night. I like how you're letting your hair grow in too. It's real cute."

I pressed my mute button and laughed silently like the Joker in Batman and Robin. *I got him just where I want him.*

I un-pressed the mute button. "Thanks, so, um, where you at right now?"

"At work. I work for Verizon doing special projects."

Cha-ching!

"So when are you trying to see me, 'cause I know you didn't call just to say hi, now did you?"

"Girl, please, this ain't Marshall State again. I got a family now. We getting married next Valentine's Day. Like I said, I wanted to say what's up."

"Mmm hmmm, yeah right, Kyle. You always did play hard to get. We grown now. You ain't gotta front no more for Shawn and Raheem and them guys. Ain't nobody chasing your butt," I stated casually.

Kyle cleared his throat. "Don't forget about Moe!"

I was going to let that one slide. "Yeah, okay. Moe too," I politely added. *Where was Moe at these days? Probably up in Brooklyn wilding out.*

"All right," he said. "I'mma stop frontin'. Ever since I ran into you, I can't stop thinking about how good you looked and how we used to kick it back at Marshall. I thought maybe we could go do a little something one of these days. I heard you're teaching now, so I know you've got the summer free, right?"

"Yeah, and?" I was liking where this conversation was going. I couldn't even concentrate on the fact that I may have given this guy, or he may have given *me* a deadly disease. All I knew was he was still fine, he was paid, and the fact that he was taken made him that much more desirable.

"I want to take you out to lunch, if that's not gonna be a problem with you coming into the city. You still stay in Jersey, right?"

"Yeah, I do." Kyle gave me the directions to his office. We made plans to meet the next day at twelve-thirty in the lobby of his building.

I had all night to sleep on the fact of whether or not I was going to tell him about my trip to the clinic earlier that week.

_____*Kyle*

"Yo Shawn, what are you doing, man?" I decided to call and ask him to ride out to Springfield so I could go look for a new system for my little 2002 Nissan Maxima that I copped from the auto auction. I knew that I needed a bigger car if I was going to be doing the whole wife and kids family thing.

Shawn sounded out of breath, like he had been running. "I just got in the crib. Why? What's going on, family?"

"What's up with taking a ride with your boy? Roll with me up to Circuit City. I want to go look at these Alpine speakers for my car."

Shawn quickly agreed, replying, "Aiight. Just come scoop me up. Let me go change, though. Give me like twenty."

"All right. One."

"One."

I hung up my cell phone and took out my house

keys. I couldn't wait to get inside, kiss Tiana and Jayda, and go run back out with Shawn. I needed to get his advice. I called Jasmyn this afternoon from work and asked her out to lunch. Her curves had been on my mind ever since I ran into her at the Gamma thing. I wasn't trying to cheat on Tee or nothing foul like that, but Jazz looked too good. Plus, she gave me *her* number so really it was just a matter of curiosity. I don't know what made me call her. Maybe it was the dress. Maybe it was that perfume. Or maybe I was turned on by her boldness. I probably just really wanted to see if I still had it. Whatever the reason, I had no plans on being physical with her.

I unlocked the door, tossed my keys on the dining room table, and headed to the kitchen. Tiana and Jayda were back in the bedroom. I hadn't been in the house five minutes when the phone rang.

I got the craziest phone call. Some guy from a health clinic in South Philly told me I was exposed to the HIV virus. I started thinking back to when and where I could've gotten it. I started racking my brain over who could've gotten my name and number. I thought it was a joke at first, but when I realized that dude was serious, I got real nervous. He wouldn't tell me who gave them my name. Something about patient privacy. Whoever it was, they had the wrong guy. I had never been locked up, never did drugs except a little chief every now and then, but who even counts that as a drug? Last I'd heard you couldn't get AIDS from smoking weed. I didn't want to get all stressed out, 'cause

Tiana could read almost every little thing about me. And I wasn't about to mess up a good thing with my baby by telling her I might have HIV. I mean, we had plans to get our blood work done before the wedding next February, so if either one of us did have AIDS, it would come out sooner or later. But what was I going to do in the meantime? *I certainly can't go up to all my exes and ask, "Was it you that gave me HIV?"*

I lied to Tiana and told her that the phone call was a telemarketer. What else was I supposed to say, that it was a health clinic telling me to go get an AIDS test? I played it off and picked up Jayda as she scooted into the kitchen alongside her mother.

After kissing and tickling Jayda, I said, "Hey, Tee, me and Shawn are about to roll out to Circuit City." I started undoing my tie and unbuttoning my dress shirt.

"And hello to you too! You didn't even speak to me. Just got on the phone and now you're talking about going out with Shawn. I was about to show you these bridesmaids' dresses I was looking at in *Modern Bride*, but never mind now!" she said, obviously annoyed. She turned away from me and went to go fix Jayda a cup.

"My bad, boo." I turned around. "Hey future-wifey of mine. How was your day?"

"Duce! Duce! Mummy duce please!" Jayda begged Tiana to refill her empty cup with a drink.

"Fine." Tiana slightly frowned at me, shook her head, and handed Jayda her cup of apple juice. "Anyway, what are you all nervous for?" She poked me in the stomach and gave me a half-smile.

My heart was still racing a mile and a minute. "Girl, you must have sniffed something working around those patients too long. What are you talking about?! Ain't nobody nervous!" I grinned and put my arms around her waist, while planting a kiss on her lips. *Tiana was sexy too,* I thought. I felt like I was still in college, looking at women and not being able to make up my mind. *I ain't even going to stress over that HIV mess. I've been feeling perfectly healthy. Whoever gave them my name, was probably somebody from way back in high school.*

"Well, what time are you planning to be back?" Tiana asked.

I wasn't for all these questions. We weren't married yet. Yes, I was really in love with Tiana, but at the same time, I was still excited about my lunch date tomorrow with Jasmyn. I admit the HIV call had me a little shook, but I knew once I had a chance to go hang with my man Shawn, maybe go get something to eat, I would be all right. He and I hadn't hung out in a long time. We were with our girls most of the time. And since Shawn's girl lived outside the city, he was always running back and forth.

Twenty minutes later, I was beeping the horn outside Shawn's house. Miss Deidre, Shawn's mom, was outside with a glass of red Kool-Aid standing over a grill, flipping one hamburger and hot dog. I said to myself, "Who grills one burger and one hot dog?" His mom, my godmother, was a bedroom slipper-scarf-and-curlers-wearing-outside-let-me-go-fix-you-a-plate kind of black mom. There was one on every block.

"How you doing, Kyle-baby? You're looking good.

Shawn told me you working downtown doing the computers for Verizon."

"Yes, ma'am," I yelled from the car.

"That's nice. You want a plate? I can throw you a hot dog on the grill right quick."

"No thank you. We'll probably grab something to eat while we out."

"Okay, baby!"

Finally, Shawn came outside, ran down the steps past his mom, and hopped in the car.

"Yo man, moms is always bugging. She needs to go back in the house and put some shoes on."

"Leave Miss Deidre alone, your mom is good people," I replied.

"Yeah well, I guess. Anyway. What's up, man?" Shawn gave me a ghetto handshake. Then, changing the subject from his mom, he asked, "Why couldn't you wait until Saturday to go out?"

"Man I was just trying to get out that apartment. I needed to get some air. Yo . . . guess who I called?"

"Who?"

"Jazz!"

"Get the fuck outta here." Shawn lit a cigarette and rolled the window down. "When'd you see her?"

"At that Gamma dinner thing they had."

"Oh yeah, Crystal told me about that. I told her, I wasn't paying no seventy-five dollars a ticket for that sorority shit. And besides, she need to save her damn money anyway! Plus, I done met some of them bourgie broads!" He sucked his teeth. "Please. I wish I would've spent a buck fifty on a pair of them tickets."

I shook my head. I didn't think the Gammas were

bad. And I didn't mind spending the money. I made almost seventeen hundred dollars every two weeks. And unlike Shawn, I wasn't afraid to spend money if it made my girl happy.

"I can't believe you still mess with Crystal. So when y'all getting married?"

"Shiiiitttt! Nigga, please. You know ain't nobody putting the man on lockdown. Not yet. Plus, we ain't talking about me. We talking about you and that trick-ass friend of Crystal's."

"Trick-ass? Damn Shawn, it's like that?"

"Yeah, it's like that. That ho is still trickin' like she used to back at Marshall. She's supposed to be a teacher and all proper and everything now. But every time I ask Crys about her, she tells me that Jasmyn has a new man."

"Well I ain't trying to, you 'nah mean?—"

"You ain't tryna what? Smash that?! Yeah right, man. You *always* liked Jazz. Even after you started going with Tiana. You know Jazz stayed right on top of that 'To do' list of yours."

"Whatever man. But look. Check this out, right. I asked her to lunch tomorrow."

"Are you crazy? Nigga, you out your damn mind!"

"Nah. Chill, man. It's just a friendly lunch."

"Well just watch yourself. You know your weak ass will slip up and kiss her or some shit like that. Knowing Jazz, she'll have you in the back of a car, trying to get you to slay that."

I shook my head in disagreement. "Man, I ain't trying to go there with Jasmyn. I'm just trying to do right."

Shawn let out a loud laugh. "How are you trying to do right and you about to cheat on your girl?"

"I already told you. It's just lunch, nigga. Lunch! I just wanna see if there's anything there. It's a test. If I can avoid falling for Jazz's game then I know I must really love my girl."

"That's a stupid test. You must be *trying* to fail. I don't know, man. You 'bout to fuck up a good thing."

I couldn't believe this was the same cat who told me to try to slay Jasmyn back at the end of senior year, after she and I kissed. And he *knew* I was with Tiana at the time. I ignored his comments.

"All right, well forget all that. Check this out. Let me tell you how some clinic called me telling me I might got the bug."

"What bug? Yo! Tee burned you?"

"No Tiana ain't burn me, man! They told me some old mess like somebody gave them my name after they got tested for HIV."

Shawn nearly choked. "What?!"

"Yo, I know, man."

"So who do you think it is?"

"I don't know. They can't tell me who gave them my name."

"Well what clinic was it?"

"Randolph; down in South Philly."

"Oh word? So who you been messing with in South Philly, man?"

"Nobody! That's just it. I have only been with a few women in my life and nobody is from South Philly. The Philly women were from West and Southwest."

"Well who would be down in South Philly at a clinic?"

"I can't think. I never messed with no chicks from South Philly."

"Are you sure? *Nobody* from South Philly? Hold up. Where did Jazz used to live before she moved to Jersey?"

I nearly ran the red light and looked at Shawn while screeching on my brakes.

"Jasmyn told me she grew up around Twenty-first and Tasker."

"*South Philly,*" we said together.

"Yo, I bet you it is Jasmyn," Shawn stated. "She's cool and I know that's my girl's best friend, but just like I was saying to you earlier; you and I both know—"

"Watch your mouth, man. She ain't like that no more."

"Man, how you know?"

"I can just tell." Jasmyn looked so elegant when I saw her. With the exception that she wasn't wearing a bra that night, Jasmyn showed no inkling of hoochiness.

Shawn sighed and responded with, "So I guess it's going down then."

"I guess it is."

We went to Circuit City and I as I walked around, I mulled over all of Shawn's comments. Even though he was harsh, he usually was right. He told the bare naked truth, no matter who it hurt. Jasmyn did used to have a bad rep. But maybe that's all changed now.

I didn't get anything for my car. But I did pick up *Finding Nemo* for Jayda and a gospel CD for Tiana. By the time we left the store, I had it already in my head that this mystery woman was Jazz. She probably knew this a long time ago and tried to act all cute and whatnot. *Wait until I see her tomorrow! I'm going to just come right out and ask her if there's something she needs to tell me.*

_____ *Jasmyn*

It was twelve-twenty in the afternoon. I was on the phone with Tarik and sitting in the lobby of 2000 Market Street.

"Hey, boo. I'm over here in Philly just doing a little shopping." Tarik and I had been talking for a little while and I had plans to see him tonight.

Kyle stepped off the elevator. I tugged on the wire that hung from my hands-free headset for my phone and discreetly said goodbye to Tarik. I loved having the hands-free wire, you could walk around and talk in a tiny microphone and it wouldn't be so obvious to others that you were talking.

I greeted him with a hug. He seemed a bit uptight and wasn't as warm and receptive as I'd thought he would be. Maybe the clinic had contacted him. Or maybe he was just anxious about work or something at home. Whatever it was, the tension was written all over his face.

"Let's go to Liberty Place for lunch," said Kyle as he approached me.

"Okay, Liberty Place is cool with me." I softly elbowed him as we walked outside into the bright warm sunshine.

We went to Au Bon Pain and ordered salads and sandwiches. We barely even spoke, aside from the obligatory small talk that people do on a first date when they are all nervous and have nothing important to discuss. Every question I asked about him—his job, his family—he answered in single word sentences. Aside from just seeming a little tense, he was now just being plain old downright rude. I wondered why he had an attitude. Whenever he talked to me, he kept asking if there was something on my mind or something I needed to get off my chest.

"No, Kyle. I'm perfectly fine," I kept telling him. A restaurant was not going to be the place that I confessed the truth to him. That is, if I decided to be honest and tell him that I was infected.

"Jasmyn, I really think there *is* something you want to tell me," he said, with his eyes piercing. You know how they say, "If looks could kill. . . ." Well, let's just say I would have been one dead woman.

I played dumb and responded with "Tell you *like what*, Kyle?"

Kyle sat back in his chair, unresponsive, turning the corners of his mouth downward and biting his lower lip. I examined his thigh go up and down as he nervously tapped his left foot under the table.

"Well, I don't even know what you're talking about," I said, dismissing his little temper tantrum.

"I'm not even hungry anymore." I pushed away my half-eaten Caesar salad along with the remains of my turkey and Swiss cheese sandwich.

We walked back to his job. I was parked in a garage around the corner from where he worked, so it made sense that we walk together.

"Jazz, look. I'm just not having a good day. Maybe this was a mistake, us going out for lunch and everything."

"Maybe it was," I agreed. I was disappointed that we didn't get to connect at all. But, I would get over it. *At least you still have Tarik,* I reassured myself.

As we turned the corner and headed up Market Street, I saw the image of what looked like Tiana walking across the street from the opposite direction, obviously headed to the same office building. She was dressed in hospital scrubs and carrying two white plastic bags in her hand.

I started to turn in the opposite direction, but I realized that she had already noticed Kyle and me walking side by side.

She jaywalked across the street in a hurry and rushed over to both of us. Kyle looked like he wanted to pee right in his drawers as Tiana handed him the bags containing white styrofoam containers of food.

"What the hell is this?!" Tiana shouted. "*Jasmyn?*"

I looked at Tiana, looked at Kyle, and then back at Tiana again.

There I was, standing in downtown Philadelphia at the height of lunch hour, busted. I wanted to turn and run away in the opposite direction. I just stood there frozen and ready to burst into tears.

What is my fiancée doing down here standing outside of my job at one-thirty in the afternoon? Tiana's practicum was at Temple University Hospital, which was at least twenty blocks away. She was the last person I expected to see. She was eyeballing Jasmyn like she wanted to drag her from there to City Hall and beat her down in broad daylight.

"Tiana? I thought you worked at the hospital today. What are you doing all the way down here?" I fixed my eyes upon the bags in her hand.

"I was going to bring you some jerk chicken and rice for lunch, but evidently, it seems that you've already had lunch." Tiana had probably gone to one of the Caribbean food trucks up by Temple to get me some lunch, and then carried it all the way down here on the subway.

Jasmyn spoke up. "Oh hey, Tiana, um, I just—"

Tiana cut Jasmyn off, turned her back on her, and began to interrogate me. "Why don't you tell me what this is about, Kyle? I mean, I see y'all two coming down the street walking all close, like you and her are all lovey-dovey."

"Tee, we weren't all lovey-dovey. Look boo, it's not what you think—"

"I mean, here I am trying to surprise my man. I said 'Okay, I got out of the hospital early today, so let me jump on SEPTA and come down here to surprise my baby with some lunch' and then I see *this*?"

I reached out to touch Tiana's shoulder to calm her down. She jumped away.

"Get your hands off of me, Kyle! I'm not playing!"

I moved away from her and pleaded for her understanding. "Jazz, I mean, uh, Tee," *Aww damn, I messed up now!*

"What?!" Tiana yelled.

"Tee, I was saying Jazz just came down—"

"*Jazz?* Oh so now it's *Jazz?* Uhn huhn, okay, okay. I see how it is. I should've known you were cheating on me."

"How are you gonna accuse me of cheating? Because of this? This little mess you see here? This—this right here ain't nothing!"

"Give me my damn food!" She snatched the plastic bags away from me. "Kyle, I want *you* and *your shit* out by tonight!"

"Soror, can I just explain myself?" Jasmyn tried to reach her hand toward Tiana. "Let me talk to you for a minute and you'll see this was all one big misunderstanding."

"*Bitch?!* Don't touch me! "I had never heard Tiana cuss like that. She was becoming a completely different person, one who was unable to contain all of her anger, right in front of our very eyes.

"Don't '*soror*'me," Tiana continued. "I should've trusted my instincts from the beginning. I saw the way you were looking at Kyle that night. And ever since then, he's been acting all funny."

Jasmyn hung her head down and began to sob.

"Don't cry now '*soror*'. You can have him!"

"Can the three of us just please go somewhere and talk?" begged Jasmyn.

By this point, I had become embarrassed. People were returning from lunch back into the building and observing the little ghetto dinner theater production we were performing in the middle of the sidewalk.

I decided I had had enough of Tiana's ranting. "Look. Let's just go out to the parking garage and talk in my car. I can't have y'all out here in front of my job like this."

"I don't have anything to say to *you*, Kyle," Tiana said as she untwisted her engagement ring.

"Wait, Tiana. Wait," I reached out to touch her hand and stop her from handing the ring over to me. "Just give me five, ten minutes tops. Please."

"You've got nine minutes and fifty-nine seconds." We headed out to the car. Tiana and I walked up front while Jasmyn followed about three feet behind us.

"Look, y'all," Jasmyn stopped as we approached the entrance of the garage near where the attendant was.

She sighed heavily and leaned back against a pillar and tilted her head upwards.

"Tiana, I know I shouldn't be out with Kyle."

Tiana, who was visibly calmer now, asked, "What's your excuse?"

Jasmyn had no response for her.

I looked over at my car, which was about six spaces away from where we were standing. *Why do women insist on having soap opera style confrontations out in the open? Whatever happened to discretion?*

Tiana and I both looked at Jasmyn, who had now slumped down and sat down right next to a parked car. "Kyle, I don't know how to tell you this. But, I got—HIV!"

We were speechless. *Where is a toilet when you need one?* Standing there for what felt like an eternity made me want to piss myself.

Jasmyn stood up, wiped her tears with the back of her palm, and smoothed out her skirt. "Are y'all happy now?"

My jaw fell open slightly. Tiana and I exchanged a nervous glance.

"And yes," she stared dead into Tiana's face as though her eyes were daggers. "I might've given it to *your* man."

I exploded at Jasmyn. "So it *was* you! You gave that clinic my name!"

Tiana looked back and forth between us with confusion. "What clinic? What are y'all talking about?!"

"Kyle," continued Jasmyn, who was bawling by this point, red eyes, snotty nose and all. "I am *so* sorry!" She looked over at Tiana who stood frozen in disbelief. "This is really awkward, I know. We can sit down and all talk about it."

Tiana wasn't having it. "Talk?! Look, the two of you can talk! I don't wanna hear nothing else. I'm done." She threw her hands up, adjusted her pocket-book on her shoulder, and prepared to leave me there standing with Jazz by myself.

Jazz touched Tiana's arm.

"Jasmyn, I already told you once. Do *not* touch me! If you touch me again, I'mma smack the mess out of you and I'm not playing. If you think I am, try me."

Jasmyn stepped away from Tiana.

"You up here telling me that you gave my man *AIDS* and me and him are about to get married. And *you*," Tiana turned and looked at me, "you better be glad we use rubbers. I swear to God, girl . . ." Tiana huffed and tried to contain herself.

She caught her breath, closed her eyes, and bowed her head. A lone tear flowed down her cheek. "You better pray."

Jasmyn gave her a puzzled look.

"What? Yes, *pray*. You both are gonna need it."

"Jazz," I said. "I think you should leave now. I need to be with my fiancée."

"What?! No, Kyle. You mean. *Ex-fiancée!* If she is just now telling us that she got AIDS—" said Tiana.

"*No! Excuse you.* I don't have *AIDS*." Jasmyn was actually catching an attitude. "I'm just infected with a virus."

Tiana rolled her eyes. "Well *whatever*! I've got a good sense about things—I can read people easily. I can just look at you and tell that you went out with my man 'cause you still like him—not just to tell him that you had AIDS!"

"HIV," Jazz protested.

"Anyway," Tiana shook her head.

"Look," I said. "All this is getting way out of control. Tee, let me go tell my supervisor I have a family emergency and that I need to leave early. That way, you and I can go home and talk."

"No, see. You forgot already, Kyle? *You* don't have a home. I meant what I said."

If the truth be told, I was the one who had the right to kick people out. It was my name on that lease. *I could be a real bastard if I wanted to, and kick her and her daughter out.* I decided to not even go there. I knew I would never go that far to throw a baby in the street like that.

Jazz went toward the exit. The parking garage attendant was one of those ghetto middle-aged black women who just couldn't say goodbye to their twenties. She must've been fifty years old and wore a young-girl wig, two pairs of big gold hoop earrings in each ear, and had her nose pierced. She had been sitting there the whole time, being entertained by us.

"Look, y'all. I parked a few blocks away. I'm just going to go. I'm really sorry."

Tiana looked at me. "Kyle, tell me the truth. Are you still attracted to her?"

"Of course not, baby," I lied. I couldn't believe we had been out here almost a half-hour. It was after two o'clock and my lunch break was long over. *I'm gonna lose my job out here messing with the Bold, the Black, and the Beautiful.*

I wasn't going to let Tiana break up with me. I pulled her in close to me and kissed her, the way the hero does in the movies.

"Tee, lets go home."

Jazz, who I thought had left, was still standing by the parking attendant's window. "I'm just gonna

leave. I mean, I wish I could say something else."
Jasmyn avoided looking at Tiana.

Jasmyn walked over closer to me. "Kyle, just go
get tested. I'm really sorry to put you both through
this." She turned and quickly walked away.

_____Jasmyn

The school year had begun and I was back to my old self. I hated that summer. All I did was sit around and think about being infected. After that afternoon I went up to Kyle's job, and seeing the hurt I brought to him and Tiana, I decided to throw away his phone number and never call him again. I could tell that his life had been happy, before I came into it. It seemed like all I did was bring drama into people's lives, especially Kyle's and Tiana's. I finally told my family about it and they were very supportive and non-judgmental. I was afraid that Adrienne would've had a nervous breakdown again, but she had extraordinary strength. It was as though she was a new person. In a year or so, she had gained a new life, a successful career, new friendships, and she even had a boyfriend.

"Jasmyn, do you want to go to church with me and Charles tomorrow?" Charles had been her "friend" since the year before. She met him through one of her co-workers at Wachovia and had started going to church with him. It was kind of good, because we hadn't really been to church on a regular basis since we lived in Philly. If I *did* go to church, it usually was TV church and involved me watching BET or TBN.

"I don't know. I'll think about it."

"Come on, baby," she hugged me. We were sitting in the kitchen. I was grading papers and she was re-lining the cabinets with shelf paper. "It'll be good for you and your brother to go."

"Well, if I can get up tomorrow morning, then I'll go. That depends on how late I'm out with Tarik."

"Well tell him to come too."

"All right, Mom, we'll see."

Later that night, Tarik came by to pick me up. I packed a bag like he had asked me to. We drove to Philly for dinner. It was our six-month anniversary. In that time, we had decided to date each other exclusively. Surprisingly, in all that time, we had only been intimate a few times. We were careful to use protection, but there was always an uneasy hesitance between us. He knew my HIV status and I knew his. He was negative; and, of course, I was positive. I thought of how that lady Nina Calderon at the clinic told me that she and her husband found ways to enjoy each other's company that did not involve sexual contact.

Most of the time when Tarik and I went out, it was to places like Dave and Buster's or Jillian's to bowl and play games. Other times, we drove up to New York to go shopping or see a play on Broadway.

Then there were times when we just went to Atlantic City to the casinos or to one of the Jersey beaches, had lunch on the Spirit of Philadelphia, and twice we even traveled down to Baltimore Inner Harbor. I spent practically every other Saturday with him. It was unlike any other relationship I had been in before. It was based on fun and getting to know each other. I knew that he was into me for who I was on the inside, not for how freaky I could turn him out in the bedroom. That gave me a sense of wholeness. That cloud that hung over me ever since I was teenager—the one that made me feel cheap and like a whore—was slowly dissipating.

That night, Tarik was taking me to the exclusive, big-baller restaurant, The Chart House. It was on the waterfront at Penn's Landing, and dinner for two there could easily add up a hundred dollars. We both had lobster that Tarik had personally selected out of the tank to be prepared just for us. As we were finishing dessert, Tarik told me he had something important to tell me.

"Jasmyn baby, you know how I told you I was in the Army reserve unit up at Fort Dix?"

"Yes." I remembered he told me that when we first met. One weekend a month, he had to go to do maneuvers with his unit or whatever it was that people in the reserves went to go do.

He pulled out a small box wrapped in gold with a big red ribbon. "Well, because it's been six months since we met at Blockbuster, I wanted to give you this before I leave."

I was so excited. The last time I had received a gift from any guy, it was Jerome. I took the box and opened it. It was a sparkling diamond open heart on a gold Italian rope chain.

"Oh my God! Tarik, this is so gorgeous. I love it!" I leaned across the table and kissed him. "But what do you mean 'before I leave?'"

"My reserve unit is being deployed to Iraq for five months. I leave the week after Christmas."

"What?! That's like six weeks away!"

"I know, but I'll be back before the summer," said Tarik as he un-did the latch of the necklace. "Come here, turn around."

I sadly walked over to him and turned around with my arms folded. He stood up and placed the necklace around my neck.

I sat back down, too upset to finish my tiramisu. Tarik placed my hand between both of his. "Jasmyn, I knew you were somebody I wanted to have in my life ever since I met you. You've got that feistiness, you're beautiful, and I know that I need to have you."

"Most guys would have left me when they found out I'm HIV positive, but you were understanding. I love you for that."

"Well, Jazz, I never told you this but my aunt died from AIDS a few years ago. She got it from her husband who was on the D.L. So, I never wanted to judge you or treat you funny 'cause of that, ma. I really do love you."

That evening, we rented a room at the Hyatt Regency right there on the waterfront. We laid in each other's arms, just relaxing and enjoying the warmth of one another's bodies. We made a decision to try to be celibate, at least for a while. I didn't want to ruin Tarik's life the way I ruined Kyle's. I let him explore me and he resisted the desire to consummate. Surprisingly enough, I had a greater euphoria and afterglow than I could've imagined.

The next morning, I called my mom and told her we'd meet her at the eleven-thirty service. We drove back to Jersey and I vowed that, in light of the way things were going, I was going to maximize every moment that I had to spend with Tarik. I never knew when our time together might end.

Kyle

The first few weeks after the Jasmyn/HIV revelation, Tiana and I walked around the apartment barely speaking to each other. Tiana was real close to her mom, so almost every day she was on the phone with her asking for advice. Whatever her mom was telling her must have eventually done some good, because Tiana finally started to come around. I had said "sorry" to her a billion times. I kept assuring her Jasmyn and I only had unprotected sex two or three times. She was mad because of that, but she appreciated my honesty, nevertheless. Sooner or later, Tiana would realize there was nothing either one of us could do about the situation but get tested. It would be a waste of time to walk around all mad. We still had wedding plans for Valentine's Day.

"Kyle, I'm not saying that I am accepting of this whole situation, but I know that you are my best friend, and I want to marry you. I'm just really afraid."

"Baby, I'm afraid too. Look, we both went to get our blood tests and HIV tests, so all we can do is pray for the best."

"Kyle, I'm not going to sit here and lie and say that no matter what the results are, I still want to marry you. I mean, I love you, but the pain of knowing that you could one day get AIDS and leave me and Jayda alone—that's just too much for me to bear."

I understood where Tee was coming from. Our tests all came back negative, so we proceeded with the wedding plans. The cakes and flowers were ordered. We already had picked out the dresses for Tiana's bridesmaids and Jayda. The suits for me, Shawn, Ty, Jamir, and my pop were the only things left to be ordered.

Tiana made her appointment with the dermatologist to get her tattoo laser-removed. There was no need for her to sport Chauncey's name, especially when that nigga had moved down to Virginia, somewhere with some chick and their new baby. As far as Tiana was concerned, she didn't even want to pursue child support from him. As long as she was with me, Jayda would always have the most top-notch of everything.

As the Thanksgiving holidays rolled around, we started feeling more like a husband and wife. We were halfway through our premarital counseling at church, and Pastor Green was helping us work through all of our drama. Even though he disapproved of our cohabitation, he let us know that we still needed to focus on God and one another. As we got closer to the wedding day, we got so busy. I had several projects at work, and Tiana was getting ready to finish up from Temple in December with her nursing degree.

Life was starting to feel pretty normal.

_____*Jasmyn*

Christmas arrived and Tarik spent it with my
family. We had dinner and opened gifts. Even JJ
was there with Jerome. It was the first time in a
long time JJ got to be with his dad's side of the
family.

I slowly became at peace with my condition.
Instead of wasting time trying to track down who
infected me, I decided not to revisit the past and
relive pain. Instead, I just lived each day to the
fullest. I was still teaching and became active with
Gamma. I chaired the Gamma Outreach project
to help women of color who were infected with
AIDS. On the personal side, I took part in a clini-
cal study for an experimental HIV vaccine, and my
family and Tarik were all helpful in assisting me
with paying for my meds, which I took every day.
And at my mom's church, I joined a support
group called the Freedom Ministry for those people who were suffering from addictions and things
that mentally depressed them.

The day Tarik left, I stood on the sidelines along with all of the other families—the wives, girl-friends, and children—who were crying. So many soldiers left home and didn't return. I didn't want to be hanging yellow memorial ribbons up and going to any funerals.

"Boo, I'll be back. You'll see. I'll call you every day. You just take care of yourself and stay healthy."

"I will. I'm not letting HIV beat me. Just come back home as soon as you can."

Five months later, he would be back home, and soon after that, he'd be eligible to retire from the reserves. I couldn't wait because I had a lot to plan with him when he came back home. I had finally found *the right man* for me and I wasn't going to let him get away.

_____*Kyle*

"Four, three, two, one! Happy New Year!"

Tiana and I stayed up late with Jayda to watch the ball drop. I kissed both of my girls.

"Boo, do you realize that in six weeks, we will be married?! Oh my God!" Tiana gushed with excitement.

"I know, I know." I smiled. The past year had been a difficult one, but we made it through. I suppose every couple needs their tests and 2004 was our season to "go through," as they say. Now, it was 2005, a brand new year, and brand new possibilities.

The music was perfect. My cousin Lamont had just finished his rendition of "All My Life" by K-Ci and Jo-Jo. The church was adorned with roses. White and pink candles flickered, creating a romantic mood. It was unusual to get married on a

Monday, but we both insisted on a Valentine's Day wedding.

The pianist played "I Believe in You and Me" as Tiana walked down the aisle with her father. She was beautifully dressed in a strapless gown, revealing her sexy, bare arms. Her father unhooked his arm from around Tiana's elbow, took her hand and placed it in mine. I had never met Tiana's dad prior to the wedding rehearsal. But, from what I could tell, he was real cool.

I never cried over a woman before, but I was overcome with emotion, as I saw Jayda walking down the aisle spreading pink rose petals, followed by her mother, whose face was behind a sheer white veil. Shawn nodded with approval at me as he saw the tear come out of my eye. I wiped it away with my forefinger and took a deep breath.

When Tiana turned to face me, I knew there was no turning back. She stayed with me despite the odds. We lit the unity candle and took our vows in front of our entire family and all of the friends we had grown up with over the years. I had placed all thoughts of other women out of my head. None of them were worth me destroying what I now had with Tiana.

Pastor Green went on with all of the "Speak now or forever hold your peace" stuff. After we exchanged rings and jumped over the broom African-style, he introduced us to the congregation.

"Ladies and gentlemen, I now present to you, for the first time, *Mr. and Mrs. Clayton!*"

EPILOGUE

Five years later

_____*Kyle*

". . . to be absent from the body is to be present with the Lord . . . "

As the minister in the pulpit delivered the eulogy, I gently caressed my wife's shoulder. I was so thankful to have her. After all of the things I had been through with women, it was a wonder that I was able to sustain such a successful marriage. Tiana was my angel, my life-mate. The past couple of years hadn't been easy, but she stood by me and honored our vows. Any other woman would've easily left. Out the door. No words. Not trying to hear any apologies. Nothing. I suppose the unconditional love she had for me was the kind of real agape love they talk about—the kind of love that is not merely sexual, but spiritual. A selfless kind of love. Tiana always told me that once you experienced God's love, it was easy to love others, despite their faults.

The preacher delivered promises of life after death and emphasized how we should be rejoicing and not mourning. I asked God why He would snatch up a life so young, but some things were not meant to be explained. Rather, they were intended to be instruments—tools that God uses to instruct us how to live quality lives. Now it was all making sense. As the choir began singing "I'll Fly Away" and the pallbearers carried the ivory-colored marble casket down the center aisle, the light bulb went off inside my head. The things I thought were meant to bring me down and make my life horrible, were the very same things that, years down the road, would build character and make me a better man, a better husband, and a better father.

We slowly followed the rest of the congregation towards the exit doors. I looked at Tee and asked her if she was sure she wanted to go to the burial.

"I insist," she solemnly nodded and intertwined her fingers with mine. The crisp March air blew as we made our way to our black Mercedes Benz C-class luxury wagon. I placed my funeral program on the backseat along with Jayda's UNO cards that she often played solitaire with when we were riding.

After a forty-five minute processional, we finally arrived at the cemetery. I didn't want to appear too noticeable. I had never really met her family, so besides Shawn and Crystal, I didn't know anyone else there. Crystal, who was cradling eight-month old Shawn, Jr. in her arms, walked over and nudged me to say hi. Shawn followed behind, grabbed my hand firmly and gave me a handshake while slapping me on the back.

"Hey Kyle, brother. Yo, I'm real sorry man," Shawn said empathetically.

"Yeah," Crystal added. "It's a shame we had to

meet back up for something like this. I mean, just when she thought she had gotten that monster under control," Crystal added, referring to the AIDS disease, "She did her meds, took vitamins, ate right, was celibate. I mean, she was only twenty-seven. And out of nowhere some mysterious blood infection attacks her body, and takes her out in less than six months!"

She handed the baby to Shawn and reached inside her bag for a tissue. Her uncontrollable tears ran down her cheek faster than she was able to wipe them. She looked at Tiana, "Oh, I'm sorry Tiana. I haven't seen you since the wedding. How are you? I didn't mean to be rude."

"Oh, please don't apologize. I'm praying for you guys. Just know that Jasmyn is in a better place." Tiana offered her a gentle sisterly hug.

Shawn and Crystal nervously glanced between Tiana's face and mine. The looks on their faces said "How in the world can Tiana be so calm when she knows her husband used to be involved with the woman that's being buried? And the thing that took her life could very well take Tiana's too!"

The truth was I never let Shawn know my HIV results, or Tiana's either for that matter. I felt that it was a private matter between my wife and me. We continued to get tested every six months. And so far, we continued to be blessed with negative results. But we weren't disillusioned. We knew the virus could show up at any time. Tiana and I matured as a couple and moved beyond panic and dread. After that first year when we learned of Jasmyn's infection, we stopped torturing ourselves with all of the what-ifs and began enjoying our lives, one day at a time. God may have set us apart and spared us from being infected, or just when we least expected it, he might spring it on us. We had no way of knowing. So what was the purpose in worrying? I preferred to just *live*.

"*. . . If we died with Him, we shall also live with Him . . .*" the minister closed his Bible and said a final prayer. Everyone began walking around the casket and dropping flowers on the top.

I wiped the tear that had finally struggled to make it out of my eye. I picked up a white rose from the basket that a pallbearer was holding. I leaned over slightly, paid my final respects and tossed the rose.

"Bye, Jazz. I'll see you on the other side, Miss Lady," I whispered.

In the last couple of years, Jasmyn had accepted her condition and started attending church. It helped her with her anger issues a lot. I noticed a slender, middle-aged woman, probably Jasmyn's mother, knelt on the ground, crying hysterically. She was being consoled by a nicely dressed guy who had to be Jasmyn's brother. I wanted to go offer my condolences, but decided it was better that I didn't. From what I had heard, at one time Jasmyn had a fiancé named Tarik who had been sent over to Iraq. He must've been the guy who was dressed in the formal army outfit standing next to Jasmyn's brother.

I talked to Shawn for a little bit as we walked back over to where our cars were parked. We quietly reminisced about the old days at Marshall, the days when I used to mess with Jazz, and how back then, I was so mad at myself for even messing with her.

"It was all for a reason, though, bro," I confided to Shawn. "I'd have to say she *did* have some of that fly-ghettoness about her that made her attractive. We had a few good times together. So, I don't regret meeting her. I just should've been more careful though."

Tiana and Crystal walked a few yards behind us. Tiana was playing with Shawn, Jr. and making small talk with Crystal. We said goodbye and promised to all get together for dinner soon.

It was a silent ride home. I glanced at Tiana, who was still teary-eyed. I turned on an old Luther Vandross CD and the track "I'd Rather" came on. He was singing about it being better to be with someone you love through the storm, rather than being alone. I used to think that song didn't make sense. I mean, who wants to be with a person going through problems? But now, I see what Luther was talking about.

Tiana placed her hands on her abdomen. "I'm just worried that this one will turn out sick, you know."

"Tiana, it's out of our hands. But look. We're both still here. We're healthy. Every day, they're coming out with new treatments. HIV isn't the death sentence it used to be."

In the past five years, science has worked miracles. We were now closer to a cure than we ever been. I was a twenty-eight year old successful project manager at Verizon, with an MBA degree. I was making over a hundred grand a year. My family and I lived on the Main Line. I drove a Benz and my wife drove an Audi. I had a gorgeous stepdaughter who was enrolled in the most prestigious

Montessori private school in Montgomery County. We were the youngest deacon and deaconess in our church. Life was good.

I didn't have time to worry about the storms, the headaches, and the bumps along the road that were inevitable. Every day was a gift and I planned on making the best of it. I kept reminding myself that later on this year, by Thanksgiving, I'd be holding a brand new baby. My very own seed. Whatever the outcome, I knew God had our back.

A smile came across Tiana's face. "What do you think about 'Nailah' if it's a girl? You know Nailah means success."

I looked over at her, and at the first stoplight, gave her a kiss. "Perfect. But what if it's a boy?"

"Then, we'll name him after his daddy." She stroked my face with her soft palm.

The light turned green and I resumed driving and envisioning all of the things we had to look forward to together as a family. I loved my wife just as much as the day I asked her to marry me, but every now and then I knew whenever anybody mentioned Marshall or college, I'd shed a silent tear inside for Jazz.

MESSAGE FROM THE AUTHOR

AIDS and HIV are plaguing the African-American and Hispanic communities at an alarming rate. It is time the young, hip-hop fresh generation takes a step back. While so many of us are out there enjoying youth, shaking it fast and dropping it like . . . .well, you know the rest. . . .many people are losing their lives. So often moments of satisfaction can determine a bitter end for us. Don't make unwise choices with your life or someone else's.

Young women of color under the age of thirty-five represent the largest percentage of new AIDS cases.

My sisters, this shouldn't be.

Ladies (and men too), please be careful. Use discretion. Be selective about who you choose to be with. Not everyone is worthy of your most intimate affections. Examine your relationships and be certain they are healthy and appropriate. We are the conduit for life and creation blossoms in us. I'm no preacher, but I've learned some lessons along the way in my lifetime. I've learned we can choose our happiness and every small decision, even the ones made in the heat of passion, can determine the path our lives take.

Protect yourself and our future generations. Don't be a statistic. Let's stop the cycle now. Ask yourself, "Is it worth my life?"

Do you not know that your body is a temple of the Holy Spirit, who is in you, whom you have received from God? You are not your own; you were bought at a price. Therefore honor God with your body. I Corinthians 6:19-20 (NIV)

Be safe!
One love,
Vonetta

About the Author

Philadelphia native Vonetta C. Pierce is making her creative debut with *Shameless*. After being inspired to write by Daaimah S. Poole (Wand G), Vonetta started penning a story in the summer of 2004. Daaimah and other writers gave her positive feedback on a prologue she sent them, so Vonetta continued to write. She soon met Mark Anthony of Q-Boro Books at Unity Day in Philadelphia, purchased *Dogism*, and was intrigued by Mark's spiritual approach to urban lit. Over the next several months, Vonetta worked diligently on her manuscript, mailing queries off to several agents.

Remembering what Mark had told her about trusting her talent and ability, she did not let five solid rejections deter her. She quickly received an offer from Q-Boro. Vonetta is a firm believer that with God anything is possible and that dreams really do come true. This is evidenced by the fact that she became inspired to write, finished a novel, and is being published—all in less than a year, an unheard of time frame within the literary industry.

Vonetta Pierce received her BA in Spanish from the University of Maryland Baltimore County, her

M.Ed. from Temple University, and is at work on her M.Ed in School Counseling. She is a high school Spanish teacher and has one daughter. She is currently working on some poetry and a second novel.

Visit her website at www.VCPierce.com.

PREVIEW

Someone Else's Puddin'

By Samuel L. Hair

Coming Winter 2006

When Melody entered room 222, Larry was lying naked across the bed, erect as penitentiary steel, and smoking a joint of chronic. She wasted no time getting naked and pouring herself a glass of vodka. As Larry relaxed, entertained by porn movies and her 38Ds, he smiled.

"You're my baby, Melody. Believe it or not, you're the best thing that has ever happened to me. I love you and I always will, no matter what."

She enjoyed hearing those words, especially coming from Larry, and not from her ghetto-fied, institutionalized husband who couldn't seem to stay out of prison for more than two months at a time.

Larry had stuffed his paraplegic wife, Pat, with tranquilizers, assuring she would remain asleep while he snuck out for his rendezvous with her beautician, Melody. Meanwhile, Melody had filled her teenage son's request for McDonald's and Taco Bell. Afterward, while watching BET, her son fell asleep. The secret lovers both had green lights. Luckily, the rich and ruthless Michelle, Melody's extremely jealous lesbian lover, had no knowledge of Melody's date with Larry. This was a good thing, since Michelle was known to kill when it came to someone messing around with her puddin'.

Larry had rented a suite at the Travelodge for the entire month—a luxury hideaway for himself and Melody to get away from life's issues, problems, and also from people who knew them and their spouses. It was a six-day-a-week ritual for the secret lovers to meet between two and six p.m. to socialize, have a couple drinks, and to have uncut, explicit sex.

They made each other feel needed and appreciated. Unfortunately, on this particular day, their date was delayed due to Pat's illness.

The fact that they were both married didn't matter to them. They had grown accustomed to fooling around with someone else's puddin'. They had kept their relationship a secret for over four years, and not once had Melody thought of saying no to Larry, dismissing him, or rejecting him for any reason, not even for her mother, who had advised her several times to break off her relationship with the married man. After all, he was the man who showered her with diamonds, gold, a variety of other expensive gifts, paid her house note, car note, dressed her son in name-brand tennis shoes and designer clothing, and gave her raw, pleasurable, uninhibited sex. Under no circumstances was she going to dismiss him out of her life. No way in hell.

After taking another long swallow of Popov vodka, she began showing her appreciation for all the things he had done for her. She fell to her knees like she was about to pray, while he sat comfortably at the edge of the bed sipping vodka. She then took his long, fat penis into her hands and began gently massaging and stroking it. Then she began sucking, licking, and slurping in exactly the way he had taught her.

"Uumhmm, yes, baby, yes. Damn, you make me feel so good," Larry moaned. Gradually, she sped up her rhythm, causing him to quiver and tremble, which is something his wife had never done. She thought about bringing him to a climax, but quickly dismissed the thought.

"No, baby, not now. I want to feel your hot, thick juice inside me," Melody said.

She brought her lips and tongue to a halt and quickly exchanged positions with him. It was now her turn. He ran his snake-like tongue up and down her legs while twirling three long, fat fingers in and out of her hot, juicy womb. He then began licking her clitoris, causing her to move rhythmically and have tremors that triggered breathtaking multiple orgasms. They had been sexing one another for so long that they had mastered each other's bodies and knew when the other was about to climax.

"I want it, baby. Now." Melody moaned, giving him the signal to immediately enter her. Suddenly he flipped her like a pancake, and she dutifully bent over and grabbed the edge of the bed. Impatiently, he thrust his rock hard penis inside her hot, wet, trembling tunnel of passion. His strokes were slow and deep and his penis touched all the right spots.

"Ooh, yes, give it to me, Big Daddy. Yes, damn, I

want it all," Melody begged. At that moment he pulled out, flipped her on her back as if he was angry, and she instinctively placed her legs over his shoulders. He thrust his hard, throbbing penis inside her, plunging into the depths of her womb, riding her with rough passion, pounding like a jackhammer, just the way she enjoyed it. Her cries of pleasure filled the room and caused a crazed, wild look to develop in his eyes. He plunged harder, deeper, and faster, and then suddenly, simultaneously, they exploded like volcanoes in full eruption. Afterward, they lay side by side totally spent, but relieved of all stress and daily pressures.

Mission accomplished. And so they returned to their spouses.

Attention Writers:

Writers looking to get their books published can view our submission guidelines by visiting our website at: *www.QBOROBOOKS.com*

What we're looking for: Contemporary fiction in the tradition of Darrien Lee, Carl Weber, Anna J, Zane, Mary B. Morrison, Noire, Lolita Files, etc; groundbreaking mainstream contemporary fiction.

We prefer email submissions to: candace@qborobooks.com in MS Word, PDF, or rtf format only. However, if you wish to send the submission via snail mail, you can send it to:

Q-BORO BOOKS Acquisitions Department
165-41A Baisley Blvd., Suite 4. Mall #1
Jamaica, New York 11434

*** By submitting your work to Q-Boro Books, you agree to hold Q-Boro books harmless and not liable for publishing similar works as yours that we may already be considering or may consider in the future. ***

1. Submissions will not be returned.
2. **Do not contact us for status updates.** If we are interested in receiving your full manuscript, we will contact you via email or telephone.
3. Do not submit if the entire manuscript is not complete.

Due to the heavy volume of submissions, if these requirements are not followed, we will not be able to process your submission.